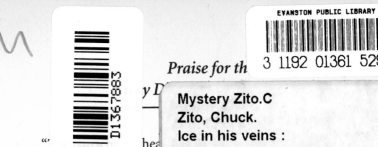

Praise for th

y D

he

a

"A laugh-out-loud romp . . . Zito's funny and lovable pro-
tagonist, Nicky D'Amico, is sure to be a favorite."

—*Booklist*

"Laugh until you weep. Zito's background in theatre is clearly
an asset—he has a great ear for dialogue and the ability to set
believable scenes both in the theatre and out."

—*Mystery Scene Magazine*

"A delightful novel, written with all the wit and repartee that
the gay community has made famous, and this book is something to be enjoyed by any fan of either the theatre or murder-mystery field, whether they be gay or straight. Packed with
humorous situations and characters all too believable, *A Habit
for Death* manages to hammer home the idea that gay people
are no different than the heterosexuals, having the same diffi-
culty with relationships, circumstances, and attractions—and
does it in a fun way. Author Zito's approach to this genre is
most welcome."

—*Who Dunnit*

"For those theater aficionados among you, Carnegie Mellon drama graduate and San Diego theater director Chuck Zito has crafted his first (hopefully of many) Nicky D'Amico mystery. Summer stock turns to summer schlock turns to stark reality as Nicky and his crew work toward a denouement that features plenty of hilarity along the way."

—Mystery Lovers Bookshop

ICE
IN HIS
VEINS

ALSO BY CHUCK ZITO

A Habit for Death

FORTHCOMING BY CHUCK ZITO

Deck the Halls

A NICKY D'AMICO MYSTERY

ICE
IN HIS
VEINS

CHUCK ZITO

MIDNIGHT INK
WOODBURY, MINNESOTA

FIRST EDITION
First Printing, 2007

Book design by Donna Burch
Cover design by Kevin R. Brown
Cover illustration © Larry Schwinger / Artworks

Midnight Ink, an imprint of Llewellyn Publications

Library of Congress Cataloging-in-Publication Data
Zito, Chuck.
  Ice in his veins : a Nicky D'Amico mystery / Chuck Zito. — 1st ed.
     p. cm.
  ISBN-13: 978-0-7387-1038-9
  ISBN-10: 0-7387-1038-5
  I. Title.

PS3626.I86I34 2007
813'.6—dc22   2007012031

Midnight Ink
Llewellyn Publications
2143 Wooddale Drive, Dept. 0-7387-1038-5
Woodbury, MN 55125-2989, U.S.A.
www.midnightinkbooks.com

Printed in the United States of America

For
Todd Lind

ICE
IN HIS
VEINS

THE CAST
(in order of appearance)

Aliza Buday . . . . Lighting designer

Al Benning . . . . Member of the Good Company

Detective Marissa Sanchez . . . . New York Police Department

Detective Dave Rampart . . . . New York Police Department

Suege Nethevy . . . . Landlord of the Brewery Arts Center

Andy and Mikey . . . . Friends of Herb Wilcox

Man Wilson . . . . Reporter, Channel 3 News

Billy, Tommy, and Sid . . . . Friends of Herb Wilcox

Sushi, Watteau, Benji, and Snowball . . . . Themselves

A store clerk, members of the cast of *A Midsummer Night's Dream*, and NYPD police officers.

The action takes place on Manhattan's West Side and Lower East Side, and in and around the campus of Baldwin University in Philadelphia.

No animals were harmed in the making of this production.

While the use of photographic and recording devices is strictly prohibited, management does recommend the red licorice from the concession stand.

The author spent his undergraduate years at a theater conservatory; however, none of his classmates are portrayed in this book, though each will, he hopes, feel the love.

If you enjoy the performance, please tell your friends. If you do not, please tell them you went to a movie.

PROLOGUE

He looked cold, stretched out on his back in the snow. A few blown flakes settled on his exposed chest and stomach, but there was no reason to worry about his physical comfort. He was dead.

He was lying not far from the door, away from the graffiti-covered walls. Cobblestone and pavement peeked through the snow and ice beneath him. It was as if he'd wandered into the wrong play. From the looks of it, his robe had fallen open when he'd fallen backward. Other than the robe, he wore only his *Midsummer* costume and his shoes. It wasn't the absurdity of his body dressed for summer but lying in the sub-freezing winter weather that grabbed our attention. Nor was it the large amount of bright red blood turning dull red as it formed a circular pool in the snow around him. It was the icicle. It was lying propped up on his neck, its tip pointing to a puncture wound in his skin. Somewhere along the way, the tip had been inside him and had melted, allowing the ice to drop out. Someone had stabbed him with that icicle.

We were doing *A Midsummer Night's Dream* in January because we thought it would lighten our winter. As it turned out, discontent had other plans.

Not even twenty-four hours earlier, everything was on track for a typical small theater production, at least the kind I seem to get involved in. We had Shakespeare, an unhappy drag queen, nasty hangovers, late-night phone calls, semi-senile neighbors, and the resurrection of failed romance. If I'd only known, I could have anticipated all the fun that was yet to come: color voodoo, overwrought local newscasters, scary art, and way too much Lycra.

I stepped back into the theater, where the rest of the company waited to hear what was happening. All they knew was that something in the alley had sent two members running back onto the stage, where they'd passed out, the victim's name hanging in air.

"Listen up, everyone," I said. "He's dead. We're going to have to call the police and—"

I never finished the sentence. My announcement caused an outbreak of hysterical grief on the part of the actor playing Titania. At least I thought it was grief, until I realized that he was shouting for the costume designer. He didn't feel he was dressed to his best advantage for a police interview.

ACT I

SATURDAY EVENING

"The neighbor, Maria Cepedes, also saw ..."

"... the face of ..."

"... John the Baptist ..."

"... in the recently purchased chunk of ..."

"... chunk of bleu cheese."

"Give the words space," the director coached his actors.

The first actor, the one who'd begun the exercise, stretched his neck from side to side and then raised and lowered his shoulders. The other looked at his watch.

"... chunk of bleu cheese."

"Mrs. Hagida is a member of ..."

"... Mary, Queen of the ..."

"Attitude," the director urged them on.

"... Universe Catholic Church in ..."

"... Kew Gardens, Queens."

"My cheese is very ..."

"... ordinary ..."

"See the cheese, guys. Share the cheese."

"... said Mrs. Cepedes."

"It makes me ..."

"... sad. I never see ..."

"... saints."

"Give and take," the director said.

"Church officials would not ..."

"... comment ..."

"... on the sighting other than to say ..."

"Color the words." The director's voice was hushed, swallowed by the empty theater.

The vocals were muffled in part by the thick black curtains hanging along the back and side walls of the claustrophobic stage. These absorbed not only the sound, but also the flickering light from the fluorescents hanging as work lights over the stage, leaving the three people center in a dingy brownish-yellow glow. They sat at a folding table scattered with newspaper clippings. I served as the lone audience member. The house lights were at half strength. In the dim light, the red leatherette seat cushions appeared to be the same dull brown color that washed the stage. The only really noticeable noise in the entire space was the whirring of the overhead ventilation fans.

"... that ..."

"... they were studying the event."

"Share."

Alex Isola, the actor with the stiff neck, tapped his foot rapidly on the stage floor. He picked up the thread of the news article.

"Mrs. Hagida charges one dollar per viewing ..."

"You know, she could have got a lot more if she'd been smart enough to see Christ himself," his partner interrupted, speaking to the theater house as if it were filled with an opening-night audience.

"Stick to the words, Herb," the director patiently urged.

"Of course." Herb Wilcox sighed. "The text. The holy, holy text."

I was huddled in the first row, a stage manager waiting to set up rehearsal. As the tension gathered onstage, I deliberately looked away, doing my best impression of detached professionalism, neither encouraging nor condemning the actors. If we'd been in rehearsal, I would have glared back with disapproval. Keeping order was part of my job, but this was a director's exercise, so I gazed meditatively at a shining red exit sign.

Alex pushed away from the folding table. "Why are we doing this?"

Marcus Bradshaw, the director, started to explain. "Well, the point of the exercise—"

"Thank you, I know the 'point' of the exercise." Alex mimicked Marcus's word choice and tone. "I was in class with you when you learned it. I want to know the 'point' of doing it with *him*."

The *him* in question was Herb Wilcox, downtown drag queen diva, better known to adoring fans in small East Village bars as "Anita Nutha." Today, Herb was out of drag but not attitude. He stood six feet four inches, thin in a way that was either genetic or the result of a lettuce diet. Even seated, he looked down at Alex.

"Doing it with me? With *me*? As if I would do *it* with someone like you." He left Alex and Marcus center, crossing downstage to ask me, "How did you do it, Nicky? Princess, how did you manage day after day, week after week, month after month, year after year, decade after decade—"

"It was only four years, Herb," I jumped in, before the millennia overwhelmed us.

"That's pretty faint praise," Marcus said. He sounded more offended than the smile on his face suggested.

"Yeah, Nicky," Alex said. "Couldn't you have said something more supportive? Like, 'It was really my pleasure'?"

Herb winked at me, then spun around to confront Alex. "That's all you think about, isn't it, prep-boy? Your pleasure. Well, I've had enough of trying to please you."

He stepped off the low rise of the stage into the front row of the house, an opening neither deep enough nor wide enough to be called an orchestra pit. "I'll be in the lobby when you're ready to rehearse."

With a grand passion normally reserved for royal coronations, Herb processed up the length of the Tapestry Theater.

The theater was part of the Brewery Arts Center, a renovated microbrewery on West 53rd Street in Hell's Kitchen in New York City. The Tapestry, a ninety-nine seater with a stage the size of a suburban living room, occupied the first floor and had rehearsal space and a dressing room on the second. There was a light booth just behind and above the audience at the back of the theater house. Here, stage managers and light and sound board operators would work during performances. From the public's perspective, the renovation was impressive. Audience seating was very comfy, with deep burgundy cushions surrounded by laminate wood. What they couldn't see was that the booth was only marginally outfitted with equipment already five years out of date when it arrived. What they wouldn't know was that the finely done detail work on the walls and molding was every designer's nightmare. In the words of Midsummer's eternally testy lighting designer, "Who the hell wants the walls to 'talk to you'?"

Herb was barely past those overdone walls and into the lobby before Marcus started laughing.

"You only encourage him when you do that," Alex said.

"But he's funny."

"Don't be so earnest, Alex," I added.

"How come he stomps out of here and I am the one at whom fun is being poked?" Alex asked.

"Oh, Alex, Alex," Marcus said. "We promise. Even though you're obsessive about not dangling your prepositions and say things like 'at whom fun is being poked,' we'll always adore you and always take your side against evil drag queens. Promise. No matter how funny they are. Swear." Marcus wrapped Alex in one of his trademark all-embracing, heart-thumping hugs, the sort of hug known to make strong men weak and weak boys faint. Believe me, I knew from experience.

"Marcus, you cannot possibly be defending him," Alex said.

"Me? No. I'm not defending him. I'm just saying he's funny."

I was fairly certain that Alex had never kissed Marcus while we were at school. I couldn't say whether or not he wanted to now. I can say that Alex didn't pull away from Marcus's embrace. For just a moment, I thought I caught a vibe that was a bit more than "former roommates and friends."

Built to match, they were solid, lean men. Alex had the same black hair and blue eyes as Marcus. If you didn't know them, you might momentarily confuse them if you saw one without the other. But if you had more than a casual familiarity with either, you would never make that mistake. Marcus retained the easy, open manner he'd had on the day I'd met him. Alex, though he'd shed much of his early shyness, was still more reserved, more cautious. In my mind, Marcus's image appeared much larger than Alex's, and not just because I knew that Marcus could screw like a bunny in springtime.

The first time Marcus Bradshaw kissed me was also the first night we had sex. This is not nearly as slutty as it sounds.

It was the Friday evening of our first week as drama students at Baldwin University in Philadelphia. We were sitting on a bench slipped into one of the many parklets dotting the campus: a sunken flagstone area, tree-lined with a small semicircular fountain at its center. Wrought-iron faux streetlamps lit the perimeter, and wooden benches sat next to each lamp. In all, a not particularly special bit of concrete fringed with some everyday trees. But to me, eighteen years old and living in a large city for the first time, it was a magical space, combining newfound urban freedom with an old-fashioned hunger. A hunger Marcus was more than happy to satisfy. With my happy acquiescence, he had been marching us toward that kiss from the moment we'd met at convocation the previous Monday.

The night was a perfect September evening—warm, without a trace of the humidity that had plagued us all week. We were sitting on that bench sharing the fifth of Jack Daniels that Marcus was BYOBing for a party. Sunset gave way to what passed for a brilliant night sky in the city—three stars and no haze. The timing was strictly freshman-year pre-party: nothing weighed on us.

"Toast," he said, after several rounds of slugging it straight from the bottle.

"No toast," I yelled. "Bagels. Bagels from here on out. I'm in the big city now."

"No. No. Not just toast. *A* toast. A toast!" He put his arm around my shoulder, explaining to me the heartfelt and deep, deep distinction between recooked bread and the exchange of civilities over liquor. "Toast is for ... for breakfast. *A* toast is ... forever!"

"Forever!" I tipped the bottle once more.

"A toast." He held up the Jack. I caught sight of the lamp light refracted through the amber liquid, of Marcus momentarily silhouetted against the glimmer of the multipaned window of a nearby dorm.

"Toast," I repeated.

"To us." He swigged.

"To us." I swigged.

He kissed me. And again. We were late to the party.

When we finally arrived at the three-story Victorian house that our classmate Rita Lombard shared with several non-drama-department friends, the place was packed. It seemed as if the entire department and then some had shown up. Rita herself, six feet tall with copper red hair, sat outside on a stool on the front porch, collecting five-dollar bills for the food and drinks, all the while flirting with the more heterosexually inclined men. As we dropped our cash in the bucket, she didn't say anything, just gave us the once-over. Then she winked at me before turning her attention to the next boy in line.

Once inside, we heard Anna Mikasa before we saw her. I'd met her at the same time that I'd first met Marcus. Tonight she was holding forth in the living room. Undaunted by not knowing anyone in her audience—undaunted even by not knowing all that much about theater history—she was in full swing, expounding her opinions of where "we should take the American theater as its next generation of creators." The rapt attention of her circle of listeners was as much a testament to her charismatic charms as to the effects of the joint passing amongst them.

She paused in mid-sentence when Marcus and I appeared, framed in the wide pocket doorway.

"Beer is in the kitchen. Try not to maul each other before you at least meet a few new people." Anna: so direct, so practical. She picked up her impromptu lecture exactly where she'd left off.

We wormed our way back along the crowded, narrow nineteenth-century hallway. In the brightly lit kitchen we found another classmate, Sean McGinn, leaning on a counter and looking a little overwhelmed. Sean was a tall, lean, rangy guy with blue eyes and a sweet smile. Eventually, we'd all grow accustomed to his pleasant, nonobtrusive presence. That night he just seemed out of place.

Sean lifted the large red plastic cup he was holding, saluting us from across the room as we entered.

"What are you doing crushed into the corner?" Marcus asked.

"I'm a kitchen partier. It's easier—more light, everyone passes through, no one ever asks you to deal with the music." Sean didn't look so much overwhelmed as baffled by the press of increasingly inebriated partiers.

Marcus and I continued our slow progression throughout the evening. We let the party carry us from the first floor to the second to the third and back again. Rita's house was tall and narrow, squeezed in the middle of the block, sharing walls with homes on either side. The structure was old and had once represented a great deal of luxury, attested to by the presence of two sets of stairs, the beautifully tooled front stair leading up from the main entryway and the narrow, winding servants' stair sneaking up from the kitchen.

About mid-evening, I escaped outside to the front porch, desperate for fresh air. Marcus had momentarily retreated to a third-floor bedroom to enjoy "a little line of coke. I'll be right back, baby." I wasn't certain how I felt about this new bit of info. I'd no experience at that point with anything more than alcohol. That night, I shrugged it off. What harm could a "little line of coke" do?

Even though the humidity was creeping back, the porch was a relief after the closeness indoors. I was leaning on the railing, looking at the now-hazy sky. The classmate Alex had been eyeing all week, whom he'd tagged "the Big One," took the open space next to me. At six feet two, with more muscle on his body than most freshmen, this guy did not look like any of the theater geeks I typically hung with. Blond with blue eyes, he was a walking corn-fed cliché. His proximity (I was almost touching his forearm) clicked the evening into focus—I was awash in beer, damp warm air, and hormones. I wanted Marcus. Now.

I was about to turn away when he said, "Hey."

My middle-class Catholic upbringing momentarily trumped lust.

"Hey. I'm Nicky D'Amico."

"Stacey Rose." He shook my hand with stiff formality. I could smell the alcohol on his breath. He'd obviously been drinking, but based on his expression and tone, I wouldn't bet he'd been enjoying himself.

Music rolled out of the front door each time it opened. I forced the image of a naked Marcus out of my mind, trying to listen to what the guy was saying. Not that Stacey ever actually made it much past stilted, but he did let loose some bits of his history as he free-associated in a fumbling approximation of camaraderie, aided by a slight beer buzz.

I'd been right to guess corn-fed. He was born and raised in a little town to the southwest of Chicago. I didn't get anything near the entire story that night. In fact, I *never* got the entire story, but I did pick up on a high school athletic career, a love of theater, and a lackluster academic background. I had the impression that there was not a great deal of family support for Stacey in any particular activity.

My mind drifted at some point and I began to imagine that Marcus was standing next to me, the damp air raising sweat on our skin as I leaned over to …

"Are you OK?"

"What?" I snapped to, with Stacey standing in front of me holding a pocket dictionary.

"You were leaning over."

He rambled on about his dictionary, telling me that he looked up words that other people were using but whose meaning he didn't know. It was a tentative, endearing confession from a man with such physical presence.

"Like that girl in the living room. I have no clue what she's talking about." I assumed he was referring to Anna. I also assumed he wasn't alone in his confusion.

Our fitful conversation stopped after that. I think he felt he'd gone too far in revealing himself. An impression he would confirm by not speaking to me for the next month.

We were well into the awkward silence when Marcus found us.

Not constrained by my sense of duty, he barely acknowledged Stacey, who seemed to become smaller and more distant when confronted by two strangers. Marcus hauled me off to the kitchen for more beer.

As we passed back along the hallway, we ran into Anna and a too-frisky classmate, Eduardo Lugo. Eduardo was at least a foot taller than Anna. He had one arm wrapped around her shoulder, loudly proclaiming, "I love this woman!" As he bent over to kiss her, Anna pushed him back. He went in for another try. Just as I was moving to help her, she gave a flat-palmed shove to the center of his chest. It was just enough of a surprise, and he was just enough drunk, that the momentum sent him tumbling first into the wall and then, as he missed his grip on a closet doorknob, onto the floor.

"Oh God," he said, hitting the carpet. "Amazing."

"Beer. Now." Anna grabbed my arm and dragged me forward, Marcus dutifully following along.

The temperature in the kitchen felt as if it had risen at least ten degrees during the evening, even with the window open. We found Alex, our first sighting of the night, leaning on the same white Formica counter where Sean had earlier perched. The room was blindingly brighter after the hazy outside air and the dimly lit hallway. Overhead light bounced off both the counter and the white tiled floor. A thin layer of cigarette smoke was all that cut the glare.

"Where have you been?" Marcus asked, while I pulled beer for all of us.

Alex ignored the question. Instead he asked, "Have you guys seen the Big One? Is he here?"

"His name is Stacey Rose," I said. "I can't believe you don't know that yet."

Alex leaned forward. "Did you talk to him?"

"Yes, I was talking to him on the porch. You should try it."

"Really now, were you?" Marcus asked. He grabbed my waist and kissed me. The kiss tasted of beer. I wanted us to leave right then. No one else showed the slightest interest in our sudden coupledom.

"He's very something, isn't he?" Alex seemed lost in his own dream.

Rita Lombard, a tumbler of something much stronger than beer in one hand and a cigarette in the other, pushed her way into the middle of our group. "Oh, you can stop right there, kid. The boy is straight, straighter, straightest. I'm Rita, I haven't met you three. Anns and I are already like old friends. Who the hell are you people?"

"How can you be so certain?" Alex asked. "You just met him too."

"I know one when I see one, OK? Trust me on this."

"Maybe—"

Rita cut him off. "Oh, you're not one of those guys, are you? Lusting after all the wrong boys? My bestest gay friend in high school—and who doesn't have one of those, huh?" She tossed this aside at Anna, who stared wide-eyed. "Trust me, baby, do not go there. Now, I'm Rita Lombard. This is my home and I still do not know who the fuck you people are."

For the five of us, it was love at first grouping.

It took another hour to pull Marcus away from the party. It was only later, after a full year of parties, that the process of disentangling him from the beer and drugs became a grinding drudgery. That night it was still a long, flirtatious cruising game.

I was very nervous. Yes, technically the confused fumblings of summer camp qualified me as a non-virgin when it came to gay sex.

But this would be my first premeditated effort. I was actually going back to someone's apartment to actually have sex.

The first round was frantic, the second energetic, and the third something few men manage after their mid-twenties without the aid of a little blue pill. When we finally exhausted ourselves and slept, it was only for a few hours before we disproved an old cliché. It's the fourth time that counts.

———————

"He's not listening," Alex said.

He and Marcus were onstage, annoyed with me for losing the thread of their conversation.

"You're daydreaming again."

"Am not." I suppressed the smirk on my lips. While I did not miss anything about the long, ugly descent Marcus had taken into his addiction, I couldn't help smiling at the memory of that first night. I forced myself to pay attention to the conversation on the Tapestry stage.

"I was telling Marcus, for those of you who switched channels, that it is not funny when Herb ruins rehearsal." Alex was nearly begging in his anxiety.

"You trust me, yes? OK?" Marcus was smiling again, working hard to blunt Alex's anger. "He's not going to ruin anything. Anyway, you look great onstage. Doesn't he look great onstage, Nicky?"

"Always has," I said.

"See?" Marcus said to Alex, as if he'd solved everything.

"You are insane. And you are no help," Alex said to me. "You always agree with him."

"Not always," I said. "Coney Island."

Marcus winced. "Oh God. Not Coney Island again."

Alex sighed and held both hands up in surrender. "All right. Please. Even I do not want to hear about Coney Island again. Just do not ask me to do that exercise with him. Ever again."

"You have my word. Promise," Marcus said, holding the hug a moment longer before stepping back.

"You know, guys, there's going to be a rehearsal in here in a few minutes," I said, focusing my attention back on the task at hand. As stage manager, I was supposed to be the responsible one. One of my jobs was to keep everyone on schedule. That duty, along with setting up the space, prompting actors who forgot their lines, and keeping a record of the blocking, filled most of my time at rehearsals.

"As your producer, I would appreciate your concentration," Anna Mikasa said, announcing her arrival from a spot halfway down the side aisle.

"Nominal producer," Marcus said.

"Temporary," Alex added.

"Titular producer?" I turned in my seat to look at Anna. "I think that one's new."

"You all suck."

"Thank you," the three of us answered in unison.

"What happened? Why is Herb in the lobby swearing that all he ever wanted was a simple frock and a garden of his own?"

"We didn't do a thing, Anna," Alex said. "He is a dick."

"There was just a simple disagreement on an acting exercise. That's it." Marcus started to collect the newspaper clippings. "It was nothing. Really."

She waited, but no one said anything more.

She turned to me. "Anything to add, Shemp?"

"Ah … we have ten minutes till rehearsal and I need the stage now?"

"Guys, you've got to be nicer to him. You know he feels like an outsider with us."

Anna was not just referring to the four of us. We understood that she was talking about "the Classmates." A term that always required the capital letter. The twenty-one of us had graduated from the Baldwin University Drama Department. There, as conservatory students, we'd spent four years working, playing, eating, and sleeping together seven days a week, a minimum of ten months out of each year. The party at Rita's that first Friday had just been a preview of the fun to come as we worked and played our way to graduation. And though at times the entire experience seemed more slumber party/summer camp than college, we did learn a great deal. After school, we'd gone our separate ways, making fitful starts at the post-conservatory life. The pull of familiarity had proven too strong for some. Twelve of the actors in the class eventually formed the Good Company.

I wasn't officially part of the company. Shortly after graduation, I'd gone to Los Angeles for half a year, but the West Coast didn't settle well with my Northeast sensibilities. Back in New York, the Good Company was being founded to keep everyone busy. They wanted me to join, but I kept slipping in and out of the City.

Now it was mid-winter—January in New York—and I was single and between work. This combination of circumstances allowed me to sign on for just one production: an all-male version of Shakespeare's *A Midsummer Night's Dream*.

Don't get me wrong, it wasn't that I disliked my Classmates. In fact, exactly the opposite was true. I knew them all too well and had, over our four years of near-continuous exposure, grown fond of each, in one way or another. It was that familiarity, that intense closeness, that even allowed me to reach some level of accommodation with Marcus after he'd trashed the relationship we'd formed that first year at school.

More immediately, Anna had wanted me for this show. And what Anna wants ...

"You know what we need?"

That question.

"What we need is better stage management." Anna had pushed her yogurt salad across her plate. In eight years I'd never actually seen her eat an entire meal.

"What we *need*"—and here she'd emphasized the word "need" as if lacking this desired necessity would result in the failure of tomorrow's sunrise—"is for someone to step in and pick up the slack. You should see rehearsals, Nicky. You know these people. They need real organization."

We had been sitting in the window of Casa da Sopa on lower Broadway. I was temping in an office around the corner and, at her request, had met Anna for a quick lunch. Outside the window, the slowly blackening remains of yesterday's snowfall were turning to slush. The sun was bright, but not overly helpful. Inside, Anna wrapped her puffy down jacket around herself and her chair, insulating herself from the cool air falling off the window.

"... order. You know this, Nicky, as well as anyone. Truly creative theater needs a certain amount of order and discipline to thrive. It's a paradox. We all live with ..."

I didn't even bother trying to speak. Eventually she would have to breathe. Or get hungry enough for at least one bite of food. I munched on my BLT.

"… not that everyone isn't doing their best. That isn't the problem. It's their focus I'm worried about. All of them are trying to keep track of too many technical questions. Things actors shouldn't be dealing with. We'd all love to have you working with us."

She paused for air. I jumped.

"What happened to Rita? I thought she was stage managing. Didn't you guys divvy all this up?"

Anna's friendship with Rita Lombard had eventually led them to share a two-bedroom in New York on East 10th, beyond Avenue B. More to the immediate discussion, Rita, along with Anna and three other Classmates—Stacey Rose, Sean McGinn, and Eduardo Lugo—formed the Steering Committee that attempted to wrest order out of the chaos of the Good Company. And, though theater is basically a team sport, running one by committee permitted only so much untangling of Anna's "paradox."

"It's ridiculous. Rita has gone to Detroit. Detroit? Who the hell goes to Detroit? In January? Rita."

I laughed. "Someone's paying her, right?"

This was always a problem with small productions. If there was any pay, it was usually just subway fare. Anyone in the production who had the opportunity to take a paying gig jumped at it. I've known actors who pulled out two days before opening to begin rehearsals for real money.

"Yes. Damn it." Anna took a breath, then launched off again. "The point is, you and I are going to make *Midsummer* happen in

Hell's Kitchen in January. We're going to do this with the people we know and love best in the theater. We need you."

"Anna, stop it." I put my hand up to ward off more words. "Just tell me—can Marcus do this?"

"Marcus is not the question," she answered, regrouping.

"Marcus is always the question," I said.

"Oh, Nicky. It was seven years ago. Are you still on about him? I don't think that's healthy. Think about this now—"

"Oooops. Wrong turn. I'm not talking about that, and you know it." I actually managed to interrupt her only because, while waving her spoon, she'd tossed yogurt into her coffee. She came to a dead stop.

"He hasn't had a drink in a year. Is that what you want to know?"

"Does he go to meetings?"

"Are you a social worker now?" She was signaling for a waiter. "You haven't seen him in years. I'm with him every day. He's staying in Rita's room while she's gone. We're helping him live cheap until he gets some cash together."

"That still doesn't answer my question." I was not letting go so easily.

"He's sober. He's sane. He can do this. He is doing this. You know he's always wanted to."

The last statement was certainly true. He'd been staging scenes from *A Midsummer Night's Dream* since his first directing class. He'd fine-tuned it, but the basic idea hadn't changed over the years. It was an all-male production, which was neither revolutionary nor revelatory. There were, however, two hooks for capturing the audience. A real live drag queen—not just another actor in drag—would play Titania, queen of the fairies. The fairies themselves would be a male chorus of incredibly hunky six-feet-plus guys wearing nothing but biking shorts. This wouldn't exactly be high culture, but then neither would it be as low as I'd already sunk in my short theatrical career. After a stint with a trained marmoset, pretty much anything qualifies as art.

"I know he's always wanted to. But he hasn't done a thing since we graduated."

"That's the point, Nicky. This will be good for him. It will be good for us. The production concept is great."

The waiter was refilling Anna's coffee while speaking with the people at the next table. This was the international waiter's signal for "You are a lot of trouble and you do not look like good tippers."

"Come on, Nicky. You're not working. We open in two weeks. It's a simple tech: bare stage, minimal props, some sound, and light. It's a showcase. It'll only run two weekends. Most of us are involved and it means everything to Marcus. It's true that we'll get it onstage one way or another. It would be a lot better if you helped us. Please, Nicky. 'Us' includes you."

Anna was small, but never easily discounted. Not just thin or short, she was close to the ground, with miniaturized features that seemed to defy function. She was dark with black hair and had a brooding color to her that accentuated the compactness of her frame. Strikingly, her eyes were two different colors. Just as strikingly was how much at odds her physicality was with her energy.

When she finished waving her arms and bulldozing conversations, Anna's biggest advantage with me was always her absolute commitment to her work. No one worked harder. No one worked longer. No one worked smarter. I found that kind of dedication infectious. I sighed. She said nothing—a strategic waiting.

So it might not turn out to be great art. At least, with the male chorus in a constant state of near-undress, I'd always have something fun to look at. And it was true that part of me missed hanging out with the old gang.

"OK. OK. What the hell. You're right. I'm not working and it's only a few weeks. How bad can it be?"

She toasted me with her coffee. Considering how it all turned out, it would have been less painful if she had just tossed the hot liquid on my lap.

———————

"You know," I said in response to Anna's defense of Herb, "I am not a member of this company."

They all three turned on me.

"Technically, no." Anna, as usual, led the charge. "Let's add it up. There are twenty-one Classmates."

"Twelve of whom are company members," Marcus said.

"Six of with whom—to the best of our knowledge—you have had sex," Alex added.

"You said, 'of with whom you have had sex.' I'm humbled. Truly humbled." Marcus bowed toward Alex, who nobly nodded his head in return.

"Let's not lose track of our math," Anna said, sitting on the edge of the stage. She fit perfectly, her feet resting flat on the auditorium floor. She'd dumped her parka in the front row. Even from two seats away, I could feel the cold coming off the blue nylon. "Two of the men Nicky diddled played both sides of the field."

"And both of them were far from shy about playing on that other team," Marcus said. He was having much too much fun. "Actually, very far from—"

"Stop," I jumped in. "I don't need an encyclopedic review of my undergraduate years." I pointed at Marcus. "And you know, the only reason I was a free agent—" I didn't get to finish.

Anna laughed at me. "No fair blaming Marcus. Be a big boy, take responsibility for your penis, Nicky."

Alex grinned triumphantly as he laid out the final piece of the puzzle. "Now, where were we? Oh yes, it follows logically that Nicky, as the health care professionals say, has had sex with all the Classmates."

"Except Molly," Anna said. "Who is ... boys?" She pointed at Marcus and Alex, who replied in unison, "Still a virgin!"

They all three bowed.

"OK. OK," I said. "Maybe, just maybe, we are a little hard to take as a group."

"That's being polite." Anna turned toward Marcus. "You. You are responsible for setting the tone in rehearsal."

"You know, I was younger back then. We should take that into account," I said.

"You're right, Anna," Marcus said. "You're right. I'll try harder. We all will, won't we?" he asked Alex and me.

"I suppose we have to," Alex said.

"And I was away from home for the first time. I think that should count in my favor as well."

"Nicky ..." Anna gave me her you-are-falling-so-short-of-expectations face.

"Yes. Yes. All right. I will be nice to Herb. Scout's honor," I said.

"Who would let you into the Boy Scouts?" Alex asked with genuine sincerity.

"You're not helping." I stood. "Let's get set up."

I jumped onto the stage to start arranging rehearsal furniture.

We heard the strangled, choking sound before we knew where it originated. Suddenly, Herb was rushing at us from the back of the house, hands at his throat, eyes bulging. From his open mouth came a staccato beat of half gasps.

"He's choking. Oh my God, he's choking." Anna jumped to her feet.

"Heimlich. Does anyone know the Heimlich maneuver?" Alex shouted.

As suddenly as he'd appeared, Herb stopped choking. "I knew a Heimlich once, Princess. He was blond and pale and so ... so ... how do you say ... ah, yes—German."

"You asshole," Alex said.

"Now who says I can't act?"

———

Oberon and his court step into the woodland grove. A bright full moon casts a blue-silvery light that shimmers in their magical fairy eyes. He stands for just a moment. A rustling from across the clearing catches his attention. Suddenly, Titania, his queen, a towering beauty of unearthly presence, appears with her retinue.

"Ill met by moonlight, proud Titania," the king says.

"What, jealous Oberon? Fairies, skip hence. I have forsworn his bed and company." She turns to lead her court away.

"Tarry, rash wanton. Am I not thy lord?"

Titania turns a slow, smoldering look toward the fairy king. With a dismissive laugh, she taunts him, "Oh, then I must be thy lady—"

Herb stopped the action. "Wouldn't it be better if right on 'lady' I let a boob slip or maybe my wig? You know, some kind of visual thing?"

After Herb's miraculous recovery, we spent the rest of the evening in the woods outside Athens. The central story of *A Midsummer Night's Dream* involves two young couples enmeshed in a love triangle with an extra spoke. One set slips away from Athens to marry against *her* father's wishes. The other follows to try to stop them. In the forest, the four of them cross paths with Titania and Oberon, the feuding king and queen of the fairies. Titania and Oberon's quarrel entangles the young lovers in a round robin of abandonment and love brought on by Oberon's magic love potion. At the same time, in another part of the forest, a group of tradesmen (tailors, tinkers, and such) from Athens are meeting. They are secretly rehearsing a play they hope to perform at the wedding of the king of Athens. These "mechanicals," as they're traditionally called, become a comic casualty in Oberon and Titania's grudge match. Even if you don't know the play, you can safely assume that all is right by the rising of the sun. As the character of Puck says at the end: "And every Jack shall have his Jill." Or, in the case of the Good Company, to every Jack another.

Midsummer is one of my favorite plays. It's funny, clever, a true romantic comedy. What can I say? I've been known to cry at the occasional sappy movie.

In our performance, cool blue moonlight would indeed wash over Titania and Oberon. I was not so certain about the rest. The forest would be the male chorus, posed as trees, each actor holding two or three branches. This distraction was not the only thing that made me suspicious. Usually *Midsummer*, which runs very long for modern tastes, is cut by trimming, among other parts, the chatter of Titania's fairy retinue. Instead, Marcus had parceled those lines out to the chorus. Literally, the trees would speak. Mercifully, not tonight.

In this rehearsal, the stage went first to the young lovers, and now to Titania, Oberon, and Puck. This meant that at the moment Herb was sharing rehearsal with Stacey Rose. As the actor playing Oberon, Stacey would be one of the two people spending the most time onstage with Herb.

"Great," Stacey growled, not taking well to Herb's wig and boob joke. "Really bad 'see-and-say' Shakespeare."

"And what the hell is 'see-and-say' Shakespeare?" Herb demanded.

"My hand, my heart, my sword." Stacey illustrated each word with a corresponding gesture: hand out, then on his heart, then miming a grasp on a sword hilt at his side.

"Oh, right, I forgot. Baldwin students don't do funny. They do art. Except, it's a fucking comedy. It says so right on the cover." Herb held up his script for all to see, just in case any of us had lost our own.

I was sitting in the front row at a low table, doing my prompting duties. Tonight that mostly meant helping Herb through dialogue he still hadn't memorized and apparently didn't intend to. ("Why can't I improvise? The damn writer's dead, isn't he?")

A conversation started up in the seats immediately behind me.

"This is bad."

"Very bad."

"We should have anticipated this."

"Magenta."

"How were we supposed to know?"

"We should have been ready. We need to keep more shirts with us."

"Right. More shirts."

"A full range of color."

"Ah, guys?" I said, turning around. "Would you mind maybe moving elsewhere so I can concentrate?"

I confronted the blank stares of the Two.

The Two were unlike anyone I'd ever met (or imagined I'd ever meet again). They were not actors, nor were they in any recognizable way connected to theater, other than through Stacey Rose. They mostly spoke to each other or him. They were small (shorter even than me, and I'm only five-seven) and thin, with voracious eyes that swallowed entire rooms whole. As impressive as Stacey had been at our first meeting freshman year, he'd added even more muscle to his frame. The first sight of the three of them together was not something you would want to experience drunk.

When the Good Company was still just one of those things "we needed," Anna had issued invitations to all the Classmates. In a very few cases, this was pro forma. No one expected Molly to show up. And no one, except Anna, expected Stacey. While the rest of us had cozied up as undergraduates and behaved in ways that the future parents among us would someday deny to their children, Stacey remained vaguely aloof, his initial outburst on Rita's porch being a high-water mark of volubility. He was more likely to simply wander off after rehearsal or class rather than to actually turn down an invitation. He attended just enough parties in a term, was around during just enough lunch breaks, and put in just enough dinner appearances. As far as any one of us knew, his one intimate relationship was an impromptu and never-repeated slightly boozy Halloween-party hook-up with our former-stage-manager-gone-to-Detroit, Rita.

The exception to all this was Anna. Their friendship began in late fall of sophomore year. We'd catch them in conversation on a bench or at lunch for two. They'd occasionally volunteer to be scene partners, another exception to Stacey's general ambivalence toward us. ("I'm an actor," he once told me. "I have to be able to work with anyone.")

During the first two years after graduation, no one saw Stacey, not even Anna. When she invited him to the first meeting of the company, she'd done so with little expectation. However, he showed up, and with the Two following dutifully behind. All three returned for the next meeting, and the next, and again and again. And though all Stacey would confirm was that they did indeed live together, it was clear that the Good Company had its very own long-term ménage. Even Rita gave up the last shred of her illusions about Stacey.

Stacey had two passions: acting and the Two. The Two had two passions: Stacey and color.

"We don't know your name," Two #1 said to me as Marcus patiently explained to Herb why neither the boob trick nor the line "Come here often, sailor?" were going to find their way into Shakespeare.

"I'm Nicky D'Amico. I'm the stage manager. I went to school with Stacey."

"He never mentioned you," Two #1 said.

"Not once," Two #2 added.

What could I say to that?

"Yeah, fine. Look, I really need you guys to move a few rows away so I can concentrate. Can you do that for me?"

Again the blank stares.

"It would be a big help," I said.

"No, it won't." This was Two #1.

"Yes, it will," I said. "Really. It will."

"No." Two #2 shook his head and sighed. "We put him in a deep blue shirt. We armored him in tranquility. But the other one is wearing magenta. A much too bright magenta."

Two #1 shrugged his shoulders. "It won't help him for us to move. This is not getting any better tonight."

"It would help me work."

I didn't think it was possible for a blank look to go more blank. I was wrong.

"Guys," Stacey interrupted us from the stage. "Let Nicky work."

"OK." The Two jumped up and moved to the far end of the row. Stacey went back to arguing with Herb and Marcus.

"Do you think he keeps them on a leash at home?" Alex asked, none too quietly, sitting down next to me.

Two #2 actually hissed.

"Like master, like dog," Alex said in a very audible pretend whisper.

The Two rose from their seats.

"Leave it," Stacey barked at them from the stage. He didn't bother to acknowledge Alex.

"You are the kinkiest uptight Mary I've ever met," Herb said to Stacey.

"Do not call me Mary." Stacey barely contained his anger.

Marcus intervened. "Can we focus here?"

"I can," Stacey said. He cast a death look at Alex.

"I see working together hasn't improved your relationship," I said to Alex in a true whisper as work resumed onstage.

"What relationship?" he answered, this time quietly enough that only I heard him.

I just shrugged. Alex's initial freshman-year fascination with "the Big One" had given way over time to the same nonthreatening civility we all shared with Stacey, only to be replaced in the fall of sophomore year with a subdued but mutual animosity. This was as old a piece of news as my relationship with Marcus. I pretended to go back to working hard.

In fact, I was doing far less work than usual, but who ever wants to admit that? Rita's notes on the production were in good order and easy to follow. What was happening onstage was moving very slowly as Marcus picked his way through scenes he thought needed a bit more polish. Other than prompting forgotten lines, my only real effort had been a mental inventory of how to arrange the stage during the performance. There was very little scenery to speak of, but the physical running of the show—where props and costumes were stored, how objects moved in and out of view—was very much a concern.

"You are so diligent, Nicky," Alex said, smirking. "It is really a turn-on. What are you doing later?"

I continued ignoring him. Onstage, Marcus and Stacey were trying to have a conversation about the nature of Oberon and Titania's feud. Herb, being far less interested in motivation than couture, wanted to discuss hairpieces.

"Nicky." Marcus turned toward me with a look that would terrify even an imaginary fairy. "Is it time for a break?"

"Time for two if you like," I said.

"Let's make it ten minutes. I'm going out back. Outside." Marcus marched toward the rear curtains. As he walked, he reached for a pack of cigarettes that wasn't there and cursed himself for giving up tobacco at the same time he'd given up alcohol. He pushed a panel of the heavy black fabric aside, exiting through the metal doors that opened onto a small serviceway behind the theater. This space was not really an alley, but rather a leftover loading area from the microbrewing days.

Stacey turned on Herb and bellowed in his best-trained, deep register, "Go thy way. Thou shalt not from this grove till I torment thee." He then stepped off the stage and took refuge with the Two. They huddled together, no doubt planning a dye job on the blue shirt.

"That's not how the line goes," I said.

"It'll do." He didn't even look up from his conversation.

Herb was alone onstage. He looked truly bewildered. "Are we at least going to run lines? OK, I guess not. So am I the only one around here who wants to work?"

I looked at my prompt book, the master script of all the blocking and technical cues that I keep during rehearsal. Alex started counting overhead light instruments.

"Whatever." Herb headed for the lobby.

"What has he got out there—a drunken sailor?" Alex asked.

"You stole that line from George S. Kaufman," I said.

"Steal only from the best."

"I don't understand," I said. "Didn't Marcus talk to Herb about what happens in rehearsal *before* he cast him?"

"I would assume so." Alex shrugged. "Everything was OK until just a few days ago. He's been getting worse. He's not much of an actor, but I suppose he can read a calendar as well as anyone. It is Saturday. We have an audience in two weeks."

"So what? He thinks he can dish out more of this shit before anyone will want a new Titania this late into it?"

"I figure it is going to be a very long week. Marcus does look good, doesn't he?"

There it was again. Just like earlier in the evening, that hint of something more intimate in the sound of his voice. I gave him my version of the you-are-falling-so-short-of-expectations face. "Alex, what have you been doing?" I asked.

"I am just saying he looks good. As in, not drinking agrees with him. He's confident. He's healthy. It's good."

"Fine."

"You are completely wrong, Nicky."

"Then what are you planning to do?"

"Nothing," he said, but he wasn't looking directly at me anymore.

"Your nothings come like bricks," I quoted.

"*The Lion in Winter.* Anyway, I thought you two were over long ago."

"Oh no. No. No," I said. "You are not going to turn this on me."

"Methinks the lady doth protest—"

Anna interrupted our war of overused quotations. She'd been out in the box office all evening. She didn't look like she was having fun. "You guys on break?"

"More accurately, we've broken," I said.

"Good." She wasn't really listening. "Look, the box-office computers are a total mess, Nicky. When is Roger coming?"

Before I could answer, the Two called out in unison, "Hello, Anna."

"Hi, guys," she said. "You behaving?"

The Two giggled, smiling extraordinarily pleased and silly grins. They went back to their conversation with Stacey, who hadn't looked up once.

"OK. That was creepy," I said.

Alex pretended he hadn't seen.

Anna just shrugged her shoulders. "You haven't met Suege."

"What's that?" I asked.

"Who. Our landlord. Creepy is a compliment. I just ran into him in the lobby. He invited me to come up to his studio to pose." She faked a shudder.

"How is it," I took the opportunity to ask, "that you managed to not mention Herb when we had lunch?"

"I didn't?" Anna actually pulled off looking innocent. She was good.

"I still don't understand why we are responsible for repairing the computers. Aren't there other companies renting here?" Alex asked.

"They don't open in two weeks," Anna answered.

"How much is this going to set us back?" Alex wanted to know.

Anna looked at me. "How expensive is Roger?"

"You make him sound like a high-priced whore. He's doing it as a favor to me, assuming it isn't too, too complicated," I answered.

"We don't have any money to spare," Anna said. She looked at Alex, who mimicked her sour expression.

"That is the truth," he said.

Since I'd signed on with no expectations and wasn't a company member, I ignored the topic.

Just then, Marcus returned from his break.

He looked at the three of us, then at Stacey and the Two.

"I want you to know," he said, "honestly, I love you all. Each of you. And no matter what happens next, you should never forget that. Ever. Now get Herb."

Oberon stood resolute above the lounging Titania. "Why should Titania cross her Oberon? I do but beg a little changeling boy..."

"There's a joke here about—," Herb started.

"Line," Marcus shouted.

I prompted just a few of the next words. "A little changeling boy to be my..."

"I do but beg a little changeling boy to be my henchman." Titania waved him away and gestured to one of her fairy attendants. "Set your heart at rest." She barely gave Oberon any attention. "The fairy land buys not..."

Herb broke from the scene. "Fairies are—"

Marcus pounced. "Line."

"Buys not the child of me...," I called out.

"Give me that boy and I will go with thee." Oberon makes one last effort.

"Not for thy fairy kingdom…"

"Y—"

"Line."

"Not for thy fairy kingdom. Fairies away."

And, in a whisper from three rows back: "Maybe that blue is dark enough."

So it went for forty-five minutes. Marcus, who must have had the best ten-minute break in the history of theater, drove rehearsal forward. At each pause in the dialogue, Herb rushed to insert his comments and, just as quickly, Marcus cut him off. If the words coming out of Herb's mouth were not Shakespeare's, Marcus was there to silence him. If he tried one bit of undirected shtick, Marcus pounced. Add in the bad relations between Alex and Stacey, and Stacey and Herb, and there was plenty of tension on which to build the Titania and Oberon confrontation. Marcus was relentless in using it. Long before the evening ended, Herb actually began to look as angry as Titania should have been.

"Yes." Marcus pointed to Herb. "See that face. Can you feel that, Herb? That's what Titania feels when she sees Oberon."

———————

Herb skulked out the moment I called an end to the evening. Stacey and the Two lent a hand cleaning up the space. The Two enthusiastically helped Anna where they could and pointedly ignored Alex. Finally, they headed out, no doubt looking for an all-night clothing store from which to augment their anti-Herb wardrobe. Just as it had on so many late nights at school, the evening ended with Marcus, Anna, Alex, and me sitting in an empty theater, the stage dark, the air chilly.

"Why am I always hungry after rehearsal?" Anna asked. She was sitting in the front row, legs stretched out.

"You weren't even in here tonight," I said.

"He is awful." Alex said aloud what we were all thinking.

"No," Marcus said, sitting on the edge of the stage, "he's not awful. You'll see. Once he's in performance, he'll be fine. Trust me."

Alex just shook his head. "Could you come up with any fainter praise with which to damn him?"

"How do you do that?" Marcus asked. "How do you automatically not put prepositions at the end of sentences?"

Alex shrugged. "I've told you—taught by nuns."

"You have to keep him from making it up each night," Anna said.

Alex was sitting in the second row. He put his head down on the back of the seat in front of him. "Oh God. And I'm going to be out there with him."

"It's going to be fine," Marcus repeated, patting the top of Alex's head.

"'Fine' is a really ugly word in this context. We need better than 'fine,'" Anna said.

"Then we will need better than Herb," Alex sighed.

Marcus tried to reassure us. "Look, I realize it's not turning out the way we'd hoped. But it's going to work. It is."

"Are you going to get something to eat?" Alex asked, having resigned himself sufficiently to his fate to at least allow for a late-night snack.

Anna couldn't imagine where he'd gotten such an idea. "Are you kidding? At this hour?"

"Then is anyone going for a drink? I need a drink."

Obviously, Alex needed a diversion. So much so that it took him a moment to realize what he'd said. Silence crashed on us like a loose, heavy piece of scenery.

"I'm not really up for one," Anna said, trying to cover the awkward moment. "It's a long day tomorrow."

"Come on," Marcus said. "It's OK. You can mention going for a drink. I'm not going to collapse into an emotional heap or rush for the nearest bar. It's OK."

"How about you, Nicky? You are my last hope," Alex said.

The next day's schedule was busy. We were starting at one o'clock. First warm-ups, then costume parade, then a full run-through, and more rehearsal after dinner. This was just the sort of schedule that should have sent me home for a good night's sleep. Considering that my home was only five blocks away, I'd every good reason to get to bed at a decent hour.

"Nope. I'm going home too," I lied. Is reason ever highly rated on a Saturday night?

Not that I didn't want to have a drink with Alex. I adored Alex. But the next day really was going to be very hectic. In fact, the entire week was going to be a mad dash. I wanted to fortify myself, but a collegial drink with an old friend was not exactly the bracing I sought. There was, however, a bar on East 4th Street—not much to look at, but in about one hour it was very likely to start filling up with exactly the kind of new friend I was interested in meeting for the night. I was a single twenty-six-year-old gay man living in Manhattan. I had every intention of exercising my subcultural prerogatives.

Alex looked dejected. "Guess I will go home. You people used to be much more fun."

Marcus stood up. "Oh, think of how happy you'll be, all rested up tomorrow."

Alex pretended to think about it for a moment, then smiled at Marcus. There it was again. I had that feeling that the guys either had crossed or were at least thinking about crossing a line. I assured myself my only concern was for the production.

"Leave it to a reformed partier to take the fun out of Saturday night," Alex said.

Just then, we heard a sound behind one of the rear curtains. Someone was coming down the back steps from the dressing room. Anna looked at me. I shrugged. I'd thought everyone but us was gone.

The curtains parted. Herb Wilcox strolled through. When he saw us, he showed a moment's surprise, which he immediately hid under a look of disinterest. It was the most captivating thing he'd done onstage all evening.

"Good night," he said, as he passed by on his way to the lobby.

Anna watched him exit. "He was in a hurry," she said, her voice edged with distrust.

SUNDAY MORNING

I LECTURED. I PATIENTLY explained. I tried bribery. Once I even threatened an intervention. Still, every so often, my futon, if not absolutely drunk, ended up less than completely sober on a Saturday night. Or was it early Sunday morning?

Wasn't it bad enough that I had failed in my search for fun? Oh sure, I'd run into one of my Classmates. A long conversation, very nice. He may have wanted more—it was unclear—but in any case there was this other guy. I just couldn't take my eyes off him, and maybe there'd been a chance, just a moment—one glance? No. I did have the good grace to leave before last call. I left alone—alone *and* sober. I had exercised restraint, but my furniture had been drinking.

I stood in the doorway, hands gripping the doorjamb. The futon, in bed formation, rocked gently back and forth in the middle of my studio apartment. I'd seen it in worse shape. I guessed it was a beer night. If it had been gin, the thing would have been dancing Martha Graham. From experience, I knew that the only solution was to toss myself, spread-eagle, across the bed, firmly grasping the sides.

Preparing to throw myself onto the futon, I began swaying in rhythm with the frame. When I was synched up, I pitched forward, hoping to catch it off-guard. The futon was ready for me, body-slamming me full force. I gasped once, holding on to the contents of my stomach. I managed to secure a grip on the edges and waited. All movement ceased. Triumphant, I raised my head to look about the room.

In front of me, the digital alarm clock was not impressed. It was deliberately obscuring information, reading either 3:35 or 8:66. How much of a fool did it think I was?

Next to it, the phone machine winked at me suggestively. I reached out and swatted the light. The machine, a never-to-be-trusted piece of electronics that referred to itself in the first person (as in "*I* will now erase your messages"), spoke in my voice.

"Hello, you've reached Nicky D'Amico at—"

I poked at another button. The devil in the box mimicked Alex.

"Nicky. Are you there? Pick up … I see you went right home. Well, I'm not going to tell this to your machine. Call me as soon as you get in. This is major. I mean truly, this will blow you away." This was followed by the machine's own voice: "Sunday, 2:45 a.m."

I woke. I was not happy. I was lying face-down on my futon, very hung over, still wearing my clothes.

It took me forty-five minutes, but eventually I was sitting by the window, coffee cup on the table, head in hand. I had barely two hours to get myself in order and get to the theater. At the rate I was moving, I'd need four.

41

I considered food but decided not just yet. I could always pick up a bagel at the corner on the way. Then again, it was cold out there, and food was probably a good idea for my body. That was two thoughts too many. I had more coffee. With my head in my hands, I wondered why it was that I hadn't just gone home after rehearsal. Truth is, I am a lightweight drinker. Now I was paying for the fun, if that's what it was. Rita Lombard, our AWOL stage manager, once told me, "Don't live it up if you can't live it down." I was feeling pretty down.

I sat very still, staring out the window at West 51st Street. It looked as if the January thaw, that strange three-to-five day period late in the month when all of North America warms up ten degrees, had ended during the night. Icicles hung from the masonry along the tops of the buildings across the street. A light snow crusted over the cars. Breath clouded the faces of the people walking below. Since this was New York City, my apartment was a hothouse. Heat poured uncontrollably from the radiator beneath the window. I didn't need to touch it to know that the riser in the corner was hot enough to blister. In winter, no matter how much the weather fluctuated, the temperature in my home never varied from "hot enough to dry fruit." I usually kept a window cracked open to let in a thin slice of fresh air.

My studio, not as small as most but nothing that anyone outside of New York would mistake for a real apartment, was cluttered. The unmade futon doubled as the couch. The long side walls that I shared with my neighbors were lined with bookcases. The short interior wall was entertainment central. I decided that a soothing piece of music might inoculate me against the inevitable onslaught of city noise waiting outside. I lurched over to the CD player and put on Beethoven's string quartets. If my morning activities hadn't included a hangover, I would have cleaned. Or at least rearranged the recyclables. As it was, having made it to the CD player, all I wanted to do was lie back down. ("Don't live it up if you can't live it down.")

My coffee sat on the table, enticing me like a willing blond surfer boy. I started toward it. After just two steps, the phone rang. The sound bounced through me, coming to rest just behind my right eye. So much for the medicinal effects of Beethoven. I stumbled to the receiver.

"Hello?"

"Jesus, Nicky, you sound like shit." Roger Parker's voice boomed in my ear.

"Sssshhh ... not so loud. I think we're being taped," I said.

"Are you hung over?"

Roger Parker and his lover, Paolo Suarez, were my best friends. They lived downtown in a SoHo loft subsidized by Paolo's trust fund. The miracle of telecommunication was pounding Roger's voice into my ear as if he were shouting at me from across the room. The global village was definitely overrated. How much nicer if Roger had nothing more than a telegram at his disposal?

"I am not hung over," I lied.

"Liar. So what time am I supposed to meet you?" he asked.

Meet me? Meet me? Meet me? When? Why? I finally recovered the thought. Roger was coming to the theater to give mouth-to-mouth to the box-office computer.

"Right. Meet me. I'm meeting Anna at noon. You can come anytime after that."

"OK. It'll probably be about then. Can I bring Paolo?"

That was no easy question. I adored Paolo. There were many reasons to do so: he was an excellent artist, a loyal friend, extremely

43

entertaining. He also had very little patience for people he didn't like or considered untalented. The last time he was loose in a theater where I was working, he managed to get into fights with both the set designer and the prop master in less than twenty-four hours.

"I know what you're thinking," Roger said. "He'll behave."

"Do you swear that—"

"I'll swear whatever you want me to swear," Roger said. "Just let me bring him."

"I don't know if I can handle this today," I said, thinking about more aspirin.

"It's not our fault you're hung over. Who was he, anyway?"

"There wasn't any 'he.' I came home alone," I said.

Roger started in on what was certainly going to be another lecture by another coupled friend on the virtues of settling down. "Nicky, you need to—"

"I ran into someone last night. I think."

"You think?"

"He's an old friend. One of my Classmates. Sean McGinn. Actually, he's in *Midsummer*. I haven't seen him in a long time. I think he's been out of town, but I swear he was interested."

"A rerun?" Roger insisted on believing that I'd spent my undergraduate years sleeping my way through the Baldwin Drama Department. Strictly speaking, this was very nearly the truth, but Roger had no solid reason to know that. He was just assuming. Yes, that's a fine distinction, but nonetheless, I was annoyed. I take my comfort where I can.

"No, not a rerun. And enough with the tone of voice. I get to choose who I date, not you."

"And how's that going for you?"

44

We both knew the unhappy answer to that question.

"Can we do this later? My head hurts."

"All right. But we worry."

"Yes, Mother."

"You know, I'm doing the computer work as a favor to you guys." He let this statement hang in front of me. The point seeped into my fuzzy brain.

"Ah, that's how it's going to be?" I gave in. "OK. OK. Bring him with you. But you're responsible."

"It's going to be OK. See you then."

"Fine. Fine." It was a measure of my hangover that I believed him.

"And drink lots of water." Roger hung up.

I reached over, picking up a small container of fish food, and drizzled flakes into the goldfish bowl. The fish had been an effort on my part to pacify Roger and Paolo after my last boyfriend, acquired while working one summer in western Pennsylvania, had decamped for the West Coast. We'd been together for only six months.

"At least get a pet. You need something alive in that apartment," Roger had said.

They were unimpressed with my choice.

"You can't take a fish for a walk, or pet it, or have it sit on your lap." Roger had sighed as he said this, as if my singleness was his personal burden.

"And naming him Sushi is beyond passive-aggressive," Paolo had added.

After feeding the fish, I saw the number 1 lit up in the display screen of the answering machine.

Right, I thought. *Alex.*

I pushed the play button to hear the message once more.

"Nicky. Are you there? Pick up ... I see you went right home. Well, I'm not going to tell this to your machine. Call me as soon as you get in. This is major. I mean truly, this will blow you away." Then the date and time stamp: "Sunday, 2:45 a.m."

I'd been too drunk to call him when I got in; now I was too hung over. Besides, what would I say to him? I'd refused his invitation to go out, claiming I wanted a good night's rest. Now he knew I'd not gone home from rehearsal. I could always try the truth. After all, why shouldn't I have gone out looking to get laid? Well, there was probably a list of reasons, but if you can't live it down, don't live it up.

———————

I finally scraped myself together and made it out the door. I'd caught a very lucky break when a cousin moved from New York to Chicago just as I was moving into the City. A good word to the management company and I was living alone in a rent-stabilized apartment in Hell's Kitchen while most of my Classmates were two and three to smaller apartments on the Lower East Side or in Brooklyn. The other exception was Alex. He was an only child whose ambiguous and often angry relationship with his mother still left room for her to help him live in a studio on West 47th Street. My apartment was in an old limestone building, five stories with only four apartments on each floor. I lived on the fifth floor.

Hoping the extra effort would contribute to clearing my head, I skipped the elevator and took the stairs at the back of the building. I wasn't paying attention to my surroundings, as I'd been up and down the modestly lit, off-white stairwell many times. Instead,

I was trying to figure out what could have happened to Alex that was important enough for him to call so late and yet be something he didn't want to tell the machine.

Suddenly, I was face to face with Mrs. Wizniski from apartment 1D. She was standing in the first-floor hallway, blocking my path. On the other side of her was the inside door of the small entranceway into the building. Beyond that, I could see the mailboxes and buzzers, the front door, and freedom.

"You must go to the store for me. I need milk." She thumped her stick—the type ballet teachers always carry in movies—on the floor as she attempted to jam a five-dollar bill into my hand. "Go to the store for me. I need milk."

Mrs. Wizniski had lived in the building for thirty years. At eighty-five, she was the senior tenant in all respects. She was a nice lady, the kind who, until she was too old to handle the volume, made Christmas cookies by the vat and passed them out to other tenants. Everyone loved her. She was four feet eleven with steel gray hair and an endless supply of housecoats. The younger tenants (God forgive us) condescendingly thought of her as "cute." She was so beloved that when, two years earlier, she'd taken to standing in the hallway and asking tenants if we might pick up a few items while we were out, no one had objected. But those two years had not been kind to Mrs. Wizniski. The situation had deteriorated rapidly in the past six months. Now she was at the door several times a day, demanding one item after another. Most of us still tried to help.

"I need milk." Bang with the stick.

"Good morning, Mrs. Wizniski," I said, attempting to get past her.

"Milk." Bang.

47

"You know, I'm really sorry, but I'm going to be late for rehearsal."

Bang. Bang. Bang.

I expected to see a piece of the black-and-white-tiled floor chip off under the onslaught. In fear of having my foot shattered, I stepped back beyond the range of her stick.

A head popped out of 1C.

"Morning, Nicky. Mrs. Wizniski."

"Milk." Bang.

"Camille, can you … ?" I tilted my head toward our neighbor.

"Yes," Camille said. "I'll take this one. But you owe me."

Camille and her boyfriend had been living in the building when I moved in. They were a cleanly scrubbed blond couple in their mid-thirties, both of whom did something in banking that they tried to explain to me at least once a year.

"Thank you." I turned back to Mrs. Wizniski. "Camille will help you."

"Milk." She shoved the money at me again.

"No, Mrs. Wizniski." Camille stepped into the hallway, pulling on her coat. "I'm going to the store. Not Nicky."

Mrs. Wizniski shifted her focus. I slipped out the front door.

On the street, grateful to be on my way (and feeling just a little guilty), I pulled my collar up, tugged my scarf over the lower half of my face, and headed west, toward the theater. I was only walking five blocks, but the temperature was well below freezing and every breeze slammed into my face like an ice pack. Still, the air was clean, the sun was out, and I was in motion. It was to be the happiest moment I'd have all day.

SUNDAY AFTERNOON

"… SPACE IS AT …"

"… a premium. An empty …"

"… high forehead is …"

"… forehead …"

"Share the words. Let them breathe."

"… is a striking placement for …"

"… advertisement tattoos …"

"Damn."

"Stay with it, Eduardo," Marcus said.

"Sorry, but on your forehead?"

Marcus Bradshaw was onstage with Phil Cook and Eduardo Lugo, the actors playing Helena and Lysander. Marcus was a great believer in the *Daily News* exercise. He swore by it as the perfect warm-up to help actors actually listen to each other onstage, not just recite lines of dialogue. Like Herb Wilcox, most of the Classmates were skeptical about its ultimate value, but as Eduardo had said, heading for the stage, "At least it'll be warmer up there."

Eduardo was the "cranky one" of us all, a misanthropic Coloradan who had still not lost his basic distrust of the East Coast despite eight years of residence. His first meeting with Anna, which had landed him on the floor of Rita's home, was a fairly typical example of Eduardo's social skills. Nonetheless, after four years at school, even he had found a niche in the insular world of Baldwin students. His personality showed in the perpetually tense lines of his body. Onstage, I'd seen him ignite that coiled energy into a slow-burn sexiness. He was playing Lysander, one of the young lovers. I fully expected that Eduardo's performance would be a high point in the otherwise spotty production. I also knew that he was usually even more stressed in the last days of any rehearsal period. Then his natural agitation would explode with the slightest provocation. This close to opening, Eduardo had two settings: irritable and scorched-earth. Under the circumstances, having him take the lack of heat with minimum fuss was a near miracle.

When Anna and I had arrived at noon, we'd expected to meet Roger and Paolo. Instead, we found that the heat was out. With the outside temperature in the low twenties, it could not have been more than fifty degrees inside the Tapestry Theater. Today being costume parade, the actors were going to try on the various pieces that our designer, Laura Schapiro, had brought together. A cold theater was never ideal for costume parade. It would be extra hard on the cast in this production. Marcus's idea for the show, combined with our own limited budget, resulted in a look that evoked "Shakespeare meets an updated *Beach Blanket Bingo*." Of course, the beach we had in mind was more Santa Monica than Nome. It was going to be particularly hard on Alex, as Puck, and on the male chorus. He wore only a Speedo and they were in spandex bike shorts.

"This sucks."

"Ah, Anna. Always to the point," I said.

She pulled out her cell phone and punched a speed dial. There was no answer.

"Suege. Anna Mikasa with the Good Company." She spoke very slowly and distinctly. "We are at the theater. There is no heat. No heat, Suege. We need heat. Call me. ASAP." She shut the phone. "He is never around when you need him."

"Thinking of posing in exchange for heat? Hey, would that be body heat?"

"You're a very sick man."

"Thanks," I said. "Look, we can turn the stage lights on to warm up the stage, but that means we're going to blow out the lamps."

"Lamp-replacement costs aren't in our contract. It's overhead for the Brewery. It's their heat that's off." Anna was referring to the cost of replacing individual bulbs (or lamps) in each light instrument hanging over the stage. If we turned them on, soon enough they'd provide a reasonable amount of comfort in that small space. The problem was, they'd also burn out sooner, probably in the middle of a performance.

"I don't think we can heat the dressing room," I said.

"Then we won't." Anna shrugged, as if this was some minor inconvenience. "I'm going to buy space heaters. When Laura shows up, you two drag the costumes down here. We'll heat part of the house with the heaters, the stage with the lights. I'll be back." Without waiting for my response, she turned and marched herself out of the building. A crisis always gave Anna a happy sense of purpose. I swear I heard her whistling as she exited to the lobby.

Laura Schapiro arrived a few minutes later. She was swaddled in oversized winter clothing and lugged bundles of costumes in plastic bags. As a group of actors and directors, the Classmates at the core of the Good Company did not have reliable design skills. Laura, like the lighting and sound designers, was a "friend of the family" acquired by one of us in the years since graduation. She had signed on for what turned out to be not so much costume design as a good "cajoling" of costumes. She was borrowing, digging through actors' closets, thrift-shopping, and stitching her way to a fully clothed cast on what she hoped was the smallest budget with which she'd ever have to work. She was mercifully good natured about the process.

"Good morning." She plopped her baggage down in the first row and started to unpeel her outer garments. "Damn, it's cold in here. Where's the heat?"

"On its way," I said, filling her in on the plan.

We decided to line one of the aisles with costume racks. Then, if we unscrewed a few mirrors from the dressing-room walls, propped them on the seats, and cranked the house lights, it might work.

We were almost set up when Anna returned. She'd found a hardware store on 9th Avenue and had purchased three space heaters, four emergency blankets, and three road flares.

"A flare?" I asked as she held one up.

"I've been known to turn a few heads." Anna smiled at her joke.

Laura and I stared at her silently.

"It was worth at least a giggle."

"Yeah. OK." Laura went back to work.

Anna scowled at us.

"The flares are for fun. When we've reached the bitching point and it looks like someone is finally going to lose it and kill Herb, we go out back. We light the flares. Pretend it's a bonfire."

"Fine." I went back to work.

"We are doing this costume parade today," she said. "I don't care how cold it gets."

For Anna, this was a pep talk.

I've seen this need in producers and directors to combat the weather. They do it not just by heating cold spaces or air-conditioning hot ones. I knew one director who would, on a hot summer day, make everyone in his cast chant, "It's hot as fucking hell." He insisted this would get the complaining "out of our systems." Mostly, the shouting just made everyone sweat.

We were just finishing the setup when the others began to arrive. They were understandably skeptical, but willing. By the time Peter Chang, who was playing Hermia, and Peter Timcko, playing Demetrius, replaced Phil and Eduardo onstage, most everyone was settled into the idea of dashing from heater to heater, then to stage and back.

"The man was found…"

"…nude in his chimney…"

"…chimney. Shit."

"That's OK. It's all right," Marcus said. "Pick it up right there."

"Police suspect…"

I was sitting in the front row with Anna. We were trying to stay out of Laura's way as she worked to get the entire cast dressed at once. *Midsummer* is a big show as written. When we added Marcus's fairy chorus, the total number of actors came to eighteen. Today was the opportunity to see all of them together in costume, a chance for the director and designer to make adjustments before the process got any further along.

"Why are the lights on? Who the fuck is burning my lamps? What the hell is going on?" Aliza Buday, lighting designer, had arrived. Aliza was not known for diplomacy. She wasn't even known for civility. Mostly, she was known for working cheap.

"It's cold in here," she said. "Turn on the goddamn heat. And turn off my lights."

"Good afternoon, Aliza," I said.

"The lights are on because the heat's broken," Anna said.

"You're running my lights to warm yourselves?" Clearly, Aliza preferred frozen corpses to burnt-out lamps.

Anna started to explain in her best calm and controlled producer's tone. "It's a costume parade, Aliza. Some of these guys are only going to be in bike shorts. I wanted—"

Aliza cut her off. "I didn't design it."

"Hey. What are we supposed to do, freeze to death?" It was Eduardo, hunkered down at a nearby heater, coming to life about the situation at precisely the wrong moment.

"Eduardo—" I didn't get to finish.

"How the hell should I know what you're supposed to do?" Aliza turned on him: cranky versus crankier. It looked as if they would start tearing the down out of each other's coats at any moment.

"The lights stay on. Everyone"—here Anna paused for effect—"chill out." She and the lighting designer glared at each other for a moment.

"OK. But don't expect me to drag my ass up that ladder all week long to replace burnt-out lamps." Aliza shot this last remark at me.

She was five feet ten with a wide girth that seemed equal in diameter at every point along her body from her shoulders to her hips. Watching Aliza work on a ladder was a suspense-filled experience. They twisted under her, but none had broken—so far.

"Not a problem," I said, perhaps too heartily.

Unable to decide if I'd insulted her or not, Aliza quietly retreated to a seat near a heater, squeezed into it, and sat there scowling at the air in front of her.

"Sorry, guys." Eduardo offered his apologies to Anna and me.

Anna put her arm around his shoulder. "Eduardo. Dear Eduardo. Please. Until we open, don't speak to anyone but Nicky and me, OK?"

He laughed. "I'm not that bad."

"Oh, but you are," I said. "In fact, talk only to Anna."

"Coward," she countered.

"All right, all right. I'll behave." Eduardo found a heater as far from Aliza as he could.

Roger and Paolo arrived during the third and final *Daily News*. This time Al Benning and Stacey Rose were onstage reading an article about a six-year-old who'd driven his parents' car to a 7-Eleven to get a Slurpee.

Paolo led the way down the aisle toward us. "It's freezing in here. Why can't you find a job with decent working conditions, Nicky?"

Anna jumped when she saw them. "At last."

"Sorry. *We* had to go back and change clothes—three times," Roger explained, making it very clear which part of "we" he was referring to.

"How was I to know the temperature had dropped ten degrees? Twenty-three degrees requires a completely different outfit than thirty-three degrees." Paolo looked to Anna and me for support.

"You looked great," Roger said. "You looked great the first time you changed. You looked great the second time. You look great now. You always look great. What does it matter what you're wearing?"

Paolo smiled at his lover. "Isn't he sweet?"

Roger shook his head.

Four years earlier, having just arrived in New York, I'd befriended Roger Parker at a temp job. We were both new in town. When another friend invited me to an art opening, I'd dragged Roger along. The sculpture on display was Paolo's. Within six months, to the complete surprise of everyone who knew them, Paolo Suarez, native New Yorker and visual artist, and Roger Parker, fresh-faced, recently emigrated Midwestern systems operator, had merged their lives and household goods.

They peeled off their outer layer of clothing—heavy wool overcoats with an extra lining that added visible bulk to even the wiry-thin Paolo. He was as tall as me, which made him a good four inches shorter than Roger.

"I know this place," Paolo said. "There are art studios for rent on the top three floors, right?"

As they settled their pile of garments, Sean McGinn, the Classmate I'd run into the night before, arrived.

"Hello, everyone." Sean was holding out a cup of coffee. "Nicky, I thought you might want this."

His smile hinted at how drunk he must have thought I'd been at the bar. I'd seen that smile on men before. They always had something in mind beyond hot caffeine. I smiled back, uncertain at best.

Sean was the Classmate easily labeled as everyone's favorite. He was, without a doubt, the nicest of us. A kind man who never lost his sense of theater as fun. No matter how late the rehearsal hour, how brutal the critique from teachers (or fellow students), Sean continued to maintain his optimistic belief that he was blessed to be able to work in theater. He wasn't bad looking either: not quite six feet, with dirty blond hair and gray eyes. A man whose sweet smile hadn't dimmed since I'd first met him.

"Hey, thanks." I took the coffee and did the honors. "Sean, these are my friends, Roger Parker and Paolo Suarez."

"Nice to meet you." Sean extended his hand to both.

Paolo shook hands vigorously. "Sean? Yes, Nicky has told us all about you."

"How nice to finally meet you," Roger jumped right in.

They'd only been in the building three minutes, and already I regretted inviting them.

Sean blushed. Anna, covering her mouth with her hand, was busy looking at her feet.

"Damn," Sean said. "I forgot to get one for myself."

Onstage, Sean was amazing: focused, funny as needed, the type of actor who electrified the space around him. Audiences had to work to take their eyes off him. In our production, he played Bottom, the lead clown, who is transformed by Puck into a donkey and provides the main comic counterpoint to the romance onstage.

Offstage there was a completely different Sean. He was the kind of guy you kept expecting to run into walls or doorjambs. He might walk through a screen door or forget where he left his backpack. Still, even for Sean, only buying coffee for me when he set out to buy one for each of us was a new level of preoccupation. I took it as further proof that I was the object of unanticipated attention.

"Well, look. I should go change. Nice to meet you." Sean went in search of Laura Schapiro.

"That's the guy from last night, right?" Roger asked.

"Last night?" Anna cocked an eyebrow at me.

"We ran into each other when I was out for a drink," I said before remembering that I'd made a big deal of needing to go home early.

Anna laughed. "I'm not your mother, Nicky. You don't need to explain to me."

"He's cute. And he likes you," Paolo said.

"We all think he's sweet," Anna said.

"Oh." Roger shook his head. "That's too bad, then."

"What does that mean?" Anna asked.

"Our Nicky's more of a bad-boy type." Paolo patted my arm. "That's OK. Everyone has their thing."

"And some are just less useful than others," Roger added.

Paolo twisted the knife. "Nicky has issues, you know."

"I prefer to think of them as hobbies, thank you," I said.

Anna raised her hands and stepped back. "I'm out of this."

I was saved, in the sense of being pushed from the fortieth-floor window before the flames engulf you, by the arrival of the Two.

"He doesn't look so good."

"Too blue and the wrong shade of it."

"He's olive. He needs some green."

"Green will balance him."

The Two had snuck up on us. I could see no good coming of Paolo meeting the color boys. I shot him a warning look.

"And betrayal," Two #1 said, continuing their critique.

"Yes. That shade of blue suggests betrayal," Two #2 agreed.

In taking off his coat, Paolo had revealed a teal sweater.

"This shade of blue suggests a sale at my favorite store in SoHo," Paolo responded. Then, to me, "What are these?"

"Guys," I said to the Two, "shouldn't you be helping Laura?"

"We're done with Stacey's costume." Two #1 gave me that blank look again.

"There's nothing more we can do." Two #2 looked equally baffled. Had I actually suggested they do something not connected to Stacey?

"Not now."

"Nothing."

They went silent and stared off at the exit sign for a moment. Then, responding to some shared internal cue, they both turned their attention on Roger.

"This one is too pale," Two #1 said.

"Too pale," Two #2 repeated, pointing at Roger's strawberry blond hair and winter-white skin.

They then simultaneously turned and walked back up the aisle, taking seats to watch Stacey onstage.

"What are they?" Roger asked.

"They're with Stacey," Anna said.

"I told you about them." I pointed to Stacey onstage. "You know, the ménage."

"Christ, you didn't come close to the weirdness in describing them," Paolo said, looking at his sweater.

"Are they twins?" Roger asked, with a lilt in his voice that both surprised and appalled Anna and me.

"They most certainly are not," Anna snapped.

"Oh." Roger's disappointment was clear enough to be read in the back of the balcony, if we'd had a balcony.

Anna raised an eyebrow in an appeal to Paolo, who shrugged and said, "Trust me. You do not want to know what goes on in Midwestern suburbs. Why is it so cold in here? And loud? Aren't rehearsals supposed to be quiet?"

Under normal circumstances, he'd have been right. But shoving everyone into one space for dressing and rehearsal was well beyond normal. As I explained our situation, scraps of conversation came at us from all directions, including the *Daily News* exercise onstage.

"We're just having utility trouble today," Anna said. "Nothing serious. Nothing that will stop us."

Alex joined us. He was wearing a very large, exceptionally comfy- and warm-looking bathrobe and a pair of Nikes.

"Hello," he said, looking at the stage, not us.

This time, Anna did the intros.

"Do you always have a bathrobe around in case the heat goes out?" Roger asked.

"Pardon?"

"The robe?" Roger repeated.

"Oh." Alex turned toward us. "No, this is my costume."

He opened the robe to reveal a pair of emerald green Speedos and nothing else.

"I brought the robe with me because I get cold even when the heat is on."

"Wow." Roger stared, marveling at the wonders of costuming, or perhaps at Alex in his Speedo. In either case, Paolo was not amused.

"You guys should get to it, shouldn't you?" Paolo said. "You never know how long these things will take."

"What things?" Alex asked.

"The computer things." Paolo placed a hand on Roger's back and began to gently push him toward the lobby.

"Oh, right," Alex said. "Well, do what you need to do, it's just money." It didn't seem as if he was paying any attention to us. In fact, he was behaving and speaking in a very un-Alex-like manner.

"Just money? Are you OK?" Anna asked.

"Yes. Yes I am. I am just thinking." His gaze remained fixed on the stage.

That's when I remembered the phone call. "You called me last night. I'm so sorry, I just remembered."

"Don't stare." Two #1 was back.

"We don't like it when you stare at him." Two #2 was right behind.

"He doesn't like ..."

"... to be stared at."

"No, he ..."

"... does not."

"Are you talking to me?" Alex's attention snapped back from wherever his mind had been wandering.

"You're staring at Stacey." Two #1 was beginning to sound like a hurt child.

"What? I ... Never mind. I'll speak with you later, Nicky." Alex headed back to the costume area.

"And he shouldn't be wearing that green," Two #1 said.

"It's deadly for him," Two #2 added.

"He's a little spacey, isn't he?" Roger asked.

"Not usually." Anna turned to the Two. "Guys, go sit down, all right? Leave Alex alone."

"OK, Anna," they practically chirped as they headed back to their seats.

"What is it with you and them?" I asked. "They never listen to me."

"Some people," she said, "are just enamored of my flair."

Aliza, scrunched in a nearby seat and buried up to her eyes in her coat, grunted.

"Let's get you set up," Anna said, and led Roger to the box office.

Back onstage, "I wanted…"

"…a Slurpee…"

"…the seven-year-old…"

"…driver…"

"What are they doing?" Paolo asked, nodding toward the reading actors.

"It's an acting exercise. People bring in news articles and then they cold-read. They're supposed to work at reading them together. Sharing the story but not overlapping. It's a talking and listening thing."

"…the parents have been charged…"

"…charged…"

"Share," Marcus coached them quietly.

Paolo was skeptical. "That actually helps?"

"To a point," I said.

We watched for a moment as the actors, who were not yet in costume, and Marcus, wearing what looked to be three layers of clothing topped by a sweater, followed the story of the very juvenile delinquent.

Behind us, among the costume racks, the noise level continued to build. Like a city blackout, the heat problem created an atmosphere that was approaching carnival in its jauntiness. Ever louder bits of conversation were overlapping with the sounds of people running their lines.

"He finally left at 1:30. I thought I was going to have to …"

"Not in two weeks, no one …"

"How chance the roses there do fade so fast?"

"No, bigger than the governor …"

"Yes, but not until he gives …"

"Could ever hear by tale or history, the course of true love never did run smooth …"

Marcus had been struggling along, trying to make allowances for the crowded conditions. An outburst of laughter from the house finally put him over the edge.

"Nicky," he snapped.

I turned around. "Folks, could we have it a little quieter, please? Thank you."

Marcus went back to the exercise.

"So that's him," Paolo said, just loud enough to worry me.

"You keep it down too," I said.

"But of course. He's cute. They always are, though, aren't they? The drunk, charming, pathological ones."

"Stop it. It was seven years ago. We're friends now."

"No, Nicky. You and I are friends. You and he are ex-boyfriends. I don't believe in all this touchy-feely crap. An ex is an ex and a friend is a friend."

"You don't have many exes, do you?"

"I don't have many friends."

"Well, don't worry about me," I said. "Marcus and I *are* just friends. That's it."

"What he is, is the reason you avoid relationships."

"I do not avoid relationships. I have bad dating karma. You've said so yourself."

"I was trying to be kind. It's my nature."

The *Daily News* exercise finally came to an end. Marcus joined us in the first row.

"Nicky, let's take a break, OK? Then we'll start with the costumes. Hello." This last he addressed to Paolo, whom he'd never met. The tone of his voice hinted at remedying that.

"Hello. I'm Paolo. My *boyfriend*"—Paolo wielded the word as if he were waving garlic in a B-rate vampire film—"is in the box office fixing your computer. I'm Nicky's best friend and I do not like to see my friends fucked with."

The residual effects of my hangover, which I'd kept at bay for hours, slammed into the space just behind my eyes.

"OK, everyone," I said. "We're on a break. Take fifteen minutes and then we'll get started."

———

Anna, who'd left Roger in the box office, and I sat in the house near one of the heaters. Marcus, having added a coat to his multiple layers of clothing, was on his feet, anxiously moving from stage to house, changing his angle of view as needed. Aliza, two rows back and to our left, was close enough to comment on the action, but not close enough to appear friendly. Having extracted a vow of silence from Paolo, I allowed him to sit behind me.

First up were the mechanicals—the hapless tradespeople whose brush with Oberon and Titania provide so much laughter during the show. Shakespeare describes them as "rough mechanicals." Puck turns their de facto leader, a weaver named Bottom, into a donkey. He then sets Titania up with the love potion so that she "dotes upon an ass." Marcus wanted them looking like the surfer boys who hung out on the beaches of Southern California. One had a wetsuit with sleeves, one without. One had his suit rolled down to the waist; another wore boarding shorts. They were in blue and black with splashes of color coming from bright red and orange stripes and side panels. To set him apart, Sean McGinn, playing Bottom the Weaver, was in yellow shorts with an aqua and white neoprene shirt. There was no question, he looked very shiny.

"Bottom, huh?" Paolo said, just loud enough for Anna and me to hear.

"It's the character's name," I said.

"It certainly explains why—," he started.

Anna cut him off. "Stop." She held up her hand. "I don't want to know what it could possibly explain. I never want to know."

"All right." Paolo shrugged. "Live with your fantasy of Nicky's machismo."

"You promised to be quiet," I reminded him.

"I'm sorry. I thought you meant about the costumes. Which, I might add, is your good fortune. Not another word. Swear." He sat back in his seat.

"We don't like them," the Two called from a few rows back.

"From out of the mouths of freaks," Paolo mumbled to himself.

"No one asked you," Marcus shouted back at the Two, walking past us on his way to the stage.

"You're being very tetchy today," Anna said.

"I'm freezing, OK? Can we get on with this?" He shifted his focus back to the stage, where Laura Schapiro and the actors were engaged in a discussion about flexibility and ease of changing. I was paying close attention. Getting these guys in and out of this stuff quickly was going to require recruiting assistance from whoever among the cast was not busy.

"Too dark."

"No. Too blue. Always too blue."

"I'm warning you two," Marcus said, this time heading back into the house.

"But she's got it all wrong."

"All wrong."

"Guys, I think you should move farther back," I said, turning and giving them my sternest stage manager's glare.

"How come they get to talk and I don't?" Paolo asked.

Anna intervened. "No one gets to talk. Everyone quiet."

"Sorry, Anna."

"Yeah."

Silence from the Two.

Paolo sighed heavily.

"That shit doesn't match the color swatch I was given." Aliza Buday pried herself out of her seat. "I picked my color based on the swatches I was given. This isn't the answer to any goddamn question anyone is asking." She stomped onto the stage as she said this, confronting Marcus and Laura.

Aliza was referring to her "light gels," the tinted pieces of clear, high-quality film that give theater lights their color. Ideally, lighting designers choose these colors armed with color swatches from the costume designer and painted renderings from the set designer.

She waded into the actors, plucking at their wetsuits and scattering them like sand before a wave. The mechanicals quickly backstepped as she, Marcus, and Laura argued.

"If she gets—"

Anna cut off Two #1 with a raised hand, palm toward him.

The exchange with the Two and Aliza had momentarily stilled all conversation in the house, which then started up again in low whispers.

Eventually the argument settled in favor of the costumes. The mechanicals and the lighting designer tromped off, replaced by Stacey Rose. As king of the fairies, Oberon has his own trusty sidekick in Puck. Unfortunately for everyone, Puck is less than reliable and prone to practical jokes. It will be Puck who, in the heat of the action, misapplies the love potion to the sleeping lovers, causing even more confusion in their already tangled romances. Puck would also play the trick of "pin Titania on the donkey" to both the queen and Bottom the Weaver. Oberon and his sidekick would be in coordinated outfits. Stacey's basic costume was a square-cut Speedo that extended partway down his thighs. On top he'd sometimes have an open cotton shirt, sometimes not. Alex, who should have been onstage but wasn't, would be wearing the deep emerald racing Speedo we'd seen him in earlier.

The Two took a breath in unison as soon as Stacey appeared under the lights.

"No," Anna said, as if she were tending to a wayward dog. "Not a sound."

"But the costume person said we could talk …"

"… about the color."

"No." Anna had no intention of letting them slow us down any further.

Marcus turned to me. "Where's Alex?"

"I saw him just before break. Maybe he got dressed and went to the corner for something." There was a corner deli that supplied us with the essentials that fuel all theaters: water, coffee, Diet Coke, and cigarettes.

"He should be here." Marcus looked very annoyed.

He had every reason to be. We were now thirty minutes into the costumes. Add that to the fifteen minutes we took as a break, and Alex had already had forty-five minutes to buy whatever he'd wanted.

"We want to say something."

"No," Anna, Marcus, and I all answered simultaneously.

There was laughter from the actors waiting to go onstage.

The Two looked to Stacey for support.

True to form, he said nothing, just shook his head.

Stacey, Laura, and Marcus got into a discussion about the need for a different act 5 costume.

"So how's it going?" Roger said, slipping into the seat next to Paolo.

"So far, it's a lot of flesh. Not bad flesh, but a lot of it. Nicky, are we sure this is what Shakespeare had in mind?" Paolo asked.

I was beginning to wonder as the chorus of fairies marched onto the stage. Marcus had recruited the guys from gyms in Chelsea. They were each wearing Lycra bicycle shorts and sandals. Aside from talking trees, they'd act as furniture (thrones or couches) and various attendants. Their real job was to make the most of catching the pale blue moonlight Aliza would pour onto the stage, dialing the level of erotic heat up or down, depending on what the boys were up to.

"Oh, I think so," Roger said. "Why else have all that stuff about the animals and the fairies having sex. You know, I didn't realize Shakespeare was so erotic."

Anna and I turned in our seats. Paolo shook his head.

"I'll take this one," I said to Paolo. Then, to Roger, "What are you talking about?"

"The plot. That tall guy, what's his name? Herb? He told me. What I don't understand is, if the two guys escaping Athens to keep the mules they love are just a dream, then why does anyone have to go to jail? And why doesn't the king take the little boy?"

Paolo placed his hand lightly on Roger's forearm. "Roger, baby, when you were in high school English class back in Smallville, what did they make you read?"

"Books."

"Books." Paolo repeated the word as if considering an entirely new concept.

"Yeah. Books. What?"

Anna started to laugh, then caught herself when she saw the wounded look on Roger's face.

"That's not exactly how the story goes," I said. "It's a little more romantic than that." I explained the basic story lines to him: how Oberon, through Puck, meddles in the lives of the young lovers and eventually settles his differences with Titania.

"Doesn't sound romantic," he said. "Sounds confusing."

"No. Not at all. And the fun really starts when Puck uses the love potion to make Titania fall for one of the mechanicals he's turned into an ass."

"See, sweets, even these asses—"

Roger glanced at Paolo without really turning. "There are limits," he said.

Paolo stopped talking.

"Even better, Oberon sends Puck to straighten out the four lovers, but Puck screws it up and causes both guys to fall in love with the same woman." I was on a roll now, trying to describe the *Midsummer Night's Dream* I loved as opposed to the flesh spectacle onstage. "Are you with me?"

"Yeah. I'm not illiterate." Roger looked at Paolo as he said this.

Paolo protested his innocence like a kid up to his elbow in a cookie jar. "I was just asking what you read in high school."

Anna added her bit for the story. "It's very, very funny. I think it will be even funnier with just men. In Shakespeare's time women didn't perform onstage. All the roles were played by men."

"I still can't believe he had this level of drag in mind," Paolo said, watching Herb get dressed for his strut onstage. I didn't have the heart to look just yet.

"So no donkey sex?" Roger asked, in a way that made both Anna and me look elsewhere.

"No," Paolo answered, in a way that made us look back.

"So who were the guys with the bike shorts?" Roger, blissfully unaware of our swiveling attention, scoped out the chorus, who were changing into something warmer.

I was about to start in on Marcus's concept for the production when the director himself plopped down in the seat next to me.

"Get ready," he said.

"What's up?" I asked.

"Herb Wilcox in all his scary glory. He's next."

"Is that him?" Roger whispered much too loudly to Paolo.

Marcus laughed and turned around. "Yes, it's me. I'm the dog that broke Nicky's heart at school. Marcus Bradshaw. You're the person we thank for fixing the computers, right? Thanks." He smiled his toothiest grin.

"Roger Parker." Roger smiled right back. Marcus's smile actually brightened as they shook hands.

"And why aren't we in the box office giving the computer mouth-to-mouth?" Paolo asked.

"It's cold in there."

"It's cold out here," Paolo said.

"I needed a break."

"Then sit back and relax."

"What the hell is that?" Marcus's comment drew our attention away from the lovers' spat and to the stage.

Titania, queen of the fairies, was to be the reigning femme fatale of the beach: long, slinky lines, legs that—as they used to say—went well past the floor, and a sultry allure that practically shouted sun, sea, and cocoa butter. Marcus and Laura had envisioned a pale, luminous green swimsuit covered with a green gauze wrap. Herb, however, had decided to raid his own closet. After all, what better clothing to drape his towering, pencil-thin figure in than his own fabulous drag? Now he stood before us in all that resplendent glory. Laura stood to one side, resigned to her fate as costumer to the crazy.

"I thought Titania—"

"Paolo." I didn't even bother turning around.

It wasn't the fishnet or even the knee-high black stiletto boots. It may have been the black crushed-velvet bustier or the big red lips with black outline. It was definitely the leopard-print jacket and the Cher hair—the platinum, waist-length version.

"Now this is a queen for the fairies," Herb said, strutting back and forth.

"No. No. No."

"No animal prints."

"None."

The Two were rushing down the aisle. It looked as if they might charge onto the stage and attempt to strip Herb. Anna was on her feet shouting at them, then shouting for Stacey.

Herb struck a defiant pose. "Oh, you will not. No, you will not."

Laura had actually begun to laugh.

Herb turned on her. "What the fuck are you laughing at?"

The remaining cast members, bunched together by the heaters, stopped what they were doing to stare at Herb. Eduardo jumped onstage. The situation did not require his particular form of jack-hammer diplomacy.

Before Eduardo could start yelling, I joined the battle. "All right, everyone settle down. Quiet, please. Where's Stacey? Stacey?"

My efforts were not successful. By now the Two were circling Herb.

Anna continued calling out as well. "Stacey? Get onstage."

"Here I am," he said, coming through the upstage curtains. He took it all in at once: Herb's costumes, Laura's laughter, the look on Marcus's face, and the Two, circling Herb like a pair of wild dogs.

"Easy, boys. Back off." Stacey stepped up to Herb's side.

"Oh, the defense of a big, strong man," Herb said, and locked his arm around Stacey's.

Stacey pulled away. "Let go of me."

The Two rushed in at once. Stacey caught one of them. I intercepted the other. With a struggling, jealous third of the ménage in my arms, I turned to Anna.

"I think we're ready for the fun now, Anna." I struggled to subdue Two #2. "Marcus, we should break."

"Yes," he said, though he was not looking happy. "Herb, while we're on break, you *will* change into the costume Laura has for you. This…" He indicated what Herb was wearing. "This is not going to happen."

By now the entire company had gathered under the stage lights. Before Herb could protest, Anna signaled for their attention.

"Everyone listen up. We're going to have a bonfire." She reached into her coat pocket and pulled out the three road flares. "Close enough. Come on out back. We'll light these."

"Anna, it's cold out there." This was Peter Chang, who was still in costume, waiting to be seen as Hermia.

"Put your coat on. It'll be fun," Anna said.

"Let me guess," said Sean, who had changed out of his surfer wear. "What we *need* is fun?"

The Classmates laughed.

"Am I the only one who cares about this show?" Herb was standing alone, sizing us up as not quite the serious professionals he'd expected. We didn't disappoint him.

"I guess I'd rather be outside faking a bonfire than in here listening to this," Sean said. He started toward the back of the stage, to the black curtains and the door that led outside. "Let Marcus solve this one."

The company dispersed for break. Most went in search of their coats as a few of the cast drifted upstage toward the door. Anna joined Sean. With her help, he found the opening in the curtains. They disappeared behind them. I heard the metal door open and close. I let go of my half of the Two, who seemed calm enough not to commit homicide.

Sean came running back inside. He stopped just a few steps from the curtain and dropped to his knees. Once there, he started retching. Anna came staggering in behind him.

"Alex..." She fainted.

It seemed as if no one moved for a very long time. Then, in part because someone had to, and in part out of a manager's habit, I started to cross the stage. My movement broke the tableaux. Marcus rushed to tend to Anna. Laura and Peter Chang, who were closest, moved in on Sean.

"What the hell are you people doing now?" Herb asked.

"Eduardo, come with me." I didn't know if I was asking for help or for protection. As I reached the black curtains, I called back to the rest of the company, "Everyone else, stay put."

Eduardo followed me through the curtains and then through the metal doors at the back of the stage. The doors opened onto the old serviceway behind the theater. A metal gate blocked the entrance to the street. The glare of the sun momentarily blinded us as we emerged from the theater. As chilled as it was inside, the outside air cut through us with a sharp, slicing frigidity.

As our vision cleared, we saw him. Alex was lying on his back, his robe open. Underneath, he was wearing only his Speedo and his Nikes. Snowflakes powdered his body. There was blood, a great deal of blood, seeping away from his head in a circular pattern, like the halos on the saint statues in my Catholic grade school. He wasn't moving.

A long, tapered icicle, probably ripped from the door frame, rested against his neck. There was a puncture wound at the end of that icicle, a hole out of which the ice had fallen when his body heat had melted the tip.

Alex might have tripped or slipped, falling backward and bashing his head on the icy paving stones. It could have happened in any number of ways. But not that icicle. He couldn't have fallen onto it, then rolled over and cracked his skull. No. Someone had jammed that icicle into his neck.

ACT II

WE COULDN'T MOVE. I would readily swear that I stopped breathing. Once we finally pulled ourselves away and staggered back into the theater, time did not move forward any more quickly. We called the police. We sat stunned until they arrived. The exception was Herb, who almost immediately lapsed into near-hysteria, demanding Laura Schapiro's help in making him look presentable for a police interrogation.

The first two uniformed officers who arrived called for more police. Men in plainclothes, some carrying cameras and other equipment, slowly spread out over the alley, then the theater. Two detectives positioned themselves on opposite sides of the stage, an empty folding chair next to each. One by one, we were called to sit with a detective and answer questions about the day's events.

The Good Company was transformed. As we each assimilated the news, and means, of Alex's death, there was hardly a whisper in the house. We sat huddled in groups around the heaters. I couldn't help but think that the sudden, collective plunge in mood was the type of transition all of us—playwrights, directors, and actors—strive to create in performance.

I watched the Two attempt to double-team one detective. No luck. The police insisted they separate, one potential witness per detective. I couldn't hear what they were saying, but I tried to imagine what it would be like for the Two not to be together. Maybe they only gave half-answers? Would the police need to compare notes back at the precinct to come up with a full conversation?

While the Two answered questions, Anna sat with Stacey. They held each other, Anna whispering in his ear and rocking him gently back and forth. She was the only Classmate who could have comforted him. He'd never allowed the rest of us to get close enough. Once the Two finished onstage, she yielded her place to them, joining Marcus and me.

Roger and Paolo sat behind us, one or the other putting his hand on my shoulder in one of those gestures of comfort that was almost more useful to the comforter than the bereaved. No one spoke. Despite the heater next to me, I started to shiver, as if I were the one lying in the cold half-clothed. The image of Alex was stuck on my eyeballs. I got up, waved off offers of help, and headed for the lobby. There were restrooms downstairs. Maybe some hot water on my face?

The lobby was both entrance to the theater and a small art gallery. In keeping with the "public" nature of the renovations, it was the nicest space in the building. The floor was highly polished wood. Two interior walls were solid white, and the third, to give variation to whatever the current exhibit, was exposed brick. The box office sat jammed into a corner next to the main entrance.

The art currently on display was dubious at best. On their way to Shakespeare's gauzy, romantic comedy, the audience would pass by a series of violent, bloody depictions of leading politicians in various states of impalement and dismemberment. Think Francis Bacon without the irony and only ten percent of the talent. If you don't know enough about Bacon's work to scale back the talent, try to imagine what you might find appealing about a car wreck. Now try to imagine all that with your friend lying dead behind the building. I felt the urge to wash my eyes.

As if the walls weren't burdensome enough, Herb Wilcox was having another panic attack, this time in front of a uniformed cop in the main entrance.

"I need air."

"Yes, sir. But we are asking everyone's cooperation in staying until the questioning is done."

"You can't hold me here. I haven't done anything. This is nothing but police abuse. You wouldn't be doing this to me if I were white."

The policeman broke his stoic expression to the point of raising one eyebrow.

"Herb," I said, interrupting him. "You are white."

He turned on me, shouting. "You know what I mean. I'm a drag queen. Drag queens never get any respect from the law. They think we're all whores." He gave up trying to bully the police, aiming himself at me instead. "Whores and drug addicts."

Herb was wearing jeans and an old sweater, a T-shirt poking through holes in the sleeves.

"You're dressed like a boy." Had he forgotten? "I don't think he knows—"

"Whose side are you on? There's a dead body back there. I want out of here. Now. I didn't sign up—"

"Herb—"

"—for dead bodies. I signed up for Shakespeare. Shakespeare— stupid words, dumbass costumes. Who the fuck speaks in poetry anyway? That is so damn gay—"

"Herb—"

"And this isn't even Shakespeare, is it? Gym bunnies in spandex. If I wanted to see gym bunnies in spandex, I'd join a fucking gym, and I am not that fucking desperate. I haven't worked out since Madonna stopped jogging in Central Park—"

"Maybe—"

"You know, I'm not that old. I read about that. That was a joke. This whole damn thing is a joke, isn't it? I need a joint. I need something. Where is Su—"

"Herb!" This time I shouted. After all, there was a policeman standing across the room from us, listening.

The situation penetrated Herb's drug-desiring hysteria.

"Oh shit," he said to me, without turning around. "I'm going back in."

I stood alone, looking at the policeman across the lobby, who was neither smiling nor cute.

"I'm going to go back in too," I said, giving up on the hot water.

As I started back, Sean stepped into the lobby.

"Hey," he said. "How you doing?"

"How are *you* doing?" I asked. His reaction to seeing Alex had been pretty severe.

We sat on one of the two backless wooden benches in the center of the lobby, the type people install in public spaces so that no one will get too comfortable.

Sean considered his state of being. "I've been better. It's … it's a lot. You were closer to him than I was."

"Well … ," I said.

"Oh come on, Nicky. The five of you were like some Evelyn Waugh miniseries thingy." He stopped, but there was clearly more to come. Sean was like that. "See … the thing is, I was actually a little jealous of you guys. It was like … well, you all looked like you were having such a good time together. And, well …" He stopped completely. "This sucks, you know."

"I know."

It was an opportunity to comfort each other, but I held back. I felt his desire just beneath the surface. I wouldn't say I was unwilling to explore those desires, but there couldn't possibly be worse timing.

"Sean, this isn't really—"

"I know. I just … I wanted you to know that I'm around."

The sound of his voice was perfect in my ears. This may seem strange, but there are some voices that make my stomach flitter. Sean's was pitched low, but not too low, strong without being aggressive. I'd forced myself to ignore it for years. Now I just wanted to hear him talk.

I put my arms around him. "I know. Believe me. I know."

We held that hug for a long time.

———

"And he didn't say why he was calling?"

"No." I answered Detective Marissa Sanchez's question without much enthusiasm. She'd already asked it twice.

"He called you this morning just before three a.m. and didn't say why?"

"No." That made it four times.

"And today, did you ask him about it?"

"No," I said. "We didn't get a chance. Things were hectic here this morning, and I . . . actually, I was a little hung over and maybe not as sharp as usual."

I could tell from the look on her face that Detective Sanchez was not happy.

"What's that mean, not as sharp as usual? As in you don't remember if you asked him, or you didn't talk about it?" She looked directly at me while writing something in her notepad. That's a pretty unnerving trick if you can manage it.

"No, we didn't talk about it."

"Did you erase the message?"

"I don't think so."

"But you were too hung over to remember?" She would have made a great Woman's Temperance League campaigner if such a person still existed. She had the distempered look of a reformer. It did nothing to improve her appearance, already hampered by what I guessed were clothes all ordered online. Nothing quite fit.

I hoped she'd get Marcus next. She'd like a recovering alcoholic.

"I'm pretty sure I didn't," I said, feeling like an escapee from detox.

We were distracted by raised voices from the other end of the stage. Aliza was working the Buday charm on the other detective. The moment passed. Sanchez turned back to me.

"We'll need the message." She handed me her card. "I'd appreciate it if you'd bring it in tomorrow."

She framed this as a request, but I just knew that if I didn't comply by the next afternoon, I'd have the police in my apartment that evening.

"The machine is digital. There's no tape."

"So? Bring the whole machine in." She seemed genuinely pleased with this idea. Did she think it would keep me sober if I couldn't pick up messages from the other drunks?

"And you didn't notice anything else unusual this afternoon?"

Where to start? Did I want to mention Herb's hysteria or the Two's aborted attack on him? I couldn't see how either had anything to do with Alex.

"Well, we don't usually use the theater as a dressing room. But that's it."

Detective Sanchez closed her notebook. "You have my card if you think of anything else."

Finished with my part of the question-and-answer session, I took a seat next to Anna. We didn't speak, just watched the police call the company members to the stage.

We each waited in our own way. Stacey sat with the Two, one on either side. He was completely broken up. His reaction seemed out of line with the barely civil relationship he'd had with Alex. Across the theater, Eduardo sat hunched down in his seat, deflated, his usual bravado missing. Marcus was answering questions, his expression alternating between a blank stare and a puzzled look of disbelief, almost as if he couldn't really wrap his mind around what was happening.

I was having the same trouble myself.

———

I first met Alex at breakfast on the Thursday morning of the first week of school, the day before the party at Rita's house. He showed up shortly after Marcus and I had settled in at the Grill, the on-campus restaurant. The place was busy, but we'd managed to find a table on the side by the wall, away from the rest of the morning crowd.

"What do you mean, you've never had a bagel?" Marcus asked as he waved one with lox and cream cheese at me. He favored the sesame type.

I'd heard of them, but bagels and lox were not something we ate in the D'Amico household. Not that the bagel didn't look tempting, but the lox had a pinkish orange color that did not appeal. I was skeptical.

We'd been through this the night before at our first dinner together. I took it all as part of the business of getting to know him. A business I was happy to engage in, since it meant I got to keep his blue eyes front and center.

I tried the bagel. Before I could say I liked it, Marcus was signaling to someone just coming into the Grill.

"There's Alex, my roommate." Marcus waved to a guy just about his same height and build.

"Alex Isola, this is Nicky D'Amico. His great-grandfather was a bootlegger, and his grandfather ran guns to the French resistance." Marcus tossed this out as if everyone was descended from a Hemingway character.

"Nice," was Alex's only response.

"It's not true. My great-grandfather was a steel worker. And my grandfather never even got out of Fort Bragg."

Marcus dismissed my family history with a wave of his hand. "I liked my version better."

"Don't worry," Alex said, sitting. "I have already learned not to believe most of what he says."

"Hey, that's not nice," Marcus protested.

"Then where is it that I come from?" Alex asked, containing a smile, daring Marcus to forgo a good opening.

I watched them happily. I was already completely taken by Marcus. Alex looked so much like him, for a moment I wondered what would have happened if I'd met Alex first. After a few minutes, it became apparent that while Alex was nice, he didn't have Marcus's charming, beguiling impact. There was a reserved quality about Alex, evidenced in both his body language and his speech.

"You're from Albany, the only child of a single mom. You haven't said anything about your dad."

"Well?" I asked.

"All true. I admire the self-restraint."

"Well, I didn't think it was right to tell him about your aunt, the serial-killer nurse, over breakfast." Marcus started laughing as soon as he said it. He was often his own best audience.

"Have you seen the Big One?" Alex asked.

"Who?" I looked from one to the other.

"We don't know his name—not yet." Marcus retrieved his bagel. "He's this big, butch, six-foot-plus blond thing that Alex is already done in for. No self-control, this one." Marcus winked at me. My heart rate picked up.

"He's in the third section," Alex added.

"I think I've seen him," I said.

The faculty had split our class into three acting sections. Marcus and I were in one, Alex in another, and, I gathered, the Big One in the third.

"God, is everyone out around here?" I asked. For me, the idea was just beginning. I still wasn't out to my family.

"It just kind of happened," Alex said.

The way he told the story, he had been a pretty quiet kid: neat, organized, bright, and not very assertive. His mother had been convinced that he'd grow up to be either an accountant or a lawyer of no special note.

Everything changed for him in ninth grade. His school (along with about two or three thousand others across the country) was performing *Guys and Dolls*. One of Nathan Detroit's lieutenants went down with a broken leg. Alex just happened to be walking past the school auditorium when the drama teacher came stomping into the hallway in total frustration.

"What was bothering him the most," Alex told us, "was that there were now more girls in the male chorus than boys."

"Would that make 'Luck Be a Lady' a lesbian love ballad?" Marcus asked, breaking out into another round of laughter. I was just loving his laugh.

Alex continued as if Marcus hadn't spoken. "He asked me if I wanted to be in a play. I said, 'Why not?' The answer just popped out. I was as surprised as anyone. And the teacher was pretty obviously not happy that I had said yes. My mother was stunned. But they were all thrilled when they heard me belting out, 'I've got the horse right here.' I think Mother was delighted I was finally coming out of my shell." And now Alex was smiling as well. "Of course, I just kept coming out."

"Not so thrilled with that, huh?" Marcus asked.

"We're working on it."

"Well, once you bring home that big blond son-in-law, she'll just be too delighted." Marcus suggested this unlikely outcome as if it were the sagest advice on earth.

Alex lit up with hope. "You think?"

Something was happening onstage at the Tapestry Theater. I drifted back to the present. Memories of that first week under the late summer sun faded away, replaced by the dark, cold interior of the Brewery. We were being sent home. Apparently, there were no more questions to be asked, no more pictures to be taken, no inch of the alley uninspected. Mercifully, they removed Alex's body directly into the street. We were spared the sight of him being wheeled through the theater.

SUNDAY EVENING

"Here. Have another." Paolo passed me a drink—long on gin, short on tonic.

"Don't kill him too," Roger said.

"It won't kill him. It helps. Oh. Sorry." Paolo tossed the "sorry" at Marcus like a brick through a Tiffany window.

"Whatever," was Marcus's barely audible response.

"Guys." My tone was enough. They stopped.

We were sitting in the living room of Paolo and Roger's SoHo loft. They'd invited Anna and me to join them when we left the theater. Marcus, as Anna's houseguest, was included by association.

Paolo stood. "How about dinner?"

"I thought the kitchen was for show?" I asked, trying to lighten the moment. "Weren't you going to rip it out and just leave the coffeemaker?"

Paolo looked past the counter island that separated the living area from a kitchen half the size of my studio apartment. He seemed to be appraising the value of the shiny chrome fixtures and burnished metal appliances, savoring the joys of family money. After a moment's consideration, he declared, "We'd need the fridge for the left-over Chinese," then headed for the phone.

"I'm sorry," Roger said. "But it's just too creepy."

"What's happened, or that we've been here for an hour not talking about it?" Anna said. She was sunk deep into a cushioned arm-chair, the Edward Gorey type that swallowed people whole.

"Both. Definitely both," Marcus replied.

"You know, I'm not really hungry," I said.

"You will be once it gets here," Roger assured me.

To the west, through a wall of glass, we could see New Jersey, to the north the Empire State Building. Outside the wind was blowing snow around the terrace. We'd dimmed the lights, allowing the sight of the city to spill in on us while the fire Roger lit kept the icy cold at bay. Each of us was nestled into some part of the over-stuffed, plush, sage green furniture. Even the cats were picturesque. The charcoal gray snuggled in Anna's lap while the calico rubbed his head against Marcus's leg in a bid for a good petting. It was the perfect setting for five friends to pass a pleasant Sunday evening. All that was missing were the happy people.

"You know, I'm sorry, but what are the cats' names again?" Marcus asked.

"The calico is Benji and the gray is Watteau," Roger answered.

"Watteau is a purebred," Paolo added from the kitchen. Then, needlessly, "He's mine."

Roger lifted Benji to his face and cooed at the cat. "You just ignore him, baby."

Conversation stopped again.

"I know a joke," Roger said, unwilling to let the silence alone.

Anna shot him a puzzled glance. Even the cats looked a bit shocked.

"You'll have to forgive him," Paolo called to us, placing the phone against his chest to muffle the sound. "This is his way of consoling the grieving."

"Is it funny? I could use a laugh," Marcus said, coming to Roger's defense. I suspected more to annoy Paolo than to hear the joke.

"OK. So this guy walks into a bar—"

Paolo almost did a spit take with his wine. "You're not serious?"

Now Anna was upset, or, rather, more upset. The conversation lapsed again.

"This is a great place." This time Marcus broke the silence. "Really."

"Thanks," Roger replied. "Anna, did you notice the new wall hanging?" He indicated a woven piece on the wall behind her.

"It's great," she said.

Anna had been here before. She'd met Roger and Paolo at that rarest of events—dinner at my apartment. It was my first attempt to mix school friends with New York friends. And my first risotto. The results were uneven. The three of them got along great. The risotto was a bust.

"I'm just going to order a selection of things," Paolo called out. "Any special requests?"

"Steamed pork dumplings," Roger called back.

"Already got them."

"That's nice. He knows what you like. I like that. So how long have you guys lived here?" Marcus was looking around with a practiced eye. He'd grown up with money, a life now past.

It wasn't that Reeve and Martha Bradshaw objected to their son being gay (though, having met them once in Philly, I'm certain they would have preferred him to be more "discreet"). Nor did they object to him taking up theater. ("At least he's not an actor, Martha.") They weren't even all that put out by his excessive drinking; after all, Martha was the one who'd taught him how to make the perfect martini. What put the Bradshaws over the edge was Marcus proclaiming himself an alcoholic *in front of strangers*. That they just could not tolerate. They now wanted as little as possible to do with him. I wondered, as he looked around Roger and Paolo's home with its two bedrooms, office space, and sweeping views, how he managed to deal with all he'd lost to drinking. In a moment of empathy, I was glad he didn't know about the space Paolo kept across the hall as his sculpture studio.

I forced myself back to the conversation, such as it was. We'd meandered our way through at least half a dozen non-starter topics. What do you say in the aftermath of the murder of a close friend?

"I think it was the two freaks hanging out with the guy playing Oberon," Roger said.

That would not have been my next choice of topic.

Nor, apparently, Paolo's. "And this," he said, rejoining us, "is how he consoles himself."

Anna said, "It's not like we all aren't thinking about it. I just can't believe one of us would even *hit* Alex."

"But if it's not someone in the company ..." Roger let the question hang in the air.

"Wait." Paolo used the tone he reserved for Roger's obsession with new (and expensive) electronic gadgets. "Are we going down the boy-detective path? Because I am not taking that walk with you."

Roger was determined. "There must have been some other way into that alley."

"Not from the building. There isn't even a fire escape back there. Maybe through the gate to the street, if it wasn't locked," I said.

"The NYPD does not need us." Paolo stood in the middle of the room, arms folded across his chest. He looked very pissed and, with the midtown Manhattan skyline to silhouette him, very dramatically lit. A formidable combination.

"We're not going to get involved," Roger said. "We're just thinking out loud."

"I'm just saying—" I stopped myself. I hadn't actually said it out loud yet. None of us had. "Alex is dead. Something has to happen."

Paolo had no answer for this. Neither did Anna or Marcus. Roger, however...

"The lighting designer is pretty mean. And how about Herb? I don't think he liked Alex."

"So? My mother doesn't like you," Paolo said. "She hasn't succeeded in killing you yet." He made this comment without looking at any of us. He sat down, gathering Watteau to his chest. Roger shrugged him off.

Marcus shot me a worried look. I shook my head slightly. I was pretty certain Mrs. Suarez had never actually tried to kill Roger.

Roger plowed on. He loved a mystery. "OK, how about the Oberon guy. What's his name?"

"Stacey Rose?" I couldn't picture it.

Marcus laughed. "What are you thinking? That Stacey ordered the Two to kill Alex? Come on."

Roger was getting excited. "He wasn't onstage. He came through the back curtain. He *said* he was in the dressing room, but he could have been out back. Right?"

"Yes, but..." I didn't finish. He was right. Stacey could have been in the alley. Then again, during the break, any one of us could have been in the alley with Alex.

"No. I don't believe it," Marcus said.

"And we all saw Alex give Stacey the evil look," Roger continued. "Even the which'ums... the Two. They saw it from several rows back. There is something not right there." He was nodding his head as he spoke.

"There is something not right here," Paolo said, looking around the room. Then he settled on Roger. "Oh."

"Funny." Roger faked a smile. "But there *is* something going on."

"Very well. Is there something between them?" Paolo asked me.

"Just can't resist, can you?" Roger was smirking.

"Oh, lover, as if I could avoid getting dragged into this once you two start. I might as well come along and try to keep you out of trouble."

I'd seen the boys work out enough problems to recognize their peculiarly rapid conflict-resolution process. Marcus, however, was not certain what to make of the exchange. Upper-class Boston breeding won out: he pretended nothing was happening.

"Well, they've never been on the best of terms," Marcus said. "But, Christ, not enough to shove an icicle in his neck. That's really out there." He dismissed the idea.

The door buzzer sounded, announcing the delivery boy at the downstairs entrance.

Roger and Paolo looked at each other. Some private communication passed between them, signaled by the slightest facial gesture, too intimate for me to read.

Roger stood. "Nicky, come help me."

After we paid for the food, Roger placed the bag on the counter, then just looked at me.

"I'm not going to cough up chopsticks, so what's the look for?" I said, unpacking the food.

"There is one other possibility." He kept his voice low, making certain the others wouldn't hear us.

"Well, I'm not whittling 'em either."

Roger didn't even grin.

"What?" I have never been a fan of the half-revelation. Get it all out, is my thinking.

"I found a half-empty bottle of gin hidden in the box office this afternoon. It was on the floor, behind the CPU tower."

I closed my eyes, took a breath, and opened them. I didn't want to hear this.

"So?" was all the response I could manage.

"So? The only people who hide liquor are alcoholics. Are you sure Marcus isn't drinking again?"

"Oh, please. There are a lot of reasons to hide liquor in a theater. Not the least of which is that you might want to actually have some of it for yourself. Theaters are full of boozers." Not exactly the best defense against the accusation, but that was my answer. What I thought was: *Please don't let this be about Marcus.*

"How's he behaving?" Roger asked.

"He's fine. Believe me, I'd know if he was drinking. And Anna would certainly know. She's been in rehearsal with him for weeks.

He's living with her." As I said this, I inventoried the past twenty-four hours for any hint in his behavior. Not a comprehensive span of time, but still, I couldn't pick out one single indication that Marcus had ended his sobriety. If anyone knew the full catalogue of Marcus's behavior when drinking, it was me. "And even if he is drinking, he was never a violent drunk."

Roger tilted his head to one side in the internationally recognized gesture of sympathetic (and often unwanted) understanding. "You're defending him too much."

"This is beginning to sound like a self-help book."

"All right." He started collecting plates and chopsticks. We finished preparing in silence. As we left the kitchen, he tossed one last comment over his shoulder: "Just be careful."

Did he mean for me to guard my heart, or did he really think Marcus had jammed an icicle into Alex's neck?

Back in the living room, I noticed that Roger caught Paolo's eye and shook his head slightly.

He was right about one thing: with my hangover hours past and my morning bagel gone even longer, I was voraciously hungry now that the food had arrived. We settled into the complete silence that ushers in a much-needed meal.

After a few minutes, Paolo spoke. Even before he finished his first sentence, I could tell we were in trouble.

"I don't understand something, Anna. You said no one would even be capable of hitting Alex, but didn't you"—and here he swung his chopsticks to point at Marcus—"smack him around at school? I remember a story." Now the chopsticks zeroed in on me. "Halloween, right?"

"Don't point those at me." I wanted to whip a dumpling at his head.

"I hate that story." Anna was shoveling shrimp fried rice onto her plate, carefully separating the shrimp from the rice. Not eating it, just sorting it.

"How come you know this and I don't?" Roger asked.

"See?" Paolo was the one smirking now. "You couldn't possibly do this without me."

"I don't think we need to get into this," I said.

After another moment, Marcus looked me directly in the eye and said, "Oh, let me." Then, to Roger, "It was Halloween, sophomore year. There was a party. I got drunk. Alex and I got into a fight—which I do not remember because I was in a blackout. We got over it. Curtain. Applause. Audience exits. End of story."

Roger looked at Anna and me for more details. Our silence crushed him. He was definitely hoping for something juicier that would produce multiple motives.

The food was doing me good.

"Not quite end of story," I said. "Rita got laid. She and Stacey had a drunken thing that night. He did look good as a gladiator." I smiled. He'd worn his breastplate well.

Paolo sat up in his chair. "Oh no, wait. This I have not heard." Murder may be fine as an intellectual puzzle, but it was good old-fashioned dirt that really warmed Paolo's heart.

"We are not going to play 'who slept with who,'" Anna said. Having not eaten her shrimp, she started on another round of Chinese.

"Which one was Rita?" Roger asked. "Did I meet a Rita today?"

"Rita Lombard," Marcus said. "She's an actress. Actually, she was supposed to be stage-managing this show, not Nicky. She's in

Detroit." He was having no trouble eating his food. Talk about being at peace with your past.

"She went to Detroit in January?" Paolo was genuinely appalled.

"So you heard this whole fight story before?" Roger asked Paolo.

"Oh yes." Paolo glanced at Marcus, then turned to me. He bestowed a "Why do you torment yourself?" look of pity upon me.

"Look." Marcus finally sounded annoyed. "Yes, I hit Alex and I have no excuse or defense. I don't even know what we were fighting about. But if he could get over it, I don't think it should be such a fucking big deal for you. OK?"

"All right then." Paolo backed off—just a bit. "Just wanted to get all the facts straight."

"All right." Marcus went back to his dinner.

Anna was now well into separating her chicken from her broccoli, neither of which, true to form, she was likely to eat very much of.

"And where were you doing all of this, Miss Anal Compulsive?" Paolo was skeptically observing her eating habits.

"I don't know. Who remembers?"

"Probably downstairs with a dwarf or two," I said.

"Excuse me?" Roger asked.

"I was dressed as Snow White. If even one of you so much as cracks a grin..." Anna didn't even bother to look up from her plate.

Marcus did his best not to laugh. "It was great. She talked seven design and production guys into dressing in sweats and hoodies and rouging their cheeks. She even sewed a stuffed bird onto her shoulder. It was great. The best."

"Wait a minute," Roger said. We could see a new idea creep into his mind. "This Stacey guy, he plays both sides?"

"I don't know. When he was nineteen, he had sex with Rita. Now he's what, twenty-six? He has ..." And here I stumbled. The image of Stacey and the Two was just not something I wanted to conjure.

"Please. I'll never sleep." Paolo stood. "Anyone want anything else?"

"Shit," Anna said. She put down her chopsticks.

"What, get some rice on your cashews?" Marcus teased her.

"Someone has to call Rita."

That stopped us. Marcus looked at me, I looked at Anna, and Anna looked down at her chicken. She pushed the dish away.

"I'll do it," she said.

That pretty much ended the conversation.

"The five of you were really close, weren't you?" Roger asked.

"Yeah," I said. Marcus and Anna didn't say anything.

We broke up just short of midnight. Everyone was exhausted. I passed on staying the night at the loft. The kind of sadness I was experiencing cried out for the comfort of my own bed, the peace of waking up in my own home. On the street, I put Anna and Marcus in a taxi headed toward the East Village and then jumped into one of my own to Midtown.

Alone for the first time since noon, I put my head back, thinking over the day. It was irrational, but it occurred to me that when Anna got home and called Rita, once she passed on the news of Alex's death, we would cross some imaginary line. The past would be irretrievably lost, even as a warm memory. Roger had asked if we were close. We were so close, we could draw blood in blackouts and still forgive each other ...

———————

As with all of her parties, Rita's Halloween bash sophomore year was packed. She was in her usual spot on the front porch, collecting cash for the beer and booze. This night she was dressed as a siren in shimmering turquoise that made her red hair pop, even in dim light. Marcus and I arrived in black, wearing white gloves and sunglasses and sporting white-tipped canes. When anyone asked, we told them we were the three blind mice. Not everyone fell for it, but enough people pointed out the obvious that we got to do our "Oh my God, where did he go?" routine at least a dozen times. What can I say? We were nineteen years old.

Alex arrived angry. He'd chosen a cowboy outfit with an inflatable bull around his waist. All pumped up, he looked as if he were riding at the rodeo. Problem was, the costume was too large to actually maneuver without sweeping every nearby surface clean. This didn't improve his mood.

"Hey," I said when I ran into him, sans bull, in the kitchen. "Nice hat."

He grabbed my arm and dragged me aside, away from the activity around the keg.

"Where is Marcus?"

"Oh my God, you mean—," I started in.

"Where is he?" Alex cut me off.

"What's with you? He went upstairs." We both knew what that meant, but Alex had learned not to dog me about Marcus's love of cocaine and scotch, and I'd learned to pretend that my boyfriend wasn't in trouble.

Alex walked away as abruptly as he'd started the conversation.

I was outside when Anna arrived in her Snow White costume.

"How're we doing?" she asked, bestowing a perfectly chaste Snow White peck on my cheek.

"Marcus is upstairs getting high, and Alex is really pissed off about something," I answered.

"It's going to be that kind of night? I love a party." She turned to her seven dwarves. "Come on, boys. Let's go find you some elves." The dwarves cheered as they swept into the house.

Around midnight, I was standing in the crowded second-floor hallway, leaning against the banister of the stairs, chatting it up with Sean McGinn. He was wearing Hari Krishna saffron robes. In an almost willful fulfillment of stereotype, Sean possessed a native Californian's interest in New Age theories and applications. He was explaining the use of the herb bayberry in preventing colds when Alex elbowed his way down from the third floor. "Hey. Hey!" Sean grabbed him as he passed. "What happened?"

Alex's mouth and nose were bleeding. The people around us partied on, oblivious.

"Nothing happened. Let go." Alex tried to pull away.

"You're bleeding," I said.

Just then Marcus appeared at the bottom of the stairs.

Alex pointed at him. "Ask him. It's his fault."

Sean and I turned to Marcus, who was trying to navigate his way past someone on the landing.

"Marcus, what's going on?" I sounded more accusatory than I intended.

"Nicky. There you are." He was clutching the newel. "Where ya been, baby?"

People were watching us now. The noise in the hallway quieted.

"Let it go," Alex said.

"Marcus..." Sean was having trouble even forming the question. "Did you hit him?"

"Hit Nicky? Never." Marcus looked around, as if he'd lost track of me.

"Marcus," I said. "Why were you fighting with Alex?"

Marcus seemed uncertain who Alex was. Then he saw him and said, "Alex is right there."

Someone laughed. I heard another person say, "Trashed..."

Alex pulled away from my hand. "Nicky, it's not—" He stopped when Marcus stumbled into him.

Marcus would have fallen if Sean hadn't caught him. As it was, he ended up in front of me, suspended in air, looking up into my eyes. "Hello." He giggled.

I snapped out of my reverie. We were turning onto 51st Street from 8th Avenue. The cab driver wanted to know where to stop.

There were happier memories, no doubt of that. This one, however, had etched itself into my mind because, as a direct consequence of that night, I called it quits with Marcus two days later. I conjured the image of Sean holding Marcus up, both of them looking at me. At the time, I hadn't really registered the expression on Sean's face. But now, seeing it again through the lens of his decision that our day had come, its import was clear. Sean had been waiting a long time to get my attention.

There was something else. We'd all taken it as given that Marcus had come down the stairs. But I hadn't actually seen him do that, and considering how messed up he was, I now wondered how I ever believed he could have. No, it was much more likely he'd been in one of the second-floor rooms instead of on the third floor, where someone had given Alex a bloody nose.

If that was true, Alex had lied. He'd covered up for someone.

MONDAY MORNING

THE PHONE RANG. I didn't open my eyes. It rang four times before I rolled over and grabbed the handset from its cradle.

"What?"

"Nice, Nicks. Very nice way to answer the phone."

I looked at the clock. It was ten a.m.

"What are you doing up so early? Isn't it like seven in the morning there?"

I myself had gotten up at seven to call the agency I was temping for. I told them I was not available for the day and immediately crawled back into bed.

"Detroit is in the same time zone as New York," Rita Lombard snapped back at me.

"I didn't know that." Yes I did.

"How's everyone holding up?" she asked.

"Well, the general consensus is you're crazy to be in Detroit in January." I knew I couldn't keep the conversation away from Alex, but at least I could delay it.

"Come on, Nicks. Talk to me."

"Fine." I pushed myself out of bed and was eyeball to eyeball with Sushi. I fed the fish, tapping a few flakes into the bowl. He darted about with joy. Fish have it so easy.

"Anns said you both saw—"

"Yeah, we did." I cut her off. Now was not the time for Rita's famous no-holds-barred conversational style.

"Can we talk about something else while I wake up?" I started toward the kitchen. It wasn't as spacious as Roger and Paolo's. Actually, it wasn't as spacious as the mudroom at my parents' house in Pennsylvania. To someone more domestic, the main selling point would have been the amount of cabinetry crammed onto every available wall surface. I didn't have a lot of use for those cabinets. To me, the prize item was the coffeemaker with timer dripping fresh-brewed into a carafe. That timer made up for the absence of shiny metal appliances. "I'm having coffee. You want some?"

This was an old joke between us. One Sunday during junior year, Rita had come over to my apartment in Philly for brunch, just the two of us. We settled in reading the paper, drinking coffee, eating eggs ("not all goopy"), and chatting, and soon it was evening. We made dinner, had more coffee. It was the longest brunch either of us have ever had, and one of the more enjoyable.

"Sure. FedEx it, OK? You know, I feel like I want to jump a plane and come back."

"Rita, something bad might be happening." I decided I had to give her the heads-up.

"Anns already let me in on your 'locked-alley' mystery."

This was one of Rita's things, her names for us. We were Anns, Marcs, Lexis, and Nicks.

"It cannot be one of the Classmates." She was emphatic.

"I won't believe that either. But—"

"How can there be any 'but' to this?"

"Well, someone killed him, Rita. And they didn't do it from a fucking helicopter, did they?" I snapped. I was pouring coffee and missed the cup. "Shit. I just spilt the coffee."

Rita was patiently silent on the phone. At least that's how I took it. I couldn't see her, so for all I knew she was crying or rolling her eyes or reading a magazine.

"We ended up talking about Halloween last night. Sophomore year?"

"Oh God, not that again. I'd love to forget it." She didn't sound like she was crying.

"Why? *You* had a good time. Alex was acting funny yesterday. There was something going on. I think it had to do with Stacey."

"Wait. Anns said you were all with friends of yours. Marcs was there too, right?"

"Yes."

"You told that story in front of him? I can't believe you."

"No one *told* the story. It just came up about the fight." I felt I owed her the entire truth. "Oh, and that thing about you sleeping with Stacey. That slipped out."

"Oh, please. That again? You know you don't have to keep it up anymore. And I hate it that strangers think I'm a slut."

"That's a privilege you reserve for your friends?"

"Very funny."

"So, what am I not supposed to keep up?" I asked.

"Hold on. I'm getting more coffee too." The line went quiet.

She was probably right. All this time with the gang was making me stupidly sentimental. Then again …

"I'm back."

"Keep what up?"

"What, were you on 'pause' while I was gone?" Rita tried to sound casual. Trying to sound casual almost never works. For Rita, it was a complete failure.

"Oh my God," I said. "Tens of thousands of dollars of acting training from one of the best conservatories in the country and that is the best you can do? You don't cover well."

"I'm not trying to cover anything."

There it was again. Definitely a false note in her voice.

"Rita, what is it you know that I don't know?" I asked.

"Well, first off, what time it is in Detroit."

"Rita."

"Look, I thought you already knew, or I wouldn't have said anything."

"Knew what?"

"Nicks, this is pointless. After all this time, what does it matter, anyway? I thought you knew."

"Stop saying that. I don't know what the hell you're talking about. And it does matter. Alex is dead." Again, tears. I pushed them back.

"And you think this has anything to do with what happened seven years ago at a Halloween party?"

"I think I want to know everything I can about anything that might even remotely have to do with this."

"The police will take care of it."

"Rita, I need to know the parts they won't even care about. Christ, it's Alex."

There was another long silence. This time I was certain I heard her crying softly.

Finally she spoke. "You'd better talk to Anns about this. I can't tell you."

I was stunned. "Can't tell me what?"

"Why do people always ask that question when someone says they can't tell them something? It makes no sense."

"None of this makes sense. You're telling me there really *is* something you're hiding from me? I can't believe this."

"Nicks, please, just talk to Anns. She'll explain all of it. OK?"

"No. It is not OK. Nothing is OK about this." I was angry. "I'm going now. I don't want to talk anymore." I hung up before she could say anything else.

I sat for a long time at my table. I tried breathing exercises. I closed my eyes and imagined a happy, warm place, with trees, sunshine, and running water. The temperature dropped, the clouds came out, and the stream overflowed. I gave up. I decided that, cold weather or not, I had to get out of my apartment.

I made quick work of a shower and dressing. I unplugged the answering machine, wrapped it in a towel to cushion it, and shoved it into my backpack. I would take it to the police after I'd had a chance to walk off the nervous energy.

"Bread." Bang. Bang. Bang.

"Yes, Mrs. Wizniski, I won't forget," I said as I pushed through the entranceway to the outer foyer.

She had collared me—literally—as I drew even with her door. I guess her opportunities were limited on a Monday morning, when most of the building's tenants were at work. At the sound of my footsteps in the hall, she must have jumped and ran. Her door flew open with me directly in arm's reach.

I bought the bread at the corner bodega. A fixture of any New York neighborhood, the bodega is equal parts convenience store, supermarket, deli, and florist. I had to push my way through the thick, clear plastic curtains hanging from the awning over the sidewalk. These trapped the heat inside, keeping the vegetables and flowers from freezing in their bins and pots. I made my way past the wide floor-to-ceiling coolers to the end of the deli counter. There, several different loaves were poking out of their white wrappers. I selected a seeded Italian. When I turned toward the counter, Marcus Bradshaw was waiting for me.

"Hey, Nicky."

He was pulling his earphones off. Even bundled up he looked good. His hair stuck out from under his woolen cap with just the right casualness.

"Hey, yourself. What are you doing here?" Anna and Rita's apartment was in the East Village. Not exactly in the neighborhood.

"I saw you come in, so I followed you."

I shook my head slightly, smiling. "A little less specific, please. Are you working at the theater today?"

"No. I'm actually kind of stuck. I was at an AA meeting in Chelsea, but I can't go home yet."

"Why not? Anna have you on limited access?"

"No." He smiled a little. "I left without my keys. I guess I'm just too distracted. It's been a really tough morning, you know?" His voice cracked. "Anyway, I started walking and then I saw you come in here."

"Here we are."

We looked at each other for a moment.

"I have to take this back to my neighbor," I said, collecting the bread and my change. "Come with me. I'm going walking myself after I give her this."

We delivered the goods to Mrs. Wizniski, who, miraculously, made no further requests. Back on 9th Avenue, I led us toward Chelsea, the opposite direction from the Brewery Arts Center.

Walking through the City—even on a winter day officially too cold for a stroll—always helps lighten whatever is weighing on me. I love urban, and New York is the best urban tonic around. I'd not made it in LA because I'd never felt that sense of "city." Now, walking down 9th Avenue had the desired effect. As we moved farther from the scene of Alex's murder, I couldn't help but feel better. The West 50s had undergone a resurgence in the 1990s. The crack houses and boarded-up businesses had been replaced by the neighborhood I'd moved into: restaurants, boutiques, bars, clubs, and a few diners still clinging to life. We passed by the Coffee Pot at West 49th Street, one of the last non-chain spots in the neighborhood. The kind of place where you could still order the traditional New York "regular" coffee and receive a cup of caffeine with just enough milk to turn it a caramel color. Then past Theatre Row at 42nd Street, the Cupcake Café at 39th, where you can buy some of the best pies in town, and on under the busway at the Port Authority. Apartments, shops, people on the street—the City's sense of purpose seeped into me. Along with the cold. We were done at 23rd Street.

We dove into a coffee shop at the corner of 23rd and 9th. The inexpensive prices were just right. We took a table in a window looking out on the avenue, keeping our scarves wrapped loosely about our necks. It was a reasonable tradeoff for a window seat.

Looking at Marcus across the table brought back my conversation with Rita. Starting with Halloween, there were just too many images of my undergraduate years...

———————

Marcus and I had our first meal alone two days after we met. On Wednesday night of the first week of freshman year, we ate at a restaurant called Lilly's, just off campus. The place was nothing elaborate—a menu full of brown rice and vegetables and a garden in the back trimmed in white Christmas lights. The humidity hadn't broken, so we relied on the light breeze generated by the fans at the back of the restaurant. The lights, hanging from leafy branches overhead, swayed in the sticky air.

Marcus lived off campus with Alex, whom he'd picked up as a roommate through student services.

"I'm a transfer student. There's about ten of us. The university has a housing shortage anyway, so they let us out of the first-year dorm requirement. Alex is one too. He's a first-year like us. An actor. Quiet type. Well, you'll meet him. You'll see."

I was pouring something called ginger-celery dressing on my salad, trying to decide if I really wanted to eat anything so liquidly green. I bit into a leaf.

"Hey, this is good," I said.

Marcus laughed. "What did they feed you at home?"

"Either chicken or things with red sauce on them."

The rest of the meal was more of the same: me oohing at food I'd never eaten, not even realizing I was near the bottom of Philly's culinary ladder, while Marcus and I swapped stories.

He was from Boston, the only son of two highly successful and, to hear Marcus tell it, highly strung lawyers. He regaled me with stories of his parents entertaining a parade of dinner guests, of cocktails at all hours. I had the definite impression that Mother Bradshaw saw the bottom of the glass a few too many times.

His parents originally had egalitarian ideas of education and had enrolled him in the public system. Where I'd found traditional shop classes less than enthralling (after six weeks in metal shop, I'd produced the handle of a hammer; after eight weeks in wood shop, two legs of a three-legged lamp), Marcus was unredeemably bored with his forced march to masculine assimilation. This got him into a lot of trouble, which he curiously left unspecified except to laugh and wink at me conspiratorially. It also got him transferred to a private school.

We both stumbled into theater as the perfect refuge for quirky, anxiety-ridden teenage homos waiting to grow up and leave home.

"So what kind of theater do you want to do?" he asked while we waited for dessert (tiramisu for him; carrot cake for me).

"Live?"

"Yeah. Yeah. Funny. I mean, what do you want to work on? You know, musicals, new stuff, are you going to do it in New York or someplace else? Like that."

"I just want to do theater. I'm not particular."

Marcus looked as if I'd spit in his tiramisu.

"You're kidding me, right? You don't care?"

I rose to my own defense. "I didn't say I didn't care. I just like it all, that's all."

He was not impressed with my answer. "I'm not certain there's a distinction in there. Not really. What I want to make is big theater. You know what I mean? Huge-ass musicals or multi-cast period repertory things. Big."

He shoveled a piece of the gooey dessert into his mouth, closing his eyes and sighing in delight. "I love this stuff."

He was giving me his full-wattage smile. There was a small piece of cream at the corner of his mouth. I gathered more courage than I knew I had, reached out, and wiped it off with the tip of my finger.

"Mmmmmm." His smile widened.

"Hello. Hello. Come back."

"What?" I blinked. Marcus was sitting in front of me, no trace of cream on his lips, the steamy Philly night replaced by the snowy New York day.

"You were daydreaming."

"Was not." I opened my menu and started talking about the production, putting freshman-year Marcus out of my mind.

We didn't get far before stumbling into the topic of who would replace Alex. We skipped over that and just talked about Alex.

"We should do something," Marcus said.

"Paolo's right. The police will—"

"I don't mean that. I mean a memorial service or something. Something *about* Alex. Something personal."

"Yeah." We were all gathering that night at the Brewery, but that meeting would be more business than tribute.

"Something that would mean something to him." Marcus was smearing mustard over his fries.

"I can't believe you still do that."

"They're great. So what was Alex into besides theater?"

"Movies."

"Yes. Yes. That's good. I like that. He had that thing for independent gay films, didn't he?" Marcus didn't acknowledge, and I didn't point out, that having to ask that question was a sign of just how out of touch he'd grown during his post-graduate drinking years.

"Oh shit." I stopped with my BLT in midair.

"What? What is it?"

"The movies. His movie collection."

Marcus shook his head. "What are you talking about?"

"He has this great collection of almost every independent homo film made in the past decade. If it's on DVD, he owns it."

"Wow," Marcus said. "He must own a lot of bad movies."

"Yeah, well. It was a collection thing. You know, trying to get all of them."

"So what's the problem with it?"

"Well, what do you think his mother is going to do with them?"

"Oh shit." Marcus put his burger down.

Alex's mother, who still had not fully recovered from his coming out in senior year of high school, was more likely to take a hammer to the movies than to cherish them.

"We could ask her," Marcus said, not very hopefully.

"Yeah, that'll get us real far," I said, remembering my one and only meeting with Marina Isola. She was not the generous type.

"This sucks. We have to get them. That's just that. We have to." Marcus took another bite, chewing and thinking.

"You know," I said, "I have his keys."

When you live alone in New York, it's smart to have someone, preferably someone who lives close by, holding a set of keys to your apartment. Someone you can call if you're locked out. I held Alex's keys.

"Yes. I like this. This is good," Marcus said.

"Is it legal?" I asked.

"I think. I mean, why not? It's not like he was killed in his apartment. It's not a crime scene or anything."

I was very skeptical. "So what, we just go over and take them?"

"You make it sound so shady. We go, and if there isn't any of that yellow police tape, we 'save' them. No one will know."

Marcus made it sound so easy. I should have taken that as a bad sign.

"Look, Nicky. If we don't do this, she is just going to throw out all those DVDs that Alex spent so much time and energy collecting. He loved them."

How would that help anyone?

"OK," I said. "We go look. But if there is anything that says keep out, we stay out. Anything at all."

"Absolutely." Marcus smiled that big toothy smile at me. "Want to hear a joke?"

No wonder he and Roger were getting along so well. The first night we spent together, each time we curled up after sex, he asked me the same question. Every time we made love, Marcus would, at some point afterward, tell me a joke. "I like to make you laugh," he once said.

In my head, I heard Roger's voice: "Be careful."

"Why don't we save the joke. I'm not in a joke mood today." I could see the disappointment on his face. "You can make me laugh another time."

"I'm going to remember you said that."

"Are you flirting with me?"

"Nicky..."

"Please don't do this," I said. "Jesus, not today."

"OK. Not *today*."

Then he gave me one of those lazy half-smiles that leading men use in black-and-white films. The type of smile that says, "I'm saying I agree with you, but I don't mean it."

"When are we going to rescue the movies?" he asked. "The sooner the better."

"It has to be tomorrow. I have to take my answering machine to the police this afternoon." Listen to me. When your reason for postponing a possibly illegal entry into a murdered friend's apartment is that you already have an appointment with the police, stop, think, change your plans.

Before I could do any of that, my coat pocket started ringing.

I'd purchased the phone two months previously, finally bowing to pressure from siblings: "If you ever bothered to be home..." and "Why is it always 1980 where you live?"

Until I owned one, I'd firmly believed there was a special circle in hell for people whose cell phones ring in public. That's what vibrate is for. I even more firmly believed that people who carry on conversations in restaurants ended up in an even deeper circle.

"Could be important," Marcus said. "Things being what they are."

Could be.

I reached for the phone, thinking I needed to either get a new belief system or at least remember to turn off the ringer.

The caller ID displayed Anna Mikasa.

"Hello."

"We have a problem."

"It's Anna," I said to Marcus. "She says we have a problem."

"Yeah, that's one way to put it," he said.

"Marcus agrees with you. So do I."

"Not *that* problem." She sounded completely frazzled. "What are you doing with Marcus in the middle of the day? Why aren't you at work? Can you talk?"

After my conversation with Rita, there was plenty I wanted to talk to Anna about, but not on the phone and not in front of Marcus. I'd let Anna toss her own topics at me.

"We're having lunch. And yes, I can talk."

That last comment raised a quizzical look from Marcus. He winked at me.

"Stop it," I said.

"What's going on?" Anna wanted to know.

"He's winking at me."

"If you two can take a break from flirting for one moment? I just talked to Suege, the landlord."

"Why does everyone think I'm going to do something stupid with Marcus?"

"Hey." He gave me a look of mock offense.

"David, Alan, the three guys named Mark, Amir, Eddie, and the busboy from Cola Novo. If I weren't in a hurry, I'd think of more. Can we talk about the landlord now?"

OK. Maybe they had their reasons.

"What about the landlord? Is the heat back on?" I asked.

"Yes."

"So what's the problem?" I gestured for Marcus to stop breaking off pieces of my bacon.

"He's not happy about Alex," Anna said.

"The landlord is not happy about Alex," I said, relaying the info to Marcus.

"Sensitive guy." He stopped fooling with my sandwich.

"He wants us to leave." Anna sounded more annoyed than worried.

"That's not his choice," I said.

"I know that, but I don't want him hanging around giving us grief," she replied.

"What? What is it? I can't hear her." Marcus leaned forward, bringing him well into my personal space. I did not back up.

I repeated Anna's news. "He wants us to leave."

"Absolutely not. No way," Marcus snapped back without hesitation.

"Marcus says, 'No way.' Maybe you two should talk?"

"I have to get back to work," she said. "You guys start planning. Come up with something to put him off."

I took a breath.

"Anna, maybe we shouldn't just assume anything here. Maybe we should talk about this."

They both erupted at once.

I waited for calm.

"All I'm saying is that we can't pretend there isn't an issue here. We all loved him. We need to talk about this tonight with everyone at the theater."

Marcus sighed, looking out the window at the remains of snow lying black along the avenue.

There was silence on the phone line, then, "Meet me early. We'll talk first. Tell Marcus too." She signed off.

I slipped the phone back into my pocket.

"What a dick. The landlord is a pain in the ass." Marcus continued to stare out the window.

"So what kind of crazy is this Suege guy? I can't wait to meet him," I said, and started back on what was left of my BLT.

"You're not missing anything." He thought for a moment. "Why are you going to the police, anyway?"

I told him about Alex's phone call.

Poor Marcus. He looked so upset at the thought of Alex's voice "still around after his death."

"But why did he call? What did he say?" he asked.

"I don't know, I didn't get a chance to talk to him about it. Did he say anything to you Sunday morning?"

He thought for a moment, slowly shaking his head. "Nothing really. I was busy onstage, he was getting ready for costume parade. We hardly spoke."

After arranging to meet at Alex's at ten the next morning, and also agreeing not to tell anyone else, we went in opposite directions.

I took the train back to Midtown. Along the way, I tried to convince myself that I wasn't interested, that Roger and Paolo were right about not getting involved, and that Rita would probably lecture me till I was an old man. Still, I could not get rid of the image of Marcus telling me a joke while we were wrapped together under the blankets. Nor the image of his body, pale as marble with the blue of his veins etching it in detail. Or the memory of his body pressed against mine that very first time and each time thereafter.

To complicate matters, every time I tried to not think about Marcus, the image of Sean's lazy smile popped into my head. Should I go back for more with one or try something new with the other? Or just walk away from both?

I've heard that grief makes people do strange things. With that in mind, I decided not to do anything just yet, neither act on my impulses nor try to quash them. This was a sound, measured response. I was being very reasonable. I was very proud of myself. I was in big trouble.

MONDAY EVENING

DROPPING OFF THE ANSWERING machine took longer than I expected. Turns out all those police station scenes on TV move along much faster than in real life.

The Midtown North Precinct was on West 54th, between 8th and 9th Avenues. The building, four stories of gray stone with a large flag flying, had "Police Department of New York" carved across the top. Except for the words, the place looked like every movie image I'd ever seen of a stolid, old-time, small-town Midwestern bank. Of course, there were the police cars too. As always in the City, each car was parked perpendicular to the curb. Across the street, tiny, golf-cart-like parking-enforcement vehicles looked like hyperactive baby strollers. The entire place, including the bars behind the first-floor windows, was uninviting. But then, who ever really wants to go to a police station? I hurried through the wide green double doors. I figured I'd just hand the answering machine off quickly, but the officer at the front counter must have been on the lookout for me. He parked me in a waiting area while he let Detective Sanchez know I was in the building. I sat for twenty minutes. When she did appear, Sanchez looked even less happy than she had onstage the day before. She walked me back to her desk and started questioning me again.

"Given any more thought to yesterday?" she jumped in without preamble. It was all business with Marissa Sanchez. It didn't surprise me that there was nothing personal on her industrial-issue gray metal desk.

"Pretty much all I've thought about," I said.

"And?"

"And?"

"Anything new come to mind about Sunday morning, before your friend was murdered?"

In other words, had anything useful risen from what I'm sure she considered the alcohol-steeped haze of my memory.

"No. Nothing at all."

"He was your friend, wasn't he?"

"Yes. We went to school together. I told you. Most of us there went to school together."

"And some of you knew him better than others?"

"I guess so. Yeah, sure. What—"

"How well did you know him?"

I had no idea where this was leading.

"We were very close friends. For four years at school and since."

"Ever have sex with him?"

"What?" She caught me completely off-guard with that one.

"Ever sleep with him. You had a relationship with Marcus Bradshaw, didn't you?"

"Yes. But that ended halfway through sophomore year."

"And never with Alex Isola?"

"No. I don't make it a habit of sleeping with my friends." She was beginning to annoy me. "Is there a point to this?"

Detective Sanchez looked at me silently. Other members of the force, some in uniform, some not, walked by, not paying any particular attention. People and business were going on as if nothing had happened to Alex.

"I'm just trying to determine the facts, Mr. D'Amico. I'm just trying to find out who killed your friend. All the information I can get will help. If you knew anything more about his phone call, that would help."

Did she mean to toss that much guilt at me, or was she just digging? I couldn't help thinking that, yeah, if I'd talked to him about the phone call before he'd met whoever killed him, we might have more of an idea of what had happened. Or better still, he might be alive. But I hadn't. I'd been too distracted by the production and too hung over. I knew his death wasn't my fault, but knowing it isn't the same as feeling it.

When I got around to asking how soon I would get my answering machine back, she didn't give me a definitive answer, looking even more disgruntled. Finally we were done. She dismissed me with suggestions that I give more thought to both what happened and drinking less. I'm sure that last part was not on her official list of duties.

I left the precinct, crossing 9th and 10th Avenues, heading toward the Hudson. There'd been nothing more than a few flurries for two days. Little mounds of the blackened snow still clung to the base of the buildings and lampposts.

My phone vibrated. I checked the ID: my mother.

My parents raised four children using the three simple rules of Italian-American parenting: feed 'em, cloth 'em, and never—ever—

let 'em forget how much you worry and worry and worry. Any conversation with my mother carried a subtext filled with the burden of parenthood. I just wasn't up to it right then, but the guilt that visits Italian-American sons who let their mothers go to voice mail is a fearsome and potent fiend. I already had my limit of phone-call baggage with Alex.

"Hi, Ma."

"Nicky, honey. How are you?"

(Translation: "I've been worried for no reason. Why am I worried, what's happening there?")

"I'm OK, Ma. There's nothing to worry about. How's everything in PA?"

"We're fine here. How's the new show? You know, your father and I were thinking maybe we'd come see this one. We haven't been in New York in over a year."

(Translation: "If you came home now and then, it would spare us the grief of traveling at our age.")

My siblings and I were scattered along the Eastern Seaboard. Not one of us had stayed in the old hometown. Despite their protest, this presented real opportunity for my parents. Their perpetual vacation schedule consisted of the joyously worrisome preparations and exhilaratingly dire risks of processing from one child to another in approximately six-month intervals. I hadn't realized my turn had come around again.

An ambulance whizzed by, heading uptown on 10th Avenue, siren blaring.

"Nicky, where are you? Was that an ambulance?"

(Translation: "Are you bleeding?")

"Yes, Ma. You caught me walking down the street. It drove right past, *without stopping*."

"Oh. OK. So how is this show? Is it a good one for us to see?"

(Translation: "If we have to travel day and night all year, at least make it entertaining.")

My parents were well trained in the vagaries of theater. After years of work, they now knew what technical rehearsals meant ("That's when Nicky's too busy to call his parents"), that not all openings are joyous and not all closings sad, and that they should always ask before seeing a show.

Explaining the fleshfest that was the Good Company's production of *Midsummer* just didn't appeal to me.

"This one's not going to be the best. Maybe you should wait for the next one. It'll be more fun." I tried to make it sound like no big deal, like just another show gone off the rails.

My mother heard right through me. "What's wrong? You sound unhappy."

(Translation: "I am not as stupid as you think I am, kid.")

It was pretty cold on the street for a long phone call. I could lie, but then I would not only eventually have to explain what happened to Alex, but why I lied about it. Talk about ratcheting up the worry meter. ("We know your friends are being murdered, dear, but that's no reason to lie to your father and me.") Best do it now and be spared the inevitable rebuke of having held back the truth.

My parents had known Alex. They knew all of my Baldwin friends. They had come to Philadelphia once a year while I was at school. Twice in my senior year: once to see a production of *Angels in America* that I worked on, and then for graduation. They'd met the Classmates, naturally spending more time with Anna, Alex, Marcus, and Rita than with any of the others.

It was their junior-year visit that flashed through my mind as I stood on the corner debating whether or not to come clean. That year our schedules worked out so that all five of us were free for dinner. My folks took us for Chinese. We sat at a big round table where Rita taught Mom to use chopsticks.

When the fortune cookies arrived, Marcus, not as drunk as usual but not in complete control, read his fortune out loud and added the obligatory "in bed" at the end: "You will reach new heights of accomplishment—in bed."

My parents looked both baffled and embarrassed. The others left it to me to explain the joke of adding the phrase "in bed" to the end of a Chinese fortune. Mom immediately read hers out: "Good news comes in threes—in bed." She giggled. My father turned red. It was the first glimpse I'd had of the three of us together as adults.

I decided to come clean.

Mom put up a brave front and minimal fuss as I broke the news of Alex's death. I knew that she and my father would be discussing the murder for the next month or ten years. They'd always liked Alex. Plus, the news would be a continual touchstone for bringing on the pleasure of late-night angst at will.

"So you're not doing the show, are you?" Her concern was genuine. No translation was necessary.

"We don't know. We're going to talk about it tonight. I'm on my way to the theater to meet Anna and Marcus now."

"That poor boy's mother. Did I meet her?"

(Translation: "Should I send a Mass card?")

"I don't think so, Ma. I don't think she knows who you are."

"Are you sure? Who was the one with the snotty attitude that never looked at me when she talked?"

(Translation: "You remember, you were no help at all.")

"No, that was Marcus's mother, Martha. I'm sure you've never met Alex's mom."

"Poor woman. You be careful. You never know who is running around on those streets."

(Translation: "Do not make me pick you up at the airport in a box, mister.")

I was not going to tell her that, in fact, in this case, I probably did know the person involved. I figured that was not the best way to keep my parents in Pennsylvania.

"Ma, I'm at the theater. I have to go now."

The Brewery Arts Center was on West 53rd Street. The building stood out by design. The brick façade was a cream color, against which were set a bright red fire escape and red doors and window trim. A large banner bearing the Brewery logo swayed from its second-floor attachment. The letters of the word *Brewery* (white on a red background) bubbled up as if rising from the frothy top of a vat of beer. The logo designer intended it to evoke the fermentation of art and ideas. Mostly, it made me thirsty.

After ninety minutes in a police station, walking into the Brewery should have been an act of joy. I almost always felt good about stepping into a theater. Sure, some productions were less rewarding than others and some just not much fun, but, more often than not, times were good. The day after Alex's murder was not good. I rushed past the gruesome lobby art.

Inside, Anna Mikasa was onstage arguing with a tall blond man. He was in his early forties, possibly older. His pale, washed-out look suggested too many hard years. He was thin—not thin like Herb Wilcox, who seemed to come by it naturally, but thin in a wasted, not-paying-enough-attention-to-himself way. I reached the edge of the stage and heard him speak. It took only about two minutes to peg him as an aging pothead.

"No. I'm getting complaints about you. I have complaints about you. I don't like taking on new companies. I told you. You talked me into it. You made promises. I told you the rules. I think you tricked me." At that point, he screwed up his face in an effort to remember exactly how Anna had fooled him.

"We didn't trick you." Anna motioned for me to join them.

Tonight the heat was working. The stage lights were off and the fluorescents were again doing duty. I stepped into the ugly pale light. Other than the three of us, the theater was empty.

"Hello," I said, sticking out my hand.

"Suege, this is Nicky D'Amico, our stage manager."

Suege squinted at me. Maybe he didn't know what a stage manager was. Maybe he thought I was a hallucination.

"This is Suege Nethevy, our landlord."

"You look like someone I know." Suege craned his head from side to side, trying to get a 180-degree view of me.

"Hope that's a good thing," I said, counting on cheery to help us out.

"I didn't like him." He turned back to Anna. "You have to … you have to go."

Marcus was right. I could have waited years and years to meet Suege Nethevy.

128

"I can't make that decision for the entire company. We're meeting tonight." Her sudden humility almost made me laugh. "I really don't think we're pulling out."

"There are rules."

"Are there house rules about murder?" Marcus Bradshaw shouted from halfway down the aisle. "Well? Does the theater have rules regarding murder? Is there a murder clause in our contract?"

"I don't think so." Suege looked confused.

"Well, if there aren't any rules, then we haven't broken any," Marcus said, now standing next to me. "The Brewery has no grounds for complaint with us."

"No. No. But ..." Suege started to think.

Marcus's intervention had a certain ruthless manipulation to it, taking advantage of Suege's easily confused thought process. At least he had the grace to cast an embarrassed glance at Anna and me. Anna looked completely relieved.

"We should set up." She grabbed a folding chair from the stack stage right and placed it, open, onstage. "Everyone will be here. We'll need twenty-six chairs."

"Twenty-eight. Don't forget the Two," I said, grabbing two chairs.

"Don't call them that," Anna said.

"Well, what are their names?" I expected the worst: Egbert and Eustace.

"I don't know."

"You don't know?" Marcus started laughing. "Well, what do you call them?"

"'Guys,' if it's both of them. 'Honey,' individually."

I started laughing as well.

"They like it," she said, defensively.

Suege, who'd been standing as if catatonic, finally got to the end of whatever he was thinking.

"You all are bad luck," he said. Then he pulled a bundle of something green from his pocket.

We each began to refuse. "No, thanks—"

"Sage, man. I'm purifying the space." He produced a lighter.

It's not that I disapprove of herbal magics and remedies. I've been known to hit the bee pollen myself now and then. It's just that I am very skeptical when they are wielded by a man who apparently devoted his adult life to a joint.

Suege began to walk the perimeter of the stage, gently waving the smoldering sage. Anna, as usual all business, paid no attention. She and I continued arranging the folding chairs in a circle. Marcus worked hard to suppress a giggling fit.

When he'd made a complete circuit of the stage, Suege confronted us again.

"I'm going to the lobby. Then upstairs. The entire building has to be cleansed. You people have seriously bad karma."

We watched his slow progress up the right aisle. Put him in liturgical vestments and he could have been a priest from my childhood, dousing a Sunday Mass with incense.

"How the hell does he run this place?" I asked, not expecting an answer.

Marcus managed one anyway. "His parents pay for it to keep him busy and off the streets. I think they live in fear of what he's going to do next."

"Really?" I was surprised. "He seemed harmless. Out of it, but harmless."

Marcus just shook his head. "You're kidding, right? Have you seen the art in the lobby?"

"Suege made that stuff?" I thought again about the paintings, which were actually mixed media: photography and paint. They were grisly: knives, ripped-open chest cavities, blood, stakes. It was impossible to dwell on the work and not see echoes of Alex's death in each of them.

Marcus had tried to make his comment about Suege's family's financial support sound like a joke, but I think I caught a sad undertone. How could he not think of his own family and the contrast between their distance from him and the efforts expended on the hapless Suege?

Anna dismissed the landlord. "By the time Suege gets another thought together, we'll be on the other side of this production."

The first company members to arrive were Stacey Rose and the Two. As soon as they stepped onstage, the Two began complaining.

"What is that smell?"

"It smells like sage."

"Is it sage?"

"We hate sage."

"Someone has been doing aromatherapy here, haven't they?"

Two #1 turned pointedly toward me, demanding an answer, as if I had lit an entire prairie on fire. Two #2 was so horrified at the thought, he just sputtered. Stacey didn't look very happy himself. For the first time, I realized that his investment in the Two must include the color thing.

"Well," I started to say, "the landlord—"

"Enough," Anna said. "The sage was the price of getting rid of Suege so we could continue to work."

"You don't understand." Two #1 held his ground. "The aroma people are crazy."

The level of insanity required to get you labeled as crazy by the Two momentarily overloaded our collective imaginations. For the first time ever, neither Anna, Marcus, nor I could think of anything to say.

As the awkward moment teetered on embarrassing, Marcus offered to turn on the fans and "clear the air." I swear he was going to pass out from trying not to laugh.

"If you want to cleanse this place and have less stress..."

"...we can paint these walls turquoise for you."

They were doing that *Twilight Zone*–ish shtick of finishing each other's thoughts. This time, they did it as they turned in opposite directions to inspect the theater.

"All the walls," they said in unison, their eyes wide with awe at the prospect.

This was too much even for Stacey. There was a reason that the walls and stage of our small theater were black. It made them recede from the audience's eye. For this production of *Midsummer*, with very little scenery but the male chorus and all the effects done by lighting, we didn't want the walls to be objects of attention. As for surrounding the audience itself in turquoise...

The Two misunderstood the expressions on our faces.

"Don't worry."

"We'll buy the paint."

"And do it ourselves."

"You'll love it."

Anna took each of them by a shoulder and began to lead them to the edge of the stage. "That is really not the issue. Stacey will explain this to you. Stacey?"

"Let's talk over here, guys." Stacey led his entourage to seats on the far side of the auditorium.

As they walked away, Two #2 was expanding on the idea. "A dark turquoise. No one will notice."

By now other company members were arriving.

We settled into the circle. As sometimes happens, the actors grouped themselves according to the roles they played. The four young lovers—Peter Chang and Peter Timcko, Phil Cook and Eduardo Lugo—sat quietly on one side. Next to them, the six actors playing the mechanicals, including Sean McGinn, were a little more animated. After he convinced the Two that the walls were best left black, Stacey and they took seats. Tonight's meeting would also involve the designers. Laura Schapiro was the first one in.

When Aliza Buday arrived, she didn't take a seat. She very ostentatiously hauled a ladder onto the stage.

"These lights won't gel themselves," she snapped when some of the cast objected.

She proceeded to make a real show of dragging her ladder and her gels across the stage.

Herb Wilcox was last. I would have bet that he'd watched everyone arrive and, once certain we were all gathered, swept himself in for the grand entrance. He brought a surprise with him.

Despite what you might see in badly made movies, drag queens do not wander around all day in evening gowns. If anything gives them away, it's the attitude. It takes a certain bravado-tinged ego for a man to cavort onstage as a woman. Herb Wilcox and his two companions may have been dressed as boys, but they were dripping with the vestigial energy of ball gowns and diamond pendants. The snap and sizzle was unmistakable: we now had three drag queens.

"This is Andy. This is Mikey." Herb introduced his friends as if bestowing a general blessing upon us all. "They will need chairs."

Andy and Mikey were both shorter than Herb, which is to say average height. I could only guess what they looked like in drag, but as guys they looked very good. The word that came to mind was *lithe*. For a moment I was back in my LA time, gazing longingly through my sunglasses at a guy walking down the sidewalk: flip-flops, baggy shorts, tight muscle tee. I stopped myself from grinning.

"They're not part of the production." It was Eduardo. Eduardo, always speaking so much faster than he was thinking.

As soon as he'd said it, both Stacey and I readied ourselves. We could see it coming like the money shot in cheap porn.

"Oh, and I suppose Thing Number One and Thing Number Two are?" Herb belted out the question with real 1930s-movie-star overkill. He even pointed—arm fully extended—at Stacey and the Two. Like the Ghost of Christmas Yet to Come, a long, bony finger at the end of a thin arm jutted from his coat sleeve.

"You know, I hate it when life imitates art," Aliza Buday shouted from atop her tenuous perch on the ladder. "Why don't you all just sit down and get on with it?" As she punched out each word, the ladder veered from side to side.

Which was more mesmerizing? Watching Aliza swing back and forth, cheating bodily harm by mere centimeters, or seeing Herb down stage left with his drag queens and Stacey down stage right, backed by his color therapists? It was Shakespeare meets *High Noon* via a Chelsea dance club.

The Two fired first.

"You look…"

"…ridiculous in purple."

The Two were not very good at the verbal shootout.

Herb fired back.

"You are ridiculous. Don't you know, surf and turf doesn't mean shrimp and beefcake?"

The Two bristled. Stacey was on his feet.

The rest of us were silent, except Aliza, who applauded as if she was enjoying a good seat in the front mezzanine.

Herb wasn't done. "I wouldn't be caught dead in green."

Two #2 actually squeaked as he covered his sweater, a complimentary shade of the green worn by Two #1.

The one I pegged as Andy said, "Oh, that's right. It's not safe around here in green." Mikey and Herb laughed.

Alex was wearing green when he died.

Laura Schapiro had the same thought. "That's a terrible thing to say. Stop it."

"Don't stop them now, Schapiro. This is the best thing I've seen onstage all week," Aliza cheered from above.

Others had put the green comment in context. The mood turned ugly.

It was Marcus who found a way out of our corner. "Yes. Exactly," he said, standing up.

Stacey turned on him angrily.

"Oh no," Marcus said. "No. Not the shrimp part. No. The confrontation itself. Titania on one side with her minions, Oberon and his on the other." He used the distraction of at least half the minions trying to define the word to step between the two feuding camps.

"They face each other across the stage, eyes smoldering with hate, their bodies tense with the pent-up energy of bearing a grudge. Their entourages are equally invested in getting the upper hand. The entire situation is fraught with the possibility of violence.

"Thank you. Thank you. Thank you. Herb. Stacey. Stacey. Herb. Thank you for showing me this. Now let's all sit down. We'll just savor this breakthrough."

It was an instant classic. Marcus had blown just the right mix of smoke and praise at the six combatants to leave them baffled but suspecting they'd stumbled into a compliment.

Anna was able to jump in and start us off.

First we needed to have a good long moment, or ten, to think about Alex.

It might seem strange that we'd want to do this in the place where he'd been murdered, but that was, in itself, a means of honoring him. Alex had found most of what he liked about himself in the theater. It was right that we were in one to remember him.

Anna and Eduardo both spoke. Marcus's usual volubility deserted him. He was as quiet as the rest of us. Eventually we started in on business.

There were two questions facing the Good Company. Does the show go on? If so, who goes on as Puck? It was 6:45.

After only fifteen minutes, I'd had enough. The debate hadn't quite degenerated into an argument, but the situation was tense. I decided to be satisfied with the final decision, no matter which side prevailed. If the "we have to go on in his memory" faction won, then I'd go on. Honoring Alex by performing his last show was a good idea. If the "we're too devastated to continue" faction won, that was OK by me too. There was plenty of mourning I would be putting off in order to continue *A Midsummer Night's Dream*. But no matter what the final outcome, there was something I needed to do that was best taken care of while everyone else was occupied.

I excused myself and slipped out of the circle. Anna, Sean, and several other company members gave me a passing glance. I moved up the aisle toward the lobby. My goal: the box office.

I didn't make it.

In the lobby, directly between me and my destination, surrounded by the bloody depictions of Suege's nasty psyche, the landlord and painter himself stood face to face with a TV reporter and cameraman. This could not be good.

"And when this tragic and senseless event took place, did you rush immediately to the theater to be on the scene?" the TV man asked Suege.

"Ah, no. I was here already. Here in the building, not the lobby."

"And there you have it." The reporter was now looking directly into the camera. "Landlord and expressionist painter Suege Nethevy telling his personal tale of agony and horror at so pointless a murder."

Putting aside the question of when a murder might not be pointless, I wondered at Suege's statement. I hadn't seen him at all the day before. No one had mentioned seeing him. Certainly, with the heat out, if he'd been anywhere near us, Anna would have pounced on him. Had he just forgotten us, or had he deliberately avoided us? It was possible to access the dressing room from the second floor of the Brewery. From there, the upstage curtains masked the path down the back steps and through the door into the alley. In our grief, we'd all forgotten about who might have been in the artist studios above us.

I retreated back toward the theater auditorium, but I was one beat too slow. The perfectly angular TV face turned toward me and said, "One of the members of the Better Company has just stepped out of the theater auditorium."

Microphone first, the reporter, with his cameraman one step behind, came barreling toward me.

"Good evening, sir. Are you with the Better Company?"

"That's the Good Company," I said, trying not to squint into the bright light aimed at me.

"Yes, it is." The reporter made it sound as if I had stated the obvious instead of correcting him. "And your name?"

"I'm Nicky D'Amico."

"Mr. D'Amico, I'm Man Wilson, Channel 3 News. We've just been speaking with Brewery landlord and expressionist painter Suege Nethevy. Can you tell us how saddened you are by the senseless, brutal murder of one of your company?"

I thought of escape. I was only one and a half feet from the auditorium door. I could be back in the theater, door locked behind me, before "Man Wilson, Channel 3 News" even realized I was moving. But I've seen enough clips of people running from cameras to know you never come off looking like anything other than a felon. Run that clip three times and I'd be the prime suspect. Anyway, I didn't think my absence would stop him littering the lobby with adjectives.

"Alex was a close friend," was all that came out of my mouth.

He glanced at a note card in his hand.

"Alex Isola, the young actor whose promising career was so dastardly cut so wretchedly short. A sorrowful blow to each unhappy, anguished member of the company. Will the show go on, Mr. D'Amico?"

Suege tried to muscle his way back into the frame.

We overlapped in our answers.

"No, they aren't—"

"We're having a meeting right now to—"

Neither of us finished. The sound of Stacey Rose bellowing in his best "fill the house to the back of the balcony" voice came bounding out of the open theater door: "I don't give a shit what you think."

"It seems the Good Company is torn between grief and duty in the face of these shocking and appalling events."

"Don't you fucking even—"

I reached back with my right arm and swung the auditorium door shut, cutting Stacey off mid-sentence.

"It's a difficult and troubling time." I mimicked the hyper-somber tone of Man Wilson, Channel 3 News.

He stepped aside, positioning himself against the exposed brick. In one well-practiced move, the cameraman framed him, found the proper distance, and continued shooting.

"A grim and demanding time as a group of young actors who came to the big city to follow their dreams grapples tonight with the heartbreak and calamity of the all-too-early and untimely end of innocence. A story to test even the most devoted 'let's put on a show' theater artist. I'm Man Wilson, Channel 3 News."

The light snapped off.

Wilson turned toward Suege and me. "Thank you very much. That will make an excellent piece. I'm afraid we've got to get going."

He handed each of us his business card. "Here's my card. You've been very helpful."

The cameraman was already heading for the exit. Man Wilson, Channel 3 News, followed him out. I was alone with Suege in the lobby.

"That was freaky." He looked around the lobby, as if something else could begin to match the strangeness of his art.

I started for the box office.

"We need to talk," he said.

I kept walking, assuming he was referring to himself and the voices in his head.

He followed me. "Hey."

I talked as I walked. "I'm not the one you want to talk to. That would be Anna Mikasa. She's onstage right now."

"Right. The Asian chick."

That stopped me. So what if Anna, her parents, her grandparents, and their parents had all grown up on Long Island? Apparently for Suege, you could never take the Pacific Rim out of the girl. The problem, of course, with potheads is that they always give you that "whatever" look, no matter how ridiculous their behavior. I just wasn't up to it.

"Yes," I said. "That's the woman."

He seemed to be pondering something. Anna as a woman? Anna as the one in charge? Why the sky is blue?

"OK, then," I said when no other comment was forthcoming. "I've got business in the box office."

"Police are bad for sales," Suege blurted out.

"Actually, I think the idea is that all publicity is good publicity when it comes to ticketing."

Again Suege switched to befuddled. "Ticketing?"

"Yes, ticketing. Selling tickets? You know those things people buy to see a show?"

"Right. Tickets."

"Nicky, what are you doing out here? Everything all right?" Marcus came into the lobby looking like he needed another one of those cigarettes he'd quit.

"I needed a break," I said, wishing I were in fact getting one.

"You all need to go," Suege said.

"Suege, we haven't exactly decided what to do just yet. OK? We're working on it," Marcus said. "Shouldn't you be upstairs, cleansing the studios?"

"Did that."

"The stairwell?"

"I did … yes, I did that."

"The fire escape?" Marcus asked in growing frustration.

"The fire escape," Suege repeated.

"Yes, out front. It is a part of the building."

"Yeah, well, it's cold."

"Hey, we all choose what risks we live with." Marcus shrugged, as if unpurified fire escapes were the leading cause of death in Americans between the ages of eighteen and thirty-five.

Suege started thinking.

Marcus turned back to me.

"Come on back in."

"I'm not ready yet." It wasn't an actual lie, just a little misdirection. I couldn't let him know what I was doing. If Roger and Paolo were wrong, it would break his heart. If not—well, if not, there were many other choices that would need to be made.

141

"Are you sure you're OK?" he asked.

"I'm fine." I felt like a real shit, manipulating grief to cover my tracks.

Once again Suege reached the end of a long thought. "I'm going outside."

He grabbed his coat from one of the lobby benches, bundled up, produced more sage from a pocket, and hit the street.

"That was mean," I said.

"But definitely fun. Don't worry, he'll be all right. Come on back in."

"You go. I'll be there. Really, I'm OK. Go."

He nodded and returned to the theater.

At last, the box office. It was not an impressive space. Carved out of the far corner of the lobby by the erection of two hollow-core walls, it was more box than office. Someone had once done their best to organize it effectively, but successive and chaotic use by one theater company after another had worn down those initial efforts. There was a table below a customer-service window that opened onto the lobby, and another table along the wall that fronted the building. Metal filing cabinets held up both of these workspaces. A low-backed swivel chair at each table and a large five-drawer filing cabinet in a corner completed the furniture. The scratched and stained wooden tabletops held a computer and printer that were not in much better shape than the tables themselves. The hardware hadn't been state-of-the-art for years.

I started where Roger said he'd found the bottle: behind the CPU tower sitting on the floor under the keyboard and monitor. Nothing. Well, what did I expect? That someone would restock the place like a liquor cabinet?

Since I was already on the floor, I checked behind the small filing cabinet that was holding up the end of the table. I crawled under, inching my way toward the wall, so that I could get my head far enough in to see all the way behind the cabinet. Again nothing.

I heard someone enter the box office. I twisted and saw dirty work boots walking toward the large filing cabinet. I'd just seen those boots on a ladder. Now, it is true that there is no rule, tradition, or theatrical superstition that prevents or discourages lighting designers from entering a box office (which is surprising when you consider that the theater has a tradition or superstition for almost every occasion). However, it's also true that in the entire history of Western theater, from the Greeks to overpriced Broadway musicals, you could count to five and exceed the number of times such a thing has happened.

"Hello," I said, and immediately regretted it. If Roger had been there, he would have given me a sharp jab with his elbow. But then he'd read many more mysteries than I, and would have immediately realized the advantage of staying quiet and seeing what Aliza was up to.

"Who the fuck is that?" She bent over to look under the table.

"It's me," I said, trying not to sound disappointed.

"Why are you hiding down there?"

"I wasn't hiding. I dropped something." Sometimes I worry that I can lie so quickly. Mostly, I'm just grateful.

"What are you doing here?" I crawled out from under the table.

"I wanted to make a reservation." Aliza was apparently no slouch in the fast-lie department. There was, however, no reason to think that anyone would be in the box office on a Monday night, the night that theaters traditionally close. She knew that, I knew that, and we each knew the other was lying. We had very little truth between us, which was just about all that could fit into the tiny space.

"I don't think you can do that tonight," I said.

"Then I'll come back another time."

I stopped her before she could leave. "How's it going onstage?"

"I'm almost done."

"I meant the meeting," I said, convinced she was deliberately misunderstanding me.

"They're arguing," was her short reply before she bolted from the room.

Once she was gone, I tried to think of a legitimate reason for her wanting access to a filing cabinet in the box office. The booth at the back of the theater house provided ample storage for light gels. The electronics themselves, the cables and light instruments, were stored on a rack of pipes behind a curtain stage left. What would she be stashing in the box office? What if she was hiding what I was looking for? If the bottle belonged to Aliza—and, as mean-spirited as it might sound, for Marcus's sake I hoped it did—maybe she'd just led me to another one.

I stepped up to the filing cabinet. The top drawer was unlocked. I pulled it out as far as I could. The papers did not go all the way to the back. I reached my hand into the empty space behind the hanging folders. I groped around. Nothing.

I repeated this procedure with the four lower drawers. None yielded up the makings of a good martini.

What was she looking for?

I turned full circle. There was a bulletin board on the wall, ticket racks, and the window for customer service. I was back at the filing cabinet. Of course, there were the cabinets holding up the tables.

I continued searching the box office with no result. No bottles, empty or otherwise, turned up.

"Hello."

I jumped.

"Anna sent..."

"...us to get you."

The Two were standing like living Parcheesi pieces, shoulder to shoulder, in the doorway.

"You know, I really wish you guys would stop doing that."

"Doing..."

"...what?"

"Finishing each other's sentences," I snapped at them.

"We never do that," Two #1 said.

Two #2 didn't speak.

I looked at them. They looked at me.

"Do you drink?" Two #1 asked.

"As in drink alone?" Two #2 added.

"No. But now that you mention it..."

"We just wondered."

"We found a bottle."

Oh, great.

"Where did you find it?" I asked.

"Well, if it's not yours..."

"...we're not telling."

They popped out of the doorway.

I followed them into the lobby, where I again found Herb ensconced in the entranceway, this time in serious, whispered conversation with a perplexed Suege. They stopped talking as soon as I appeared. Suege smiled at me, a gruesome, toothy smile that fell far short of nonchalant. Herb muttered a single "Shit." He dashed past me into the theater, leaving Suege alone in the entranceway.

Suege looked at me. I looked at him.

"What's up, Suege?" I asked, beginning to form a guess of what business could bring our stoned landlord and Herb together.

"Nothing, man. I got to go." He left the building.

First bottles of booze, now this. The word *playhouse* popped into my head, and not with happy connotations.

———

The general company meeting was over. The Steering Committee, plus designers and Herb—who had no intention of missing out on anything—were still onstage. Naturally, Herb and Stacey's groupies were also present.

"Are you OK?" Anna asked as I joined them.

"Yes. I'm fine." My inner Catholic schoolchild reminded me that there were people on other continents in real need of sympathy. I was just lapping it up to sneak around and spy on my friends.

"So what's it going to be?" I wanted to get on with this.

"We're marching forward, no matter who the fuck drops," Aliza said, and chuckled.

Eduardo started to say something, but restrained himself.

Anna took a deep breath. "Aliza—behave. If you cannot behave, you go. For good."

Aliza considered it for a moment. She'd come to us at a cut-rate price. I could guess why. Not many theater companies were up to more than one helping of the Buday charm. She made a coy "locking my lips" gesture and smiled.

"We're going to go on." Anna looked around the room. "This means a new Puck." Before anyone could say anything else, she added, "That is a decision for the director and the Steering Committee. That is, Eduardo, Stacey, Sean, and me."

Herb immediately objected. "If the color midgets get a vote, I get a vote."

"No one votes," Marcus said. He peremptorily waved his hand to silence the Two, and Andy and Mikey. "I don't care how many cheerleaders you bring with you, no one votes. Not even the Steering Committee. I'm the director. I cast the show. I choose who replaces Alex." He stood his ground, waiting for Anna to disagree.

"I agree with Marcus," Eduardo said. "It never works to cast by committee. Let him choose."

Anna looked to Sean.

He shrugged and said, "I don't have any business casting anything. I guess it's all Marcus."

"Stacey?" she asked.

With Rita, the fifth member of the committee, in Detroit, if Stacey sided with Anna, the vote would be tied two to two. This difficult night would only get more complicated.

"I'm with Marcus," Stacey said. As usual, few words, but in this case, decisive.

"But we have an idea," Two #1 whispered to Stacey.

"Not for this, guys." He was very gentle with them.

Anna was outvoted three to one.

"Then that's how it will be." She loved to win, but give her credit: she knew when to fold. "Who's it going to be, Marcus?"

"Eduardo," he said without hesitation.

"How very convenient for both of you," Herb snapped. "Eddie sides with Marky and Marky promotes him."

Herb stood up. Andy and Mikey did likewise. As soon as Andy and Mikey were on their feet, the Two sprung up. Stacey tugged them back down.

"You're overreacting, Herb." Anna tried to calm him down with her usual gasoline-on-fire brusqueness.

"Me, overreact?" Herb managed to look genuinely surprised at the idea. If he could only do that in performance. "I never overreact. If I'm overreacting, may God strike down the little gnomes."

Now Stacey was on his feet.

"Oh, don't go all he-man hero on me," Herb said. "I've had enough for one night. We're leaving." He turned to Eduardo. "I just hope you know your lines tomorrow."

"I just hope you know yours."

Everyone turned at once. I couldn't believe I'd said it. Stage managers are supposed to be the Switzerland of theater, remaining neutral in all artistic disputes.

"He speaks." Herb flicked his eyes, taking me in, top to bottom and back. "Why don't you worry about keeping all the props in order? Let the talent worry about the art."

Both Sean and Marcus started to object.

Herb laughed them off. "Two gallant defenders. My, my, Princess. Busy, busy."

He swept out as he'd swept in, another grand-procession gesture. In this case, one that felt very similar to a common one-fingered gesture. Andy and Mikey followed him, laughing.

I turned to Anna. "Sorry," I said.

"For what?" Stacey asked. He looked as disgusted as he sounded. "Piece of shit."

"You don't need to apologize," Sean said.

"None of us needs to apologize," Anna said. "Let's get the rest of this done." She opened her notebook.

"I'm all for that. Let's get done and get out." Aliza Buday had seconded Anna with way too much good cheer. Anna shot her a warning glance.

"What?" Aliza protested. "What? I'm agreeing with you."

The Two settled down in their chairs. They dug out a notebook.

Dismissing Aliza, Anna started at the top of her list. "OK, costumes first."

Two #1 jumped right in. "Good. We have many notes on the costumes. Starting with the color of the biker shorts." He flipped pages, trying to find costume notes.

"But don't worry." Two #2 turned to Aliza. "We took notes on the lights too. We didn't forget you."

"I am such a lucky girl," Aliza said.

Anna put the brakes to the Two. "Laura and Marcus are going to talk about costumes. You are going to listen. Put the notes away."

The Two didn't like Anna's order, living as they did with the firm belief that everyone wanted to hear their every opinion. Was conversational space part of the glue that bound them to the usually reticent Stacey? Now they looked to him for support. When he made no move to help, they settled unhappily back into their chairs.

After reviewing what we'd seen the day before, Marcus and Laura set priorities for the time remaining: what needed to be done immediately, what could wait a few days, what we could live without if we had to. In fact, the costumes were well enough along that Laura could afford a peace offering. She asked the Two if they wanted to help her the next afternoon in assembling several costumes that were ready to be sewn up. Anna displayed a truly unnatural enthusiasm for the idea that convinced me she and Laura had cooked up the plan in advance. They needn't have bothered.

"We don't sew."

"We're not seamstresses."

"We're consultants."

We moved on.

Marcus had met with the sound designer on Saturday to review cues and music. The designer expected to have something to play for us by the end of the week.

Surprisingly, for all of Aliza's grumbling, the lights were in the best shape. All the instruments were hung, and almost all were completely focused and gelled. Aliza would be refining the setup during the week. She'd be more than ready for technical rehearsal on the weekend.

Saturday was the big day. The first time the actors, costumes, props, lights, and sound all occupied the same stage. No one could ever be too prepared for a technical rehearsal. No matter how hard everyone planned, that first test of all the elements of a show was always a grueling stop-and-start procedure. The process was especially harrowing on the actors. For the time it took to get through a tech rehearsal, they would be expected to forgo acting or rehearsing and be little more than scenery as lights were refocused, sound cues sharpened, and props moved on and off the stage.

I sat through the meeting, asking questions and taking notes. When the time came, I would be at the nerve center of getting and keeping everything moving. It was my job to set up the stage and the props before the show, to get everyone in place to start, and to signal the light and sound cues. Tech rehearsals were the time when stage managers were at their busiest.

As we finished the last item on Anna's list, Two #1 spoke up again. "We have an idea."

All heads turned in dread anticipation.

Two #1 mimicked Anna's signature phrase. "What this group needs is a color-therapy session."

"And soon," Two #2 said.

There was a moment as we each waited for someone else to take the hit. Finally, Anna stepped in front of the bus.

She forced out the words. "What is a color-therapy session?"

"We have everyone bring an object from home."

"Something special to them. Whatever they want."

The Two grew more animated as they explained.

"They bring it in and we analyze it. We talk about what the colors mean to them and what each color's intrinsic value is."

"How having this object near them affects their lives."

"And what they can do about it."

"What we need," Aliza said, "is better heat, a more cooperative landlord, more time for the new Puck, and fewer drag queens."

"I don't understand. What will this do for us?" Anna asked, still trying to keep the peace.

"It's really very therapeutic," Stacey said, choosing this moment to make his longest statement in two days. "Color is very indicative of your nature—how you use it, wear it. Knowing what works for you is good."

The Classmates shifted uncomfortably in our folding chairs. If Stacey noticed, he didn't let on.

"And knowing what …"

"… *doesn't* work for you is very important too."

None of us were buying it.

Then Two #1 added, "Like Alex and green. We told him it was a bad color for him. He didn't listen."

"If he'd listened, he'd still be alive." Two #2 had added just enough extra information to cross the line.

Everyone started shouting again. I'd lost track of how often that had happened since I'd stepped into the Brewery two days earlier.

Eduardo went at it, pouring out a full twenty-four hours of grief. "Who the fuck do you think …"

Laura accused the Two of being inhuman.

Sean accused her of misunderstanding them.

Anna shouted for everyone to stop shouting.

The Two were silent, baffled by the heat of the emotional response.

Stacey was on his feet. "All you people ever do is make fun of them." His anger was physically intimidating. The muscles on all six-feet-plus of him tensed.

This didn't faze Eduardo, who jumped to his feet as well.

The Two seemed to shrink as Stacey grew more agitated. "We warned him. Green is Stacey's color."

Stacey turned on them, barking for them to shut up.

Aliza Buday cheered.

Eduardo, red-faced, fists clenched, lashed out at a folding chair, kicking it across the stage. The sudden violent act stopped everyone. His fury abated as quickly as it had built. He went silent.

No one seemed to know what to do next.

Marcus spoke first.

"There will be no color-therapy session. And not," he quickly added, "because I think it will or won't help, but because I'm not giving up any of my rehearsal schedule for it. We have a new Puck, remember? We need all the time we have."

The Two were ready to keep arguing. Stacey, however, was far more familiar with the time constraints involved in mounting a show.

"All right," he said grudgingly. "We can accept that."

The Two did not look at all accepting. I watched them fight the urge to keep arguing, wondering what they'd warned Alex about. Maybe that they wouldn't tolerate him wearing green? It wasn't lost on me that Stacey had cut them off.

It was just after nine o'clock. There was no more business for the production meeting, but there was still work to do. Marcus wanted to sit down immediately with Eduardo and start in on Puck. As for me, I'd been waiting all day to be alone with Anna and talk about Rita. This would be my chance.

Aliza bolted for the exit. She was gone before anyone could even pretend to wish her a good night.

Again, Stacey and the Two helped clear the stage, but this time they barely spoke to one another. The tension between them was extreme. There would be no joy in the Rose home tonight.

Laura headed up to the dressing room to check on a few details for her notes.

Anna, Marcus, and Eduardo stayed onstage to discuss money issues. Sean and I strolled out of the theater.

"Shouldn't you be in on that conversation?" I asked once we'd reached the lobby.

"Yeah, but the whole money thing goes right by me. Herb was way out of line, you know."

"I shouldn't have said anything. We don't need any more trouble." He looked so sweet. That was always the word that came with Sean: "sweet." Did I want sweet? "Thanks for jumping in, though."

"Well, I guess Marcus had your back. Old habits, huh?" There was a question in his eyes.

"The key word is 'old.' As in, old news." I decided this was as good a time as any in the endless parade of chaos to ask the question I'd been considering for two days. "Look, I have to ask, and I'm sorry if this is awkward, but—"

"Why now?" he said, finishing my question.

"Yes."

"OK. Not easy, but here it is. The truth." He stopped.

I waited. Sometimes that was best.

"OK. I've always thought you were great. In school you were always about Marcus, even when you weren't. Then, I never saw you after we graduated. And … well, you know, I'm not usually this direct."

That was true. The man in front of me was very different from the quiet Sean of the Philadelphia years.

"So last month, Stacey and the guys and I—"

"I didn't know you guys were friends."

"Oh yeah." He said this as if it were common knowledge. "So the four of us did this color thing."

He had no trouble reading my thoughts.

"Yeah. Yeah. It's pretty much what you think. But it did make me think about some things. You know, about putting myself out there for what I want. Then with Alex. I mean, who knows what Alex maybe was putting off till later. And now he's got no later. Have a drink with me."

"I think I like the new Sean," I said. "But I'm still pretty weirded out tonight. I hate to 'put it off,' but why don't we do this later in the week, OK?"

"Very OK." Then he leaned forward and kissed me. Not too long, not too hard, just a lip-lock that was very clear with intention and desire.

"I'm going home," he said, pulling away and backing into the bench. I reached for him, but he caught himself before falling to the floor.

"Damn. You know, I never do that onstage. Never."

"Hey, guys." Eduardo joined us.

"OK, I'm off. Good night." This time, Sean carefully checked for objects as he exited the building.

Eduardo scowled at Sean's exit. "You know, I saw that."

"Oh."

"Grief sucks, and everyone does it their own way. Kiss whoever the fuck you want, if you think it will help."

Everyone does it their own way. I thought of Roger trying to lighten our moods with a bar joke, or Stacey's intense reaction to Alex's death even though they weren't at all close.

"You really think it's just grief?" I asked.

"You've known him for eight years. Ever kiss him before?" He had a point, at least about me. Sean had had some revelatory experience, however temporary it may prove to be for him. My actions, however, could very well be a product of Alex's death. I hadn't even cried yet.

"How do you do it?" I asked.

"Weren't you watching? Good thing folding chairs are cheap." For a moment the cranky exterior cracked, offering a glimpse of that part of Eduardo that made him a part of us. "I got to tell you, Nicky, this sucks more than anything I've known. If kissing Sean helps, go ahead. Hell, if I thought it would help me, I'd do it."

He hugged me. Eduardo's hugs were mercifully free of any erotic tension.

"I'm just on a quick break," he said. "Marcus and I are going to try to get some work done. I think work is what he does for grief."

I wasn't alone for more than a few seconds before the Two came charging out of the stairwell. Without pausing to look around, they were out the front door. A moment later, Stacey came racing after them.

He stopped when he saw me.

"You should know better," he said, stomping right up to me. "I don't expect anything from the rest of them, but you should know better."

"What are we talking about?" I asked.

"Yeah, right." He practically spat the words at me. "It was always so easy for you, wasn't it? Oh, look at me, I'm gay. Everyone knows. Look, look! It's not like that for everyone, Nicky. It was never like that for me. It still isn't. Meeting them was the best thing that ever happened to me. I know you call them names. Like they're some kind of freaks. I know that. They aren't. They just aren't like you or Marcus or Alex." At Alex's name, his voice cracked.

I hadn't heard Stacey say this much at one time since the night I'd met him. I was stunned.

"I'm sorry?" I half-asked, half-said.

"Then act like it." He waited for some kind of answer. I didn't know what to say. I was completely confused. I could see on his face that he was having some sort of internal debate. Then he seemed to settle with himself.

"Don't you understand? I owe them my life."

I was running out of patience with my Classmates. First Marcus was flirting with me like we'd just met, then Sean was macking on me without warning, and now Stacey was blaming me for not understanding something that I wasn't even aware of. And since he rarely spoke, this was particularly annoying. I was in mourning too and beginning to feel the need to claim just a little emotional space for myself.

"No, I don't understand. I don't understand anything that is going on here. I don't even know what the hell you're talking about. I don't even know why you're talking."

"It was a really bad time, OK? I was depressed. I met them one night, drunk. Online."

"You met them online?" I pictured a door opening and the Two, standing shoulder to shoulder, taking their first look at Stacey.

"Yeah. So? They were different, they treated me differently. It was . . . I didn't want to do this show. I didn't want to work with him. Anna talked me into it. Now this shit." He stopped.

I was about to ask who he was talking about when his tone changed abruptly to one more harsh and demanding.

"I mean this. No one hurts them."

I thought I'd known Stacey too long to find him physically intimidating, but for just a moment, as he loomed over me, face red with anger, I was one step toward fearful. He'd been unable to say the word "love" out loud, but there was no mistaking his feelings. What would he do if he thought the Two were truly in trouble?

"Hello." Anna was standing in the theater entrance.

Stacey spun around to look at her full on. I couldn't read the expression on his face. Surprise? Embarrassment? He was suddenly his usual speechless self, turning away from both of us to leave the building.

Anna followed him out onto the street. She wasn't long.

"How is he?" I asked when she returned.

"He's no better than the rest of us."

"I don't get it. He didn't even like Alex."

"You think that makes it OK by him for Alex to get killed?" she asked.

"That's not what I meant."

"I know," she said, apologizing. "What did he say to you?"

"More than he's said in the past eight years. And that he wasn't going to let them get hurt. He really does love them, doesn't he?" I started to think about the three of them differently.

"I am so tired of this. Why did I think it would be a good idea to get all of us back together? I do not need this." Anna sat down on one of the benches.

"This may not be the best time—"

"Please don't say that. It's like a threat. Just stab me or shoot me or choke the life out of me. Just make it quick."

I plunged right in. "Have you noticed Suege and Herb hanging out at all? They were in the lobby tonight having some serious conversation."

"About?" Her tone conveyed nothing but suspicion.

"I don't know. I found them whispering together. When they saw me, they stopped. You don't suppose Suege's dealing, do you?" I sat next to her.

"Shove the knife in and twist it, why don't you? *Dealing?*" She thought for a moment. "I have no idea. I do not like anyone in this company buddying up to the landlord. Especially Herb. This can't lead to anything good."

Having finished her work in the dressing room, Laura entered the lobby from the stairs by the main entrance. "Good, you're still here."

"What's up?" Anna asked in her weariest, leeriest, dear-God-not-another-problem voice.

"Look, I'm sorry to have to do this, but I think I have more bad news for you guys." Laura dumped the plastic bag of costumes she was carrying on the floor, reached in, and pulled out a pint of gin.

"That looks like the first *good* news of the day. Let me find cups," Anna said.

"I found this in the dressing room, stuffed into a costume bag. And we're not talking top-shelf. This stuff is barely more than lighter fluid."

First the box office, now the dressing room. I had visions of bottles tucked into every corner of the theater, folded into every audience seat.

"You tried it?" I reached to make a joke of it.

"Didn't have to. Just the stench. Anyway, I thought you guys should know."

No one spoke. Someone was definitely hiding liquor around the theater. The most likely candidate was Marcus. Anna didn't yet know about the first bottle. I didn't want to get into it in front of Laura. I just shook my head.

"Thanks for telling us, Laura," Anna said. "We'll look into it."

I nodded in agreement.

"You guys talk. I'm going home." Laura left us alone. In the dim, recessed overhead light, the lobby was mostly shadow. If you were kissing a cute man, all those shadows were romantic. If you were contemplating the possibility that your director was a lush, they were more ominous.

I started to speak. Anna interrupted me. "I really need to clean my apartment. I'm going to go home. I'll call you while I mop. We can figure out what to do."

Was she kidding?

"Anna, the last time you mopped a floor, it was with a freshman actor who couldn't learn his blocking."

It's true. Anna and Rita were staging an independent project ... I can be slow, but not that slow.

"Rita called you, didn't she?"

She didn't say anything. She didn't have to. The answer was apparent in the way she plucked at the end of the scarf she wore loosely wrapped around her neck.

"It's not what you think."

When someone makes a point of telling you, "It's not the money, it's the principle," you know it's the money. When a guy makes a big production out of telling you that the man he's dating "isn't anyone serious," you can be pretty sure they're nearly married. And when someone uses that simple phrase, "It's not what you think it is," you can bet all the money the first guy is losing and all the sex the second guy is trying to have on the side that it is *exactly* what you think it is.

"Are you sure? Because I was thinking we could probably take all these paintings to a Dumpster and convince Suege they were never here. What do you think?"

"It *is* what you think. But it's not *why* you think it is what you think it is."

I'm sure I looked confused. "Fine," I said. "Maybe it isn't. But are you telling me it isn't why I think it is because it actually is why I think it is and what? Because I'm thinking you're pretty desperate to avoid it and that makes me think suspicious thoughts. So let's stop the 'Who's on First' routine and tell me what the goddamn secret is."

"Shit. I don't want Marcus or Eduardo to hear." Anna dragged me into the box office. She closed the door behind us and then pulled down the service window. The tiny office felt even smaller completely shut up.

"Do you want to sweep for bugs?" I asked.

"I know you're pissed, I'd be too. Just listen. This is not easy." She stopped.

"You know," I said, "it's more expressive if you say it out loud instead of just thinking." No, I wasn't being fair, but I was angry.

"This is not easy," she repeated. She maintained her usual self-control, but there was the barest hint of a tremor in her voice.

"Just say it. Please."

She blurted it out in one long sentence. "Alex and Stacey were having an affair, but Stacey was way deep in the closet, and that night, Halloween, he and I got drunk and had sex and Alex found out and they had a fight."

I did a quick 360 of the box office. I was pretty confident that I was not on reality TV.

"Alex and Stacey?" I couldn't believe it.

"It was very, very closeted."

"Yeah. No shit."

Now I knew who Stacey had been so reluctant to work with. His reaction to Alex's death made more sense. It was the entire idea that made no sense.

"Wow. But you knew?" Just how much was everyone keeping secret?

"Not till that night. I don't think anyone did. Well, except Marcus. But he found out by accident."

"So you knew and Marcus knew. And then Rita found out. And nobody told me?" My reaction was childish, but I couldn't help it.

Very carefully, Anna spelled out exactly what she thought. "This is not now, nor was it *ever*, about you. Got it?"

"Fine." Was this worth the effort? Maybe Rita was right. Why not just let it go? Who cared about any of it now? I might even have reached such enlightened disengagement, but the distress that Anna was trying (and failing) to keep off her face made me think a little harder.

I asked, "So how did Marcus get into this?"

"That was Alex. It sort of was Marcus's fault. He was going on earlier in the evening about the two of them. You know how he was when he was drunk and coked up. You couldn't shut him up.

It freaked Stacey out. I was trying to calm him down. To help Alex. One thing led to another—"

"And, ooooops, you had sex?"

"Do you want to know or don't you?"

I knew that Anna was perfectly capable of walking out mid-story. I held my hand up. "No more snarky comments."

"Alex couldn't say Stacey hit him, because then people would want to know why. He wouldn't out him. He really did love Stacey. He just picked Marcus out of the crowd. He was angry enough at Marcus anyway. It worked. It was completely believable he'd get drunk enough to hit someone, and Marcus was always blacking out."

A true, if not very flattering, portrait.

"So how did you avoid getting on Alex's shit list?" I asked.

"He blamed Stacey."

"Oh, lucky you." Now I was angry. "Why would you all keep this a secret from me? Christ, Anna, we spent every day together, all five of us."

"What did you want us to say? 'Hey, Nicky, we framed your boyfriend. Fun, huh?' You were so blind to everything he did."

Yet another truth that hurt. I had a brief insight into how I must have appeared to the others. Not pretty. I shoved it aside.

I was leaning against one of the tables, wishing we weren't in such a confined space. Anna stood just inside the door. She was barely in the room.

"What about Rita?" I asked.

"What about her?"

"Everyone thought it was Rita and Stacey. You even said it was Rita. Why?"

"Can't we let this go? It was a mess. We were wrong to lie to you. I admit that."

"What about the crazy little midgets? Do they know about Stacey and Alex? Stacey can barely say Alex's name. Is that why they hated him? Christ, what do they think about Rita? Good thing she's not here, maybe she'd be dead too."

Anna didn't say anything.

The silence stretched on. I tried to imagine the scene in an upstairs bedroom at Rita's house in Philly: Anna and Stacey fumbling around more drunk than horny; Alex walking in on them; the fight; Alex coming down those stairs; Alex, blood on his face, running into Sean and I; Alex pointing at Marcus.

"What have you left out?" I asked.

"What?"

"You've left something out, Anna. There is no need for Rita in that story. What have you left out?"

"Nothing. No one deliberately made Rita part of this. You know how rumors start. Stacey bragged about getting laid. He used it to keep Alex away. Rita's name got wrapped up in it somehow."

"And she just never denied it? How nice for your image. You were even dressed like Snow White."

They were both talented, yet very different people. Anna: always so focused and straight-laced. Rita: the wild woman, loving sex, always working in a frenzy.

"So you humped a drunken Stacey, broke the heart of the man he was having a closeted affair with, smeared my boyfriend as some sort of violent drunk, and pinned it all on Rita?"

"When you say it in that tone, it sounds very evil."

164

"Well, then say it in a different tone. Which tone makes it sound like a picnic, Anna?"

"I got pregnant."

I sat down.

"Anna ..." I had no idea what to say.

"It got very complicated. Rita was good to me. She said she'd let the rumors ride. She said Stacey looked good in his breastplate and she would have fucked him if she could, so why not? She didn't care. You remember that I went to Rita's for Thanksgiving and got so sick I was late coming back?"

I did. Our schedule was demanding. You didn't miss class. You didn't miss rehearsal. You didn't miss performance. A cold, the flu, broken limb—it didn't matter. You showed up. But Anna was late coming back from Thanksgiving.

"Oh, Anna. Did Stacey know?"

"Yes."

A sudden friendship born out of crisis.

"The Two, they don't know about ..." I didn't even know what word to use.

"No. But you're right about Alex. They know about that, but I do not believe they would hurt him. It's just not like them."

Talk about being blind.

She was still clinging to the door, trying to keep as much space between herself and me as possible. Anna Mikasa, whom I'd always thought of as one of the most competent and strongest people I knew, clutching a door frame in a dingy box office for fear of what I might say next. Anna, who loomed so large in my mind, suddenly looked her five-feet-four height.

"Nicky, I was too young. It was the wrong time, and I did what I had to do. I'm not going to apologize to anyone for that. I am sorry that I lied to you."

I went to her, took her in my arms, and hugged until she pushed back.

"I'm sorry," I said.

We held each other for a bit longer. It was getting stuffy in the box office.

"Let's get out of here," I said. "Oh shit."

"There can't possibly be anything else."

"Oh, but there is. The bottle Laura found?"

"Right. The bottle." Good old Anna. I could see her already shifting gears to deal with the problem at hand.

I broke it to her as easily as I could. "It's not the first. Roger found one yesterday in here. Behind the CPU." I pointed under the table. "I didn't want to say anything till I checked it out. But if there are two ..."

"Then we have a problem."

I agreed. "The question is, how big and who?"

"Nicky." She gave me the look of pity reserved for loyal, foolhardy lovers.

"Don't. If it's Marcus, it's Marcus. He's our friend—nothing more—and we'll deal with this as friends."

We emerged from the box office to find Suege once more in possession of the lobby.

"Leave," he said.

"Suege, you're like a ghost haunting this place. We are not leaving. We have a contract," Anna said.

"Suege," I said, "what were you doing here yesterday afternoon?"

He scrunched his eyebrows together.

"What?" Anna asked.

"Tonight I heard Suege tell a TV reporter he was here yesterday when Alex was killed." I filled Anna in on Man Wilson, Channel 3 News.

Suege spoke at last. "No way. I had nothing to do with that. I was upstairs painting. All day."

"In the freezing cold?" I asked.

"I have a heater. No, man. I had nothing to do with that. Nothing. I'm out of here." Suege turned and ran out the front door.

"Nicky, you don't think he could have done it?"

"I have no idea what to think," I honestly answered.

The night was finally over. At the corner of 53rd Street and 9th Avenue, Marcus begged off a cab ride. Considering that the temperature had dropped again, his excuse of wanting to "walk a little off the night" seemed pretty lame to me. Anna gave me a warning look as she pulled her cab door shut.

We walked down 9th Avenue and turned onto 51st Street.

"So what are you up to?" he asked.

"I'm going home," I said.

"To bed?" He smiled at me.

"Marcus, what are you doing?"

"What I've been doing for more than a year now, ever since I got sober. Regretting the way I treated you. Regretting the missed opportunity. I'm sorry, Nicky. I really am."

We were standing in front of my building, a streetlight directly overhead. It was all too schmaltzy for me.

"You don't have to apologize. And certainly not here. What's next, a string background?" I laughed, but easily, showing no rancor.

"Then can I do this?" Marcus leaned in and kissed me.

He took me completely by surprise. The kiss lasted longer than casual but not long enough for compromising.

"Whoa." I finally pulled back. "Wait. I'm not—" I stopped. I'm not what? I'd already noticed the appeal of a sober Marcus. But there was also Sean, with whom I'd made a date only two hours earlier. I'd always believed that stage managers should not get involved with anyone in the production. Now I'd kissed two members of *Midsummer* in one night. Of course, in this case they were both old friends. Did that make it better or worse?

"What about Alex?" I asked.

"Alex?" he asked back.

"Yes. What about you and Alex? I thought I saw, you know, on Saturday night…" Maybe it was more than a little hypocritical to question him about Alex while keeping Sean in reserve, but he was the one who'd broken my heart, not the other way around. I figured that gave me room to maneuver.

"No. And Alex would tell you the same." Marcus kept his gloved hands on my upper arms.

"He did. He said nothing was going on."

"See?" He tried to kiss me again. This time I backed up.

"Wait. Not tonight, OK?" There were questions. Were the bottles his or not? Did I want the nice guy or the bad boy? Did I want either?

"OK. I can live with 'not tonight.' That's actually pretty encouraging, all things considered."

168

After promising to meet at ten the next morning for Operation Movie Rescue, we said good night. Watching him walk away toward 8th Avenue and a subway, I realized that if I was going to survive *Midsummer*, I needed a stronger defense than "not tonight."

TUESDAY MORNING

A FRESH LAYER OF snow coated the streets. Blinding sunlight reflected off the patches not already darkened by the exhaust of morning traffic.

I'd been out earlier. Having called off another day of temp work, I decided to get my life back to something resembling a normal routine. I went to the gym, stopping on the way home to buy the *Times*. Back in my apartment, the phone was mercifully silent. I had until ten o'clock before I needed to meet Marcus at Alex's apartment. Clutching a freshly brewed pot of coffee, I retreated into the paper. I was never so happy to read about world mayhem.

Somewhere between the day's troubles in the Middle East and a blizzard in North Dakota, I made two decisions. Until I was certain that Marcus was not responsible for the stashed liquor, I wasn't going to act on any of his overtures. No matter how much he romanced me, flirted with me, or drove every hormone in my body south, I was going to stand firm against his advances. Until I was absolutely convinced he was still sober, I was going to keep him at arm's length. No dwelling on the topic at all. From that point forward, I was officially dwell-free.

As for Sean, there was no reason not to at least have a drink with him, maybe even dinner, and see how the evening went. After all, I counseled myself, dating was nothing more than doing research. How could I possibly make any choice between them without sufficient research? The fact that I had done eighteen months of close-quarters research on Marcus and had known Sean for eight years did not prevent me from convincing myself that I was doing the right thing by leaving open the possibility of either of them.

I was fully at peace with myself by 9:00 a.m. At 9:30, I was dressed and ready to go. At 9:40, I turned around, walked back up the steps to my apartment, and changed clothes. Just because Marcus wasn't getting near me didn't mean I had to dress like I didn't care. I reevaluated the contents of my closet and dresser. The Two had told me I looked good in red. Did I put much faith in that? I'd like to think not, but I did choose a red sweater to replace the khaki green I'd originally selected. I changed into my brown and black Steve Maddens and replaced the belt. The pledge was to be dwell-free, not fashion-free.

On the way down 9th Avenue, I stopped at the Coffee Pot Restaurant for a morning latte. Armed with another round of caffeine, my sunglasses, and a growing certainty that this was a bad idea, I trudged on. The only good omen was that in going in and out of my building, I'd avoided Mrs. Wizniski four times in a row.

I turned onto West 47th Street. Alex's apartment was between the same avenues as the Brewery—10th and 11th. My relatives, none of whom live in New York, imagine it to be eight million people jammed together in one large, undifferentiated urban mass. Any New Yorker, however, will tell you it's all about the neighborhood. We're notoriously wedded to the immediate vicinity. I didn't think it at all unusual that Alex, I, and the Brewery Arts Center were all within six blocks of each other. No more than I thought it odd that my grocery store, gym, drugstore, video store, dry cleaners, and favorite bodega, diner, and coffee bar were all within four blocks of my apartment. Proximity is a perk of urban living.

I stood in front of Alex's building, a limestone very similar to my own. There were more steps to the front door than at my building and one more floor, but in the basics they were both one of many such structures on the West Side. This building was also divided into four apartments per floor. There were twenty-four buttons on the call board at the top of the steps. I carefully surveyed the paint job on the concrete stoop. I was stalling.

There was no police tape in sight. Why should there be? Even if the apartment was under wraps, there wouldn't be any tape out front: the other tenants had to come and go. In fact, one of them was going right then. I was so preoccupied, she had to step around me, giving me a surly look. I suddenly felt very conspicuous.

I decided to go inside. Marcus could ring the bell when he arrived. I took the steps one by one, slowly and deliberately.

There was no police tape on the door of 3C. If I felt exposed on the street, this was worse. There is really no explaining to the neighbors why you are lurking in the hallway. Torn between not wanting to be seen and not ready to face Alex's empty home, it took me three tries to get the key into the lock. Taking a deep breath, I pushed open the door.

"Stop right there. I'm armed."

I could hear her, but I couldn't see her. I thought I recognized the voice. "Mrs. Isola? Is that you?"

Marina Isola, wielding a kitchen knife, poked her head out from behind the wooden supports of the loft bed. Her eyes were wide with fear. I guessed she hadn't had many opportunities to pull knives on strangers.

"Who are you? What are you doing in my son's apartment? You're not with the police. You should get out. They're on their way here. I know how to use this." She waved the knife about randomly, convincing me she might not even know how to chop a carrot.

"Mrs. Isola, please. It's OK. I'm a friend of Alex's. We've met before. In Philly? At Baldwin?"

"Thank you, young man, but I already know where my son went to school. You do look familiar. What's your name?"

"Nicky D'Amico. You met me when Alex was a freshman?"

"Don't repeat yourself. It's rude. You're a homosexual too, aren't you?"

"Uh, yes." You never do realize just how infrequently anyone asks that question until someone actually does.

Marina Isola was a sturdy woman, already gray when I'd first met her during freshman year. She had a sweet, round face with dimples, warm brown eyes, and a disposition that didn't match any of it.

"Complex" was the most gracious word for Alex's relationship with his mother. After he'd come out, she'd gone into a true rage. During the college years, she'd calmed down considerably—even to the point of helping him live in the City after graduation. Alex was heroically sympathetic to her continued ambivalence: her threats to cut off the little cash support she offered, the pleadings to come

173

home to visit at holidays, the curses and the Bible passages, the intermittent birthday gifts. "I'm her only kid," he'd say. "She has issues."

"What are you doing here?" she asked, not lowering the knife. "Issues" was putting it mildly.

Then again, considering that I was making myself at home in her son's doorway, keys in one hand, latte in the other, it really wasn't an unreasonable question.

"I had Alex's extra set of keys," was the first thing I could think of. I put the latte down on the nearest flat surface.

"Yes, I can see that. Now, what are you doing here?" She'd regained confidence now that she realized she knew me, however vague the memory of our meeting might be. Her hands were no longer shaking.

"Mrs. Isola, could you lower the knife, please?" I asked.

"What? Oh." She looked at the knife as if she wasn't certain when or how it had found its way into her hand.

Lowering the point, she muttered to herself, "I guess homosexuals are afraid of knives. I never thought of that. It makes sense."

This was going to take a lot of patience.

"Now that's much better. Thank you," I said.

"Well, see now—I don't really care. I'm calling the police." She'd forgotten that she'd already told me they were on their way. I didn't point out the error.

What do you tell the mother of the murdered person whose apartment you were about to raid? Nothing that wasn't completely callous came to mind. And where was Marcus? This was his idea. He should be explaining it to the armed mom, not me.

"I'm very sorry for your loss," I said.

She looked stunned for a moment, then started to slowly shake her head from side to side.

"Sorry for my loss?" she repeated. It looked as if she was calculating the death of her son, whom she'd often just barely tolerated since his coming out, against the value of my sympathy. "This was just the final insult," she said bitterly.

I had no answer for that.

"You didn't come here to offer me condolences. I know why you're here. I've heard about this. You want to de-gay the place, don't you? Take away the porn and the sex toys so the family won't be shocked? You can't shock me. I know what my son was." She sniffed at the end of this, as if trying to catch the scent of porn hidden on the premises.

I looked around the apartment. Even if Alex had a porn or sex-toy collection—and knowing Alex, I didn't think it would amount to much if he did—I had no idea where he'd hide it. His apartment was even more compact than mine, which is the polite way of saying smaller than small. His also had more character. While mine was a classic '50s white box, reminiscent of the inside of a flashcube, Alex's had one wall of exposed brick, a loft bed, and hardwood floors in need of refinishing. Two large windows on the wall opposite the door saved the space from darkness.

What I did see as I looked around were the other parts of Alex. On a small desk, in two neatly arranged stacks, were a set of well-worn play scripts and a set of new, untouched ones. The only other objects on the desk were a lamp and a laptop. Clothing hung from two bars under the loft bed, grouped in loose order by type: coats, pants, shirts, and pullovers swept left to right. I could only see the last few discs in the movie collection, the rest hidden from view behind Marina Isola. Then there were the photographs. A cluster of them hanging under the loft featured several shots of the five of us: Anna, Marcus, Alex, Rita, and I in cap and gown, champagne bottles in hand; the five of us crowded together on one side of a restaurant table, making faces at the camera; Marcus and Alex in costume for *A Little Night Music*; Alex and I, laughing, squeezed together into an armchair at Rita's. In all those pictures, he looked happy.

Did his mother notice any of these things?

"Actually, I came for the movies."

"I knew it."

"Not porn movies. His independent movie collection. Movies with gay characters and stories."

"Oh, well, that doesn't make any difference, does it?" She was getting more agitated as she spoke. "Who are you to come in here and take anything? Anything at all?" She was waving the knife around again.

The door buzzer sounded. Finally.

"Who's that? Are there more of you?" she asked, as if I were part of a gang of marauding homosexuals.

"It's probably Marcus Bradshaw. You won't need the knife, I swear."

"Bradshaw? The roommate?"

"Yes. Do you mind?" I pushed the door button on the call box before she could answer. I could have pressed talk and warned him, but this was his idea. Why shouldn't he be as surprised as I?

"Did you take his license too?" She stepped back a bit, bracing herself on the sink.

"What license?"

"What do you mean, what license? His driver's license. I wish he'd done anything as normal as hunt. The police said his driver's license was missing from his wallet."

"No," I said, ignoring the "normal" crack. "Why would I do that?"

"How should I know what you people get up to?"

The front door opened, sparing me the need to correct Mother Isola's no doubt many misconceptions about being gay. Marcus stepped inside and froze.

"Oops."

"Oops?" Mrs. Isola repeated after him. "Hello, Bradshaw."

"Marina." Marcus had adopted a first-name basis back when he and Alex were roommates. ("I'm sure it pisses her off," he'd told me.)

Marina, as Alex's mother, had never been much impressed by the resemblance between Marcus and her son. Yet in the moment he entered the apartment, her faced twitched with agony, then returned to an impassive glare. She was mourning, fighting, cursing her son, and missing him all at once.

"You're looking good," she said.

"I'm sober," Marcus blurted out, as unnerved by the knife as I was.

Marina had trouble gauging the significance of this confidence. "Well, it's not even noon." She lowered the knife. Again, I breathed easier.

Marcus turned to me. "How's this going?"

"If you mean, young man, are you going to waltz out of here with my son's belongings, think again."

I'd shed my scarf, hat, and gloves on the way up to the apartment but was still wearing my coat. Between the heat and my adrenaline response to the knife, I was well baked. I would have removed the coat, but then there would be just that much less fabric between me and the cutlery.

I made another effort to console the grieving mother. "Mrs. Isola, really, you have to believe us. We did not mean any disrespect. We realize this must be very hard for you. Having Alex murdered. Stabbed. I can't begin to—"

"Stabbed?" She shook her head. "That icicle didn't do a damn thing. It barely punctured the skin. He died because he was lying with his head cracked open, bleeding to death in the cold. It was all show. You people love the drama, don't you?"

"What does that mean?" Marcus demanded.

"You people. The gays. One of you bastards left my son to bleed to death in an alley while you played dress-up." Tears collected in her eyes as she focused on the image her words created. "I've had enough of both of you. Get out of here."

She raised the knife again. I had no idea how Marina Isola was going to reconcile her son's death with the memory of the child she'd loved, then rejected, then loved and kept at arm's length. I certainly didn't want her working out her grief by lunging at me. I pushed Marcus back toward the door.

"And you tell whoever spent Saturday night with him—you tell him for me—I hope he rots in hell. I hope you all go to hell."

I decided right then that my parents' perpetual anxiety was really no big deal.

"What? How do you know someone was here?" Marcus stopped me from dragging him through the doorway.

"Isn't it enough that we can barely afford this place? I wanted him to be happy, but not to drag God knows who home from wherever you people meet. He didn't even do the dishes. There was breakfast for two just lying around. I told him, if he didn't do his dishes, he'd get roaches." She began to cry in earnest.

"Marina..." Marcus reached his hand toward her.

She raised the knife once more. "Get out. Get out!"

With one good tug, I pulled Marcus into the hallway. Marina Isola slammed the apartment door shut.

"Nicky, I—"

"Not here," I cut him off, heading for the stairs.

We walked east along 47th Street, passing several buildings before he spoke again. Our breath clouded between us. We must have looked like two agitated smokers rapidly puffing through our cigarettes.

"That wasn't pretty," Marcus said.

As understatements went, it was subterranean.

"God, why did I think it would be a good idea to be in his apartment?" I asked. My heart was racing. I saw the pictures on the wall, all of Alex's possessions spread out in his home. And that crazy woman. "How did he put up with her?"

"What did she mean about Saturday night?"

"That's what's got you?" Maybe he hadn't seen the framed production photos of shows we'd done as undergraduates.

"If there was someone—"

"You're asking me?" I remembered the lingering looks and smiles. What angered me more? Marina Isola's attitude, or the possibility that Marcus and Alex really were involved? They had both denied anything was going on, but circumstances continued to say otherwise. Wasn't this exactly the kind of bullshit I'd put up with the entire time Marcus and I were together? I asked myself why I cared. Then

I decided not to answer myself. I have no idea what a shrink would make of that.

"You think I spent the night with Alex?" Marcus started to laugh. "Not that he isn't a sweetheart. Wasn't. Shit. Look, sleeping with Alex would have been like sleeping with my brother or something equally disgusting."

"You don't have a brother."

"If you have to know, I went to a late AA meeting after rehearsal. Then I went home. Ask Anna. She was still up when I got in."

I didn't respond.

"You're really upset about this, aren't you? Damn. You know what? I'm going to take this as a compliment, because that's what it is." Marcus grabbed my arm and spun me around. "Look at me. Look at me and tell me you don't want to give it another try. Go on."

He was bundled up in a battered pea coat, a wool cap, and what looked to be some heavy-duty home-knitted scarf, no doubt purchased on the street in the East Village. Very retro. Very cute. Very smart. Very passionate. The bingo combination. I'd thought so the first day I'd met him and I thought so right then. He was also trouble. I didn't know that the first day I'd met him, but I knew it firsthand standing on West 47th Street.

Anyway, I had no intention of being some interchangeable leading man in his Julia Roberts chick flick. There would be no teary-eyed scene of emotional reconciliation on a cold street beneath the flurrying snow.

"What I want is to go home and forget about this little adventure." I started walking, crossing 10th Avenue.

"You're evading the question. That means you are seriously thinking about it."

"I'm not a character in a play, Marcus. Don't try to come up with motivation for me."

He laughed.

"If you say so, Nicky."

We were at the corner of 9th Avenue. Time to take a firm stand.

"Do not follow me," I snapped at him.

"Would I do that?" He smiled, following me up the avenue. He was always smiling at me.

"Nicky. Nicky. Nicky." Mrs. Wizniski stood in the doorway of a bodega facing 9th Avenue, just north of the intersection.

"Nicky." She was shouting as if I were blocks away instead of standing four feet from her.

"Mrs. Wizniski," I said, walking up to her. "What are you doing here?"

She wore a winter overcoat unbuttoned over a thin cotton housecoat, which was decorated with a pattern of small roses in bloom. The sneakers on her feet could not have been keeping her warm. The gray and white hair on her uncovered head spiked in all directions. This was not good.

"I needed a lottery ticket, Nicky."

"Ah," Marcus said, placing her from the day before. "The bread lady."

"Mrs. Wizniski, you should have asked someone." I took her arm and started to lead her from the door.

"No." She stopped me. "I need a lottery ticket."

She handed me a dollar bill. "Quick Pick, please."

Why she had passed the three other stores that sold lottery tickets along the way from our building to 47th Street, I did not know. I did know that she should be indoors as soon as possible.

"I'll wait here with her," Marcus volunteered.

Great, I thought, *someone to babysit her while she gets frostbite.* At least she wouldn't wander off. The faster I got the ticket, the sooner I could bundle her into a cab.

I went inside. I'd never bought a lottery ticket.

The man behind the counter, who to all appearances was completely engrossed in reading the *Post* until I interrupted him, said, "Your grandmother is not well, no?"

"She's not my grandmother," I said.

"Ah. She is still not well, bubba." He used a term of familiar endearment from his native country. I'm sure he meant it kindly, but I was in a hurry.

"No, she's not. I need a lottery ticket."

He offered me a choice between the New York Lotto and the Mega Millions drawing. Jackpot size seemed the best criteria.

"Which one is worth more?"

"This week, the Mega Millions drawing. They draw it every Tuesday and Friday. Fill out a card, please." He indicated a stack of white computer cards with red print sitting in front of his register.

"The lottery is not a proper way to plan for elder care," he continued while I read the instructions. "Even if you win, they get confused, they lose the ticket."

I handed him my card, deciding that if I said nothing, I might get back to the street by spring.

"Oh, you don't need this for Quick Pick," he said, tossing the card aside. Pushing buttons on what looked to be a miniature cash register, he started in again. "My sister runs an extended-care facility. In Queens. Nice and clean. Affordable too. I can give you her number. This is no way to plan."

I was getting the face-to-face equivalent of the telephone solicitation.

"Thanks," I said, wishing I could hang up.

"Of course, you have one year to claim the prize if she wins and you cannot find the ticket, but bubba, let me tell you …" He leaned forward and lowered his voice. Did he suspect the lottery commission of listening in? "It is a scam. They say I sold the winning ticket for the New York Lotto on Saturday night but that no one has claimed the prize. But I ask you, who doesn't claim thirty million dollars, huh? The truth is, no one ever wins. It is all a fake. It is like the moon business. All of it." He nodded his head solemnly, suspicious of everyone.

I reached forward and plucked the ticket from his hand. "Thanks." I sprinted for the exit.

He shouted after me, "You didn't take my sister's number!"

Outside, Mrs. Wizniski was telling Marcus how she planned to spend her winnings: a house on the beach, a house in the mountains. She called her real-estate ambitions her "secret desire." She sounded perfectly normal, except for insisting that Marcus was her grandson, and now that she had a house on the beach, he and all his siblings would have to come visit. It was not a good day for Mrs. Wizniski. I shamelessly used her to cover my escape.

"I need to get her home." I stuck my arm up for a taxi. Traffic was not heavy, but then neither was demand. We had a ride in moments. "I'll see you later." I helped her into the back seat.

"Let me—," Marcus started.

"Nope. See you tonight." I jumped into the cab.

I asked to be taken around the corner to 51st Street. As we pulled away, Marcus stood on the sidewalk waving—and smiling.

TUESDAY AFTERNOON

"Why make an accident look like murder?" Roger Parker asked. "Why pretend to stab someone who's fallen and cracked their head? That's backward."

"What makes no sense to me is why every time you have a problem at work, I have to ransack a theater," Paolo Suarez said to me, standing center stage. The only thing keeping him from total misery was the grande Starbucks in his hand.

I'd asked the boys to join Anna and me at the Brewery to conduct a serious search for more liquor bottles. Roger eagerly jumped at the chance. Paolo, however, had to be dragged away from his latest project, a few hints of metal shavings still clinging to his collar. I didn't want to involve anyone else from the Good Company. If it turned out that the bottles were the leftovers of another tenant or in some other way not connected to us, why worry the others?

"No one said it was an accident," I answered Roger, ignoring Paolo's lament. "She just said the icicle wasn't what killed him. She called it 'gay drama.'"

"Drama?" Paolo pulled his dumbest-comment-I've-ever-heard face. "She should know. No one waves around a carving knife unless they're in a Wes Craven film."

It was just after one o'clock. We'd spent almost thirty minutes accomplishing nothing more than me filling the guys in on my morning with Marcus.

Once he'd heard Marina Isola's info on the icicle, Roger formed a theory. He now had it that Alex and someone argued. The argument escalated until Alex—accidentally or otherwise—ended up on the ground, head cracked open. Then the mystery assailant jammed the icicle in Alex's neck. Everything about this idea seemed pretty straightforward until the icicle. Why bother doing that?

"You know, if I had to work in this light, I'd drink too," Paolo said.

I was so used to sitting in theaters for long hours, the absence of natural light didn't even register. I'd made the transition from the blinding winter sun to the dingy yellow stage light without comment.

"Does this mean you guys are going on with the show?" Roger asked.

"Of course," I answered, as if there had never been any doubt. The business of stage managing requires immediate assimilation and enforcement of even the most outrageous of decisions.

I filled them in on the meeting from the night before, including the fighting, Herb and Suege, and the antics of the Two. I left out the more personal revelations about Anna and Stacey.

"So we can add Eduardo to the list of suspects. See, if it's just a fight that escalated to a bad end, then he's just the lug for it."

For a moment, I thought Roger was going to pull out a small notebook and pencil and start actually writing down names.

And did he really say "lug"?

"We don't have a list," I said.

"Maybe you don't," he said, and sniffed at my lack of organization. "What about Herb? What's with this Suege guy? Maybe the entire thing is drug related. Maybe they have some big-time thing going on."

"You'd have to meet Suege to know how unlikely that is. I don't think he's capable of big-time anything." And yet, what if there was something bigger here than just the Good Company? What if Herb and Suege were up to something that was out of control? I had no idea how long they'd known each other. Was it even long enough to set up any kind of operation?

Paolo was through with speculation. "It's getting late. I want lunch. What say we just toss wet brains into a drunk tank and go eat?"

"He does not have wet brain."

"You're just falling for him again," Paolo shot back at me.

"I am not. You know, I have choices here."

"What, that other one? Sam?" Roger asked.

"Sean. He's definitely interested." I knew just how to get them off the topic of Marcus. "He kissed me last night."

"Hold it. Stop. Details." Paolo was all attentive. Once again, dirt trumped homicide.

"There are none. He kissed me. I agreed to have a drink later in the week. That's it."

Paolo was happy. "Oh, I like this. Much better than the ex-drunk."

"So we're free and clear of Marcus, right?" Roger asked.

"Absolutely," I lied. It never worked on them.

"You're lying. Oh, Nicky. What did you do?" Paolo asked. Roger shook his head sadly.

"It was nothing. He kissed me too."

"Where did we go wrong?" Paolo asked Roger.

"You kissed both of them?" Roger seemed unsure whether this was impressive or whorish.

"No. They kissed me."

He settled on whorish. "That's a pretty fine distinction, don't you think?"

"Anyone else take a number?" Paolo sighed as he asked.

"OK. Enough. I don't know why I tell you two anything."

"I think it's our nonjudgmental attitude," Paolo said to Roger.

"That and the unconditional love," Roger replied.

"Can we please focus? This is serious," I said. "We need to search this place thoroughly. I want to know if there are any more bottles stashed in the theater space. That's the house, the stage area, the dressing room, the lobby, the light booth, and the box office. OK? We're looking everywhere. Anything we find we'll bring here to the stage. No more about my personal life. No more pointless speculation about anything."

"No problem." Roger continued on, undeterred by anything so ordinary as other people talking to him. "As fascinating as your love life is, there are still a lot of other unanswered questions. This license thing is very suspicious. I don't like any of it."

"Are you listening to me?" I asked.

"These are the times he only hears his inner Holmes. Where do we start searching?" Paolo asked.

"I am serious," Roger insisted. "Can we take a minute here to talk about this? If it was an accident—and unless you guys think it was death by alley, it's an accident—why would the person involved stab him? You don't get charged with croaking someone if it's an accident." Roger's point was well taken, as far as it went, even if he had used the word "croak."

"I think it's called manslaughter if it's an accident," I said. "And if there's a fight, you can still be in big, big trouble."

"Then again, maybe whoever it was wasn't trying to make it look like an accident," Roger said. "Maybe he just stabbed him in a rage. How angry would you have to be to do something like that?"

"I am never getting lunch, am I?" Paolo sat down in a folding chair. "All right. Since we're doing this, let me say that I think if I had tipped Alex like a cow in a pasture—"

"Paolo," I snapped at him.

"Sorry, I was thinking of a hamburger. Cheeseburger, actually. Medium rare. Mmmm. Anyway, imagine this. Alex is on the ground. I just pushed him there, or he fell while we were fighting—no matter. The point is, blood is seeping from his brains. I'm not going to be thinking very clearly, am I? So maybe, just maybe, the entire thing doesn't make sense because there is no sense behind it. Maybe it was just panic?"

"What do you know about cow tipping?" Roger asked.

"Could we forget the cows, please?" It came to me that maybe these two were not the best people for this job.

"I'm sorry." Paolo gave me his best contrite look, but his periodic attempts at something other than skepticism and outright disdain never worked.

"I don't buy it," Roger said. "You really think that whoever popped Alex gave him an icicle shiv just 'cause it was there?"

Lug? Croak? Shiv? I turned to Paolo for an explanation.

"He started re-reading *The Thin Man* yesterday," Paolo said. "Roger, sweetie, you have to speak English to Nicky. It's all he knows."

Roger repeated himself. "I don't think an icicle ends up in someone's neck just for the hell of it."

Now *that* I understood.

"And what about the license? None of this explains the license." Roger then added, with smug satisfaction, "Until we know who scammed the license, we're just bumping gums here."

"He could have lost that anywhere," Paolo said, dismissing the comment. "And stop talking like that."

"I don't believe in coincidence," Roger said.

"Thank you, Obi-Wan Poirot. Obviously, we aren't eating until we search, so can we get on with this?" Paolo stood, gesturing for me to lead on.

"God, I hope so." I led the way to the stairs at the back of the stage.

With Roger continuing to urge us to consider the murder (accident?) from different angles, we climbed to the dressing room. My plan was to start at the top and work our way down and forward, through the theater to the lobby. I love planning ahead. In this case, the plan had no intention of returning my affection.

The size of the dressing room surprised Roger and Paolo.

"It's so small," Roger said.

"That's polite," Paolo added.

In fact, the dressing room of the Tapestry Theater was not that unusual. It even compared favorably to other ninety-nine-seat theaters I'd worked in. The other thing the boys noticed was that there was only one. The men and the women changed together. I don't think many people outside the business ever think about this. Mostly what they know of dressing rooms they get from movies, where, inevitably, even the least-funded operation has separate facilities. The reality is that most small theaters offer only one room. I've seen dressing rooms that were barely more than a ten-foot square, stuffed with actors bravely trying to change, apply makeup, and still maintain some modesty. If we were a union production, Actors' Equity would require separate rooms, but the Good Company was a long way from paying union rates.

The dressing room was oblong: ten feet by twenty. The full length of one wall held a shallow table with mirrors and high-wattage vanity lights above. The opposite wall supported a long bar with hangers. Small cardboard signs, cut to fit over the bar, hung between every few costumes. Each sign had an actor's name printed in Laura Schapiro's precise block lettering to indicate whose costumes were hanging to the right. The walls, originally a pale yellow, were now faded beyond even that limp color. The general unkempt look was one more reminder that the Tapestry, and the entire Brewery Arts Center, had been designed primarily for public consumption.

"Hello." Anna Mikasa entered from the front door, the one that opened onto the second-floor hallway. She was just finishing unbundling her coat and scarf. "Sorry I'm late."

She didn't look so good. Whatever she was doing to grieve was taking its toll on her. She looked weary. I was sure she'd been up most of the night crying.

Roger, seeing the state she was in, autopiloted into another joke, this time in '30s mystery mode.

"These two groundhogs are looking out of the groundhog hole, see? And the first one says to the second, 'When I give the signal, jump.' And the second says, 'What's the signal?' And the first one goes..." He let out a long whistle.

Anna freaked. "Get out. Get out. Go. Go."

"What? I didn't even get to the punch line. It's funny. Promise."

Anna appealed to me for help. "Nicky, get him out of here." She was backing away from us, along the costume rack.

"What is this?" Paolo may not have enjoyed Roger as a Hammett knockoff, but he wasn't going to let anyone, not even Anna, toss his boyfriend out of anywhere—at least not without a good reason.

I translated Anna's hysteria. "Roger, you whistled in the dressing room. That is tremendously bad luck. You have to go outside, turn in a full circle three times, and then ask to be readmitted."

"Now. You have to go now." Anna was a perfect example of how theater superstitions took root in even the most rational people. "This show has enough trouble as it is."

"You're kidding, right? I didn't even get to the punch line." Roger laughed. "I swear, it's a good joke."

"I'm not kidding," I said. "Please. It will only take a moment."

"Actually, I've heard the joke," Paolo said. "I think this little interruption may have been very good luck."

"This is insane," Roger said.

"Yeah, well, they call it superstition, not superfact. Now please, Rog. Just do it."

He tried to appeal to my rational self. "You believe this?"

I tossed a condescending look at Anna. "Not really, but it keeps the peace."

"Make *me* out to be the crazy one," she said. "Don't let him fool you. He has plenty of superstitions. Go." There was no diverting her.

"Oh, go ahead." Paolo added his encouragement. "This is what you get for pretending to be Bogart. And please, be careful and don't say that Shakespeare play name, what's the one—Mac—"

"Don't." Anna and I jumped simultaneously.

Even I have my limits, and no one was going to say "Macbeth" aloud in any theater I occupied.

"Oh, so Nicky, just keeping the peace?" Paolo teased.

"Ha," Anna snorted from her corner of the dressing room.

It is true that I have very few superstitions. However, saying the name of the Scottish Play in a theater, outside of using it as a line of text in the play itself, was one taboo I would not transgress.

"OK, I'll go." Roger stepped into the hallway and out of our line of vision.

"How do you know if he actually turns in a circle? And if he comes back without doing that, is it extra bad luck?" Paolo asked.

"OK," Roger called out. "I'm done. I'm coming back in."

"You have to ask permission," Anna reminded him.

I could actually hear Roger's annoyance in the silence.

"May I come back in, please, Ms. Mikasa?"

"Yes, you may," Anna answered.

"May we continue searching now?" Paolo asked. "I really want lunch."

"Yes. Let's get this done." The actors' makeup kits were scattered across the full length of the table. Arranged among the kits were a few small pictures taped to the mirrors, a slip of paper from a fortune cookie, a miniature stuffed animal: random tokens of individuality.

Anna had worked her way along the costume rack during the whistle scare. She was now at the far end of the room, where Laura Schapiro had tossed several plastic garbage bags of unused costumes.

Roger and Paolo were at the other end of the costume rack. As I opened makeup cases, they rifled through and patted down the costumes.

"Not that there's many places to hide anything here," Paolo said, surfer wear in hand. "Just how sure are you two about this show, anyway?"

"Very," Anna said, sticking her hand into a garbage bag. She began pulling out costumes.

"I think there are a lot of good ideas in this production." I was methodically moving from one makeup case to another, lifting lids and then interior trays.

"Ideas like a blind date has personality? Or ideas like Einstein is in the room?" Paolo held up a pair of impossibly small biker shorts. "And tasteful ideas, I'm sure. No wonder there is so much kissing going on around here."

"Kissing?" Anna asked, her head almost buried in a bag of costumes.

I shot Paolo a warning look that turned to pleading, but he was never one to pass up fun.

"Well, not all of us. Just Nicky."

"I'll kiss you if you want." Roger reached out and pulled Paolo to him. They locked lips.

"Nicky?" Anna now had her head out of the bag, focusing all her attention on me. "Who are you kissing?"

"No one. They kissed me." Why did it always sound so lame when I said it aloud?

Anna was giving me her sternest schoolmarm glare. "Who in my production have you been kissing?"

"I really don't think it's your production," I said.

She just kept staring.

"Fine. Sean and Marcus both kissed me." Then, to Paolo, who was still hugging Roger, "Happy?"

"Ecstatic," he answered.

Anna considered my news. "I would not have guessed Sean."

"Oh, tell us, who were *you* betting on?" Paolo asked.

"We don't need any more trouble, Nicky." Anna stopped short of wagging her finger at me.

"Your concern for my emotional well-being is touching. But not to worry, I'm fine. Really."

"Be careful," she said.

OK, so she did have a right to be concerned. We didn't need anyone else at odds in this production. I tried to look suitably apologetic.

"Anna, I promise. I'll be careful."

"Like I'm believing that look." She went back to searching. We all did.

"Here we go." Roger held an unopened airplane bottle in one hand, Titania's second-act gown in the other. "It was in the pocket of this thing."

"That costume belongs to Herb," Anna said.

"Doesn't mean the bottle is his. Here." Paolo held up another, pulled from the costume of one of the mechanicals.

"Shit," I said, lifting another top tray from within another makeup case.

"Damn," Paolo said. "It's a wonder you people get anything done around here. Anna, you find anything at your end of the liquor cabinet?"

"Yes." The tone in her voice made us stop and turn.

"Look." She held up a thick wool sweater.

"You can't drink that, sweetie," Paolo said.

"You could test it for DNA, though." She held out one sleeve. The cuff was matted with a dark brown substance.

"Is that blood?" I asked.

Paolo reached for the sweater. "Sure looks like it."

"Stop." Roger grabbed his arm. "No one else touch it. That glad rag could be important. You'll contaminate it. They can test these things for fiber and trace evidence."

Now it was my turn. "Glad rag? You have to stop, Rog."

"He's right about testing it." Anna was holding the sweater at arm's length. Expecting spontaneous combustion, maybe? "I don't know what they'll find. This bag is full of costumes. If there is anything on the sweater, it could have come from the stuff in this bag. God knows who wore what on Sunday."

"We'd better call the police." Paolo pulled out his cell phone. "Anyone have one of those cards the detectives left?"

"Wait. We can't call yet." I grabbed his wrist.

"Why?" Anna asked.

"I know this is going to sound crazy," I said. "But we need to finish searching for bottles. We may not get a chance after the police arrive."

The three of them thought for a moment.

"Yeah, that's crazy. I'll call 911." Paolo opened his phone.

"I think I have the card." Roger started rooting through his wallet.

"Wait." I must have sounded desperate. Everyone stopped again. "Just listen. I know there isn't really a good reason for this, but I'm asking as a favor. We need to collect any bottles before the police come. I can't believe there is any connection between them and Alex."

No one said anything.

"Please."

Roger broke the silence. "Nicky, you've always had a bit of a thing for playing savior, but this is too much. It's going to really hurt you someday."

"But not today. I just know this, OK?"

I had to do more pleading, but in the end they agreed. We carefully sat the sweater on the stack of garbage bags. After finishing the dressing room, we searched the prop cabinet stage left, the scenic and lighting materials stored in the aisles, and the light booth and made one more pass at the box office. In all, we collected the two airplane bottles of gin from the dressing room, one pint of Southern Comfort from the prop cabinet, and two fifths of scotch from the light booth. The minis were intact, but the others were all more than half empty. We placed the entire haul on the folding table center stage.

"And yet it just doesn't feel like a party," Paolo said.

Roger was having second thoughts. "I don't know if this is a good idea. We shouldn't be hiding anything from the police."

I offered a perjurer's comfort. "We're not, really. If they ask, we'll tell."

There was no other sound in the theater. Not even the ventilation fans were on. There was nothing to distract us from making the inevitable connection between Marcus and the bottles displayed before us. Images of the first years at Baldwin flooded in on me: Marcus drunk, falling down, throwing up, apologizing, drunk again. The others, as if by prearranged consensus, waited patiently for me to take the lead.

I chased the memories out of my head. "There are large shopping bags in the prop cabinet. Let's put them in one and stick them in the cabinet. Then we call the police."

Detective Marissa Sanchez and her partner showed up almost half an hour later.

"Well," she said, surveying the four of us onstage, bottles carefully hidden, "what's going on here?"

"We found something. In the dressing room." We'd chosen Anna to speak for us. Roger and Paolo weren't really representative of the company, and I didn't trust myself to say anything until I'd had more time to take in the evidence of Marcus's drinking.

"And what is that, ma'am?" Sanchez's partner was a middle-aged man named Dave Rampart. He wore an off-the-rack jacket and barely coordinated shirt and tie. Sanchez herself looked more put together than she had on Sunday and less unhappy than the day before at the station. Having a solid lead to track down was lifting her spirits.

"It's a sweater. We think there's blood on the sleeve."

"Where is this sweater?" Sanchez asked.

"We left it upstairs where we found it."

I don't know what four people who are keeping information from the police look like, but I'd guess we were a fairly representative example.

"So you found a sweater with what you think is blood on the sleeve?" Detective Rampart repeated the information. He pulled a small notebook from his coat pocket.

"Yes." Anna nodded her head.

"Where?" he asked.

"In the dressing room."

"Where in the dressing room?" Detective Sanchez suddenly turned on Roger with this question.

"Um. In a bag."

"A bag?" Rampart turned to Paolo. "What bag?"

"A garbage bag with costumes in it."

"Ones we're not using," Anna added.

"And why were you looking in a garbage bag of unused costumes, Ms. Mikasa?" It was Sanchez's turn.

I jumped in. "We were looking for a missing prop."

The detectives clearly did not approve of anyone answering questions asked of other people. They focused their attention on me.

Sanchez started the new round. "What prop, Mr. D'Amico?"

"A squirt gun." It just popped into my head. Roger and Anna were impassive. Paolo rolled his eyes. Had the police seen that?

"In a garbage bag of costumes?" Rampart took his turn with relish. Oh yes, they'd seen.

I gamely defended the indefensible. "It's small. These things wander off."

"Who's responsible for keeping track of the props?" Sanchez asked, following through.

"I am—"

Rampart interrupted me. "Lose many?"

"No. I never ..." I stopped.

"Except this one?" Sanchez jumped in, seeing a way through to whatever it was we were hiding.

"Well, sometimes," I said.

"Look, all of you." Sanchez eyed each of us in turn. "I don't know what you're up to here, but I'm telling you, it is not smart to hide information in a homicide investigation. Now, what is this about?"

No one spoke. Again, the others waited for me. I was touched by their display of loyalty. I also realized, belatedly but definitely, that we were in a bad position. I'd gotten us into it, so ...

I walked over to the prop cabinet. Opening the double doors, I reached in and grabbed the handle of the large white, red, and blue plastic bag that held the bottles. Placing it on the table, I lined the bottles up for inspection by the police. When I was done, I stepped back. Seeing them all neat and orderly drove home the effort it took to keep that kind of consumption hidden.

Sanchez watched me do all this with a smirk.

"They're not mine," I said.

She shrugged. "You don't need to explain your drinking to me."

"OK. Can someone explain any of this?" Detective Rampart asked. "What are we looking at here?"

"We found these bottles hidden around the theater—in the dressing room, the prop cabinet, the light booth." I wasn't ready to give a name.

"This is what you were searching for?" Rampart asked.

"Yes," Anna answered.

"And you think it has something to do with the murder?" Sanchez was peering carefully at each bottle.

"Don't you?" Roger asked. He couldn't take it any longer. "See, the murderer tips a few, gashouses it with Alex, who drops and takes it on the conk. What I can't figure is the license angle."

Paolo closed his eyes and sighed.

"If you called us out here for a prank..." Sanchez's eyes narrowed as her temper rose.

"Who told you about the license?" Rampart asked.

"What license?" This was Anna trying to keep up.

Paolo smiled at Detective Sanchez. "You have to excuse him. He was dropped into a cotton gin as a child."

"I grew up in a suburb of Bloomington, not on a farm."

"Baby, I wouldn't be so eager to give up a good excuse."

"Guys, could we wait until later for this?" Anna tried to reassure the police. "I don't know what this license thing is. There is a sweater with blood on the sleeve in the dressing room. We were looking for the bottles because we think the director of the production may have a problem. I have no idea if it has anything to do with Alex. None of us do. That is the truth."

The detectives did not respond directly to her admission.

"How did you hear about the license?" Rampart asked again.

"Alex's mother told me. I ran into her this morning." I didn't want to say where.

"Where?" Sanchez asked.

Why do I never get what I want when I deal with the police?

I considered lying, but the situation was way too far out of control already. "At his apartment. Marcus and I went there to pick up his movie collection. His mother was there."

"You broke into his apartment?" Rampart was not amused.

"I didn't break in. I have a key."

"On you?" Sanchez held out her hand.

I pulled Alex's keys out of my pocket and dropped them in her opened palm.

"All right, this stops now." Rampart straightened his tie in an effort to look more authoritative. "We were not releasing the information about the license. I don't want to see this in print anywhere. Understood?"

"Yes, sir," Anna answered.

"So the license is the hot rumble?"

Rampart peered directly at Roger's eyes. "Are you high, kid?"

"If only," Paolo muttered.

"Look, all of you. No more Nancy Drew, got it?" Sanchez said. She was well over our little mystery-cabaret act.

Paolo jumped to the defensive. "Don't call me Nan—"

I stopped him. "I think we've put on enough of a display for the police."

"Smart move. Now take us to the sweater," Sanchez said. "And you,"—she pointed at Roger—"stop with the . . . whatever it is you're doing. It's creepy."

Paolo opened his mouth to object. I put my arm on his to restrain him, but I needn't have bothered. At that moment, Marcus Bradshaw came striding down the left aisle. He stopped just short of the stage. He took in the tableaux of the police, the four of us, the bottles.

"Whoa," he said. "Where's the party?"

"This is the director," Paolo said, shooting me a quick "now you'll see" look.

202

"Are you waiting for me?" Marcus asked. He dropped his backpack and coat in the first row. Stepping onto the stage, he tried to catch my eye. I focused on the floor.

"Mr. Bradshaw, are these bottles yours?" Sanchez asked, as if it were nothing. As if she'd asked, "Are these your shoes?" or "Is this your newspaper?"

"No," he answered.

"They were found around the building. Your coworkers think you have a problem." Rampart continued the two by two—a routine that seemed so comical when the Two did it, but didn't even rate a grin now.

Marcus didn't respond.

"Look." Sanchez adopted a confidential, friendly tone, the tone your lawyer warns you to watch out for when speaking with the police. "Hiding your drinks isn't a crime by itself. It's not good, and you should seek help. But it's not a crime. And if it has nothing to do with Mr. Isola's murder, then it doesn't concern us. Understand?"

Marcus spoke directly to me. "Those aren't mine. I have not had a drink in one year, two months, and five days. I go to AA meetings almost daily. Your belief isn't required to make it true, but you know, Nicky, it would have made it easier."

It didn't take much detective work to catch the crosscurrents on stage. Paolo had lost all control and was looking quite pleased. Anna was pained. My own misery reflected Marcus's sorrowful tone. Only Roger seemed undisturbed, but then he was probably trying to translate "We've got you" into noir slang.

"What the fuck is this?" Aliza Buday was now standing at the edge of the stage. "I come in early to get something done and you people are taking up space. Don't any of you work for a living?"

"I'm here to rehearse with Eduardo," Marcus said. "But we got sidetracked." As he spoke, he moved stage right, clearing the line of sight between Aliza and the table full of booze.

"Oh, thank Christ. You found them," she said.

"What?" Sanchez spun around, confronting Aliza. "What did you say?"

"These are yours?" Anna looked at the bottles. Relief spread over her face.

"Hell, yes. I can never remember where I leave them. Anyone want a shot?"

"Aliza, you're a drunk? Yes!" I cheered, and slugged Paolo's shoulder.

"I don't think anyone's drinking just now," Sanchez said.

"Ow. Cruel to both her and me." Paolo was rubbing his shoulder.

"Sorry," I said to Aliza. "Not sorry," I said to Paolo.

"I wouldn't say 'drunk.'" Aliza joined us at the table, looking at the bottles with the desire of several drunks.

"You've been drinking at rehearsal?" Anna asked. If Aliza had known Anna as well as I did, the quiet, controlled tone of that question would have sent the lighting designer running for an exit.

Roger called for our attention. "Wait a minute."

I braced for another onslaught of Marlowe-speak.

"Does this mean he's innocent?"

"Innocent of what?" Marcus exploded. "You think I killed Alex? That's it, isn't it? You don't even know me. Oh, but that doesn't matter, because you two"—and here he turned on Anna and me—"were just as happy to blame me, weren't you? This is great."

"Marcus, you know—"

"What, Anna? Tell me, what do I know? Do I know how much you both love me? Do I know how little you trust me?"

"OK. Everyone settle down." Detective Rampart had no patience for this. As far as he was concerned, we could fight on our own time. "We have no idea what these bottles mean, if anything. Why don't you take us to the sweater now."

"Sweater?" Marcus asked.

"Apparently, someone tucked a bloody sweater away in the dressing room. Either of you know anything about that?" He directed this question at Marcus and Aliza, who shook their heads.

"Excuse …"

"… us."

"We don't …"

"… mean to interrupt."

The Two stood at the foot of the aisle, clothed in identical forest green wool coats with attached hoods. They had identical backpacks stuffed to capacity. They looked like Hobbits.

Two #1 took the lead. "We didn't think anyone would be here."

Sanchez and Rampart shared an eye roll and shoulder shrug. I don't think they wanted any of us there, particularly the Two.

I may have been up to my emotional eyeballs with Marcus, but I was still cognizant enough to find it suspicious that the Two were *planning* on an empty theater. "Why are you guys here?" I asked.

They gave me the blank-stare treatment again.

Detective Sanchez wanted an answer as well. "That's a very good question."

They looked at each other, then at Anna, then back at each other.

"It was supposed to be a surprise."

"We don't want to spoil your fun."

"Oh, we're just about done with the fun," Paolo said. "Go on, finish us off."

The Two placed their bags on the stage apron and began to unpack an assortment of multicolored items: construction paper, spray paints, sidewalk chalk, tinted light bulbs.

"Oh no. No. No. No." Aliza kicked the construction paper aside. "You are not changing anything on this stage. I have been hanging lights all week. Everything is set."

"You are very hostile," Two #1 said. "You shouldn't drink so much."

"You knew she was drinking?" Anna asked, echoing everyone's surprise.

Detective Rampart made another mark in his little spiral notebook.

"Of course." Two #2 gathered the paper back into a neat stack. "We thought everyone did."

"We never told." Two #1 glared at Aliza. "You should be nice to us."

"We didn't know," Anna said, turning on Aliza. "That doesn't matter, because she is not going to do it again, and she is never coming here drunk, is she?"

Anna's oblique approach reflected her dilemma. She couldn't keep threatening to fire Aliza without eventually following through, or she would lose control of the situation. At the same time, she couldn't afford to replace Aliza, and she certainly didn't want to go without a designer. At this point, all she could do was hope for the best.

Two #1 jumped right in. "We could design the lights."

"Light is just liquid color," Two #2 added, enraptured at the thought.

"These two are not touching my lights." Aliza was not going to be sidetracked into letting the Two anywhere near her work.

"I think we've had enough liquid today," Marcus said. "And no one is replacing anyone—yet. Now, what's with all the stuff?" He eyed the colored chalk.

"It's for the dressing room," Two #1 said.

Two #2 looked around as if to see that we were alone, as if somehow the ten of us didn't already constitute a crowd. He lowered his voice and whispered, "It's pale yellow, you know."

They nodded their heads in solemn unison.

Anna closed her eyes and took a deep breath. Maybe she was thinking of my conversation with Stacey, maybe she had a thing against pale yellow, or maybe she was just too preoccupied to care.

"You may put the paper on the walls, but no spray paint, no chalk, and no changing the light bulbs. Go and do your … whatever it is. Just be certain that it's nothing we can't clean up later."

"Nothing *you* can't clean up later," I said, amending Anna's instructions and pointing at the Two. "Understand?"

"Don't worry, Anna." Ignoring me, Two #2 stuffed everything back in the bags. "We're on it."

"Hold on." Detective Rampart stopped the action.

He and Sanchez had quietly listened to the conversation. Now, surely having seen enough of the Good Company in action and wanting the first crack at the dressing room, he reasserted their authority.

"First we go up and get the sweater. Which of you actually found it?" Sanchez asked.

"I did." Anna raised her hand like a schoolgirl admitting to a prank.

"Then lead on," Rampart said, gesturing for her to proceed.

"The rest of you—wait here." Sanchez stressed the "wait here."

The pause has a long, checkered theatrical history. Both young and bad actors favor it. The first outgrow it, assuming they aren't also the latter. Poor productions of Chekhov employ it to distraction. In talented hands, a well-timed pause can bring on hysterical laughter or deeply felt tears. At school, one of our acting teachers, in the hopes of discouraging us, insisted, "Every time you pause, a sparrow dies." In the minutes after Anna escorted the detectives to the dressing room, flocks of dead sparrows gathered at our feet.

Finally, driven by his natural abhorrence of all things calm, Paolo spoke up. "I don't know about anyone else, but I could use a cocktail." He stepped toward the liquor.

"Me too. I could use a good belt." Aliza lit up in anticipation of getting lit up.

"Anna said you weren't supposed to drink at rehearsal," Two #1 said.

"How cute, temperance midgets. Pour me a shot," Aliza said to Paolo.

Roger, whose Midwestern instincts for avoiding ugly scenes were as strong as his lover's for creating them, tried to slow everyone down. "Maybe we should just wait for the police to get back."

"Oh, baby, I don't think they're allowed to drink on duty, but you're sweet to think of them." Paolo had his hand around the neck of a scotch bottle.

As much as I didn't care at that moment, I felt obligated by my job responsibilities to intercede.

"No one is drinking," I said. "Put the bottle down, Paolo." He was looking around for glassware.

"Very well," he said. "But don't complain to me if you aren't having fun." He retreated from the table.

"We're…"

"…having fun."

That comment brought on another long pause. If we had been working from a script, the director would have fired us.

Finally, Anna returned, without the police.

"They went out the front," she said in response to my question.

"Can we go upstairs now?" Two #1 asked.

Two #2 picked up the backpacks.

"Yes, but remember the rules," Anna said, relieved to get rid of them.

I cast a meaningful look at Roger and Paolo, which Paolo ignored but Roger mercifully acknowledged.

"We'll go with you," he said.

The Two stopped their progress toward the rear of the stage. They shared one of their cryptic eye-to-eye, nonverbal communications.

"We'll take the pale one," Two #1 said.

"But we don't want the other one." Two #2 started to walk away.

I looked at Paolo. If my expression had been any more desperate, I'd have strained my eyeballs.

"Oh, all right," he relented. Turning toward Two #2, he said, "Unfortunately for you, we're not choosing sides for gym. You get us both."

Stuck with help, like it or not, the Two pushed their way through the back curtain, followed by Roger and Paolo.

"We need to start with the ceiling…" was the last we heard as they disappeared into the velvety darkness.

There were only four of us left onstage.

Aliza and I both spoke at once.

"Anna, I never—," she said.

"Marcus, let's go—," I said.

We were both cut off.

"I don't think so." Anna marched right up to Aliza. She was shorter than the lighting designer by a good four inches, and probably fifty pounds lighter, but you'd never know that from the way Aliza shrank back.

"Go?" Marcus asked. "You are fucking kidding me, right?" He didn't even look in my direction. "I have rehearsal."

"How can you possibly justify this?" Anna asked Aliza. "You have been drinking in rehearsal."

"You never noticed," Aliza said. "You never noticed anything. I do a good job."

"Marcus, will you look at me, please?" I asked, standing beside him.

"That is not the point, Aliza," Anna said. "You know that is not the point."

"You want me to look at you," Marcus said to me. "OK. How's this. Want to know what I see?"

We probably would have sounded better as opera (what doesn't?), but we didn't have the music, lights, or costumes. Marcus once said he preferred his drama onstage. As our imbroglioed quartet fought on, I wished we'd been able to keep it that way.

"What does it matter if I can do my job?" Aliza asked. "What do you care?" Out of the corner of my eye, I could see her trying to back away from Anna, who was now in full fury and pursuit.

"How about what I lived through?" I was getting angry. Who was he to blame me for not trusting him? "You have no right to expect anything from me."

Anna was shouting, her self-restraint spent. "I do not want you fucking up my show. I do not want you fucking up my insurance. I do not want you fucking up my audience when a goddamn instrument falls because you are too fucked up to do your job. That's what I fucking care about."

Marcus stepped off the stage into the house. "I don't expect anything from you." He started to root through his backpack.

The girls were both red-faced and looked like they would gladly have sucked up a fifth, if that weren't already the problem.

I started putting bottles back into the plastic bag.

"I don't suppose...," Aliza said wistfully, watching her stash disappear.

"No." Anna stepped off the stage. "You and I are going to the lobby." This time she didn't wait for Aliza to say anything, just started for the exit. Aliza sighed and followed.

Marcus stayed in the house. "Eduardo will be here soon. I need to work."

"This won't take long," I said.

"You know, you can't stop her from drinking by taking away her liquor."

"Oh, believe me, I know." I regretted it as soon as I said it.

"You have to let it go, Nicky," he said. "It was years ago."

"You have to rehearse." I put the bag in the prop cabinet. "I'm sure these will be safe here." It was a gratuitously mean comment. "I'll be upstairs if you need anything."

I really was sorry I'd suspected him, but he should have been more understanding. After all, I told myself, I was the one taking the bigger risk. It was Marcus who'd screwed me over in the first place. I took the steps to the dressing room two at a time. If I'd been taller, I'd have gone for three at a clip.

Two #2 was standing on the makeup table while Two #1 offered instructions. They were taping one sheet of green paper after another to the ceiling. More frightening, Roger was standing next to them sorting out various shades of green, one from another, and handing them over as Two #1 called out a color.

I watched for a few sheets. When I was convinced that my anger at Marcus would not seep into my voice, I spoke up.

"Do I want to know?" I asked Paolo, who was standing just inside the door at the top of the steps.

"I couldn't tell you anyway. Mostly they've ignored me."

"We can hear you," Two #1 said.

They turned simultaneously to look at Paolo.

"We just don't think you are funny," Two #2 said.

Still moving in unison, they went back to their work.

Two #1 held out his hand. "Jade."

Roger handed a square piece of paper, maybe ten inches by ten inches, to Two #1, who passed the paper up to Two #2, who taped it to the ceiling.

"Olive." They repeated the process.

Again for asparagus, spring, deep forest, and celadon (which I'd never heard of and which looked, well, green).

"It's a green rainbow." Paolo yawned. "I'm still hungry. In fact, I'm hungrier."

"Can you make him go away?" Two #1 asked me.

"Not usually," I responded.

"He's not going to go until I do," Roger said, and passed along another sheet of asparagus.

The Two looked at each other for barely a second.

"You can go," they said in unison.

"Hey, that's—"

"Come on, Rog. I need to talk to you anyway." Taking Paolo by the arm, and with one hand on Roger's shoulder, I maneuvered us into the hallway.

I shut the door on Two #1 calling out colors as he passed them up to be added to the ceiling: "Drab olive, pine green, sap green, vert, verdian …"

"Where do you think they get it?" I asked once we were safely on the other side of the door.

Paolo shrugged. "They probably picked it up from some trick when they were just little pervs, and now it's in the tertiary stage."

"I meant the paper. Who knew there were so many shades of green?"

"Forget the paper. Start chinning. What's the skinny?" Roger asked.

We were in the long, narrow hallway that ran the length of the second floor of the Brewery. From front to back it passed, first, a small office from which Suege ostensibly managed the property, then a rehearsal hall we were no longer using, and then ended at the dressing room. Like all the nonpublic spaces, it was slightly shabby.

Cheap, industrial carpet covered the floor. The walls were the same sad yellow as the dressing room.

"What's a 'skinny'?" I asked.

Roger sighed. It was lonely in noir land. "Tell us what happened downstairs, OK?"

"Pretty much what you'd expect. Anna and Aliza are having it out. Marcus doesn't want to speak with me."

I decided to leave it at that. Once I had more time, I could better sort through the situation.

Paolo added a new twist. "You know, some of those bottles could very well be his. If she's such a drunk, why wouldn't she claim them all? Maybe she thought she'd get some free booze."

"Let it go, Paolo. He's not drinking. You'll just have to accept the bad news and move on."

He grunted, not quite conceding the point. I had a passing awareness of how much easier my choices would be if Marcus actually were drinking.

"So what are we talking about here?" Roger asked.

"I need you guys to do me a favor."

"Ooh. What? What are we going to do?" Roger started bouncing on the balls of his feet. I placed a hand on his shoulder to steady him.

"I just need you to come to rehearsal tonight and keep an eye on the Two and, well, just generally keep your eyes open. I'll be stuck on the book all night, prompting. I just want someone watching what's going on. OK?"

Roger was smiling. "You got it."

"You cannot wear a deerstalker cap," Paolo said.

Roger sighed. "I don't own one."

"If he comes in costume, you have no one to blame but yourself, Nicky," Paolo said. He turned and walked down the hallway. "Now I am going to lunch. With or without the two of you."

———————

The Renaissance Diner on 9th Avenue at 53rd Street is what the locals call an "upscale diner." This is a finely graded designation I've never heard used anywhere but in New York. The "diner" part indicated that the prices were low and the menu included the basic American and Greek dishes common to all New York diners: hamburgers, salads (chef, Cobb, and Caesar), gyros, moussaka, and an assortment of specialty dishes that came with vegetable and potato ("veg" and "pot" on the menu). The "upscale" meant you could get grilled seafood on the Caesar and sit in the back garden, and the bread was fresh.

The place was nearly empty in the middle of the afternoon. We snagged my favorite spot, a booth in the front window. The guys were quiet for a few minutes while they looked over the menu. I was a regular and knew exactly what I wanted. Instead of perusing the menu, I gazed out the window, wondering how much stress it would entail to ban the Two from rehearsal at this late date. Almost certainly more than any of us were willing to bear.

The waiter arrived. His nametag read "Michael." He pronounced it "Mikhail." Dark, curly hair topped a head from which two onyx-black eyes solicited our orders. The look, the name, the muscles, the tightly stretched red pullover with the diner logo on his left pec—everything conspired to focus our attention.

"What'll it be, guys?"

Paolo, as always impervious to the charms of strangers, ordered a Caesar and Coke without looking up.

Roger, never one to miss a cute boy, asked, "What's good? What do you recommend?"

Responding to Roger's tone, Paolo looked at the waiter, then at Roger, then straight at me and said, "Order, will you?"

I had no boyfriend at the table. I had no boyfriend anywhere, only an ex sniffing around for a rerun and an old friend suddenly struck with romance. I ordered a BLT with extra-crispy fries.

"Are the fries really crispy?" I asked.

"They can be, if you want." Michael winked at me.

Roger was ready. "I'll just have a hamburger, medium rare. And a Diet Coke. Thanks."

"Wait, I need a drink," I said.

"Or two?" Michael did a semi-leer thing with his lips that was both cute and provocative.

"Just one Diet Coke, thanks," I answered.

"Just one," he repeated. "For now."

Once he was gone, Paolo said, "You really are going to have to start giving out numbers to line them up."

"Oh, please." Roger dismissed Michael as so much scenery. "He's a waiter. Waiters don't count. Everyone flirts with them."

"You certainly do," Paolo said, turning to his lover. "Endlessly."

I'd seen their jealousy routine way too many times to find it at all entertaining.

"Don't start. I'm not in the mood for the jealousy game today. It's too rough on me."

"Oh, Nicky. Don't you know? The best games are rough and tumble." Paolo and Roger both laughed at Roger's comment.

"Really. Not in the mood," I countered.

They gave me the overly sympathetic look they trotted out when they thought my heart was broken.

"Stop it."

"Stop what?" Paolo came as close to innocent questioning as he genetically could, which is to say as close as New York is to LA.

"You know what. Stop the 'look.' I am not devastated. At best, I'm undecided."

Michael returned with our drinks. He placed mine last.

"Here's number one." He smiled at me before leaving.

I smiled back.

"Enough with the waiter. Undecided about what?" Paolo wanted to know.

"What do you mean, 'what'? Sean. Marcus."

"Do you really want to work this out with him?" To Paolo, the idea was inconceivable.

"I didn't say that. The thing is, Sean is very sweet, but I really haven't given it all that much thought. With Marcus, I don't know. I've been there, haven't I? It's just that I never felt like it had a real ending, you know? The actual breakup was very ugly, but then we sort of had to come to terms with each other. We had two and a half years left at school. We couldn't spend them not talking—like Anna or Rita would have let us."

"Please do not tell me you're looking for closure. I hate that word." Paolo dipped into the bread basket the busboy had deposited in front of him.

"I might be. I don't know. It just… the way he looked at me today." I really didn't know what I wanted to do.

"Remember, a still-unidentified somebody murdered Alex," Roger said. "It could be one of the two of them."

"Oh, please. Sean wouldn't even trap a roach. Marcus is sober. Sober people don't commit murder—it's against the rules. If it was anyone, it was the Two or Herb," I said.

Paolo pointed at me with the butter on the end of his knife. "'If'? What 'if'? You said yourself, no one could get into the alley except from the building. The gate to the street was locked."

Michael returned with our food. We went silent on the topic of murder as he sorted plates. I watched him reaching across the table, mesmerized by the workings of his tricep as his arm moved back and forth in front of me.

Alone again, Paolo asked, "What is it with you all of a sudden?"

I pulled my innocent face: eyebrows and shoulders up, mouth in a twisted line. "Eduardo says grief makes people do strange things."

"Horny is not strange. But it will get you in trouble with these people," Paolo said.

"The thing is, no one has a motive, do they?" Roger asked while pouring ketchup on his fries.

"Depends." Paolo played at inspecting a crouton. "Tell us why Alex and Stacey didn't speak. Tell us why Anna and the Two are so friendly. Tell us why Stacey and Anna are so friendly. You've known these people a long time, and excuse me, but I don't think you're telling us everything you know."

"I am not—"

"And don't lie to us." Paolo gave me his you-are-pathetic-if-you-think-you-are-fooling-me look. "That may work with your theater friends, but we *know* what a liar you are when you're in work mode. So out with it."

I settled back into the red vinyl cushion that covered the booth. The two of them were my closest post-Baldwin friends. I thought about Alex. He certainly couldn't object. I didn't care what Stacey thought. Telling them might make them see Marcus's position in this differently. I could use their support there. Only Anna would object. I weighed it all out and decided to come clean.

I told them the truth about the Halloween story and Anna and Stacey. For good measure, I threw in my suspicions about Herb and Suege and the drug dealing.

"OK," Roger said. "I think we can safely say there are any number of people who might have found their way into a violent argument with Alex. We have Stacey, with a long, difficult history. He says he was in the dressing room, but we don't know that for certain. We have the Two, who hate Herb and, if Sunday was any indication, Alex—probably by extension from Stacey. We have Herb, who hates everyone. What if Alex found out that Herb and Suege were dealing and wanted to do something about it?"

"Like what?" I asked. "I can't see him trying to get in on the action."

"I'm just speculating." He went back to his burger. "They make a good burger here."

"So everyone has opportunity, and a lot of people might have a reason," Paolo said.

"The landlord." Roger stopped with the burger halfway to his mouth.

"Suege?" I asked.

"Yes. The landlord. He must have keys to the gate. The landlord could have come in that way." He smiled, very happy in his realization.

I looked at Paolo. "He's right. And Suege was there on Sunday afternoon. I heard him tell the TV guy."

"Huh," was all Paolo could manage.

Humming to himself, Roger flagged the passing Michael. Pointing to the still-silent Paolo, he said, "The love of my life here is overwhelmed by my deductive powers. He needs a gin and tonic."

TUESDAY EVENING

UNIFORMED POLICE FILLED THE lobby. No one objected, so I walked directly up to Detectives Sanchez and Rampart. They were in conversation with one of the uniformed officers. Two other plainclothes officers stood a few feet away, watching the action around the front door. There, several more police were systematically conveying pot after pot of plants out of the stairwell and through the front door.

"Hello." Detective Sanchez greeted me with a tone that telegraphed disappointment.

"Hi. What's all this? Did you find something?"

No surprise, instead of answering my question, she asked one of her own. "Do you know where we can find Suege Nethevy?"

I may be slow at times, but I am not hopeless. Once I heard his name, I realized what the potted plants were. Suege must have been doing some serious farming somewhere in the building. So far, I'd seen at least two dozen plants go by.

"I don't know," I said. "But Anna will have his number, maybe his address."

"Thank you. We've already spoken to her." Sanchez watched the seemingly endless parade of plants.

Suege was not going to be happy once the police caught up to him.

"Perhaps you'd like to join her? She's in the theater," Rampart told me. His unsolicited advice was as unequivocal an invitation to depart as the blast of light after last call. Never being one to be found under the fluorescents at four a.m., I excused myself.

Anna sat alone in the front row.

"Hey. What's going on?" I settled into the chair next to her. "The police look like they're having a great time in the lobby."

She didn't answer immediately. She let out a sigh, leaning her head back on the chair.

"What I wanted was to have fun. Winter in New York, looking for a few laughs. An excuse to hang out with my friends. 'Now is the winter of our discontent.' Blah, blah, blah." She reached over and took my hand in hers. "Sometimes I actually miss having all of you around. Not today."

"What's happened?"

"Finding a bloody sweater in the building next to a crime scene sets off all sorts of bells and whistles. Who knew? They came back and searched the entire place. What does it say that having a police contingent rooting through everything barely fazes me? Shouldn't that leave more of an impression? I don't want police searches to become a common feature of my life, Nicky." She was so deadpan serious, I laughed.

"I'm pretty sure that we can say this is an unusual situation for us," I said.

She laughed too, one quick, short burst.

"I almost feel sorry for Suege. I don't think this is going to go well for him."

And if the landlord was in trouble...

"What about us?" I asked.

"The police didn't say anything about us. They're not likely to want to tell us much. As far as I'm concerned, unless someone shows up with a court order, we're not budging." She didn't let go of my hand, but the tone in her voice grew sharper, a complete contrast to that quiet physical contact. "Tell me again why you were in Alex's apartment? What were you guys thinking?"

There was no easy explanation, so I didn't even try. "Yeah, well, it was probably not our smartest move."

"How was Marina?" she asked.

"Armed with a carving knife. You should have seen her. She was like the anti-PFLAG poster mom."

"Nicky, you broke into her son's apartment. Her *dead* son's apartment."

"I didn't break in. I had a key. It seemed like a good idea at the time."

Now Anna laughed for real. "It was Marcus's, wasn't it?"

The way she said it was almost accusatory.

"It could have been mine." What a lame defense.

"I don't think so. This one has Bradshaw all over it. You have got to be careful, please. I know he's sober, but, Nicky, sweetie, I don't think you guys are a good combination."

That made it unanimous among my friends.

"Unfinished business?" was the best I had to offer.

"Doesn't look like it to me." She continued before I could offer any counterargument: "Now Sean ..." She shook her head. "Actually, I have nothing to say about Sean and you. What is that all about?"

"Eduardo says it's grief."

She considered this. "Grief." She shifted in her seat to cast her gaze across the width of the stage. "Let's be quiet. I need quiet. I need a few minutes where absolutely nothing out of the ordinary happens."

We sat like that, hand in hand, staring at the stage, not speaking, for ten minutes, until the clock forced me to start setting up for rehearsal.

"They're reproducing."

"Not likely," I said.

I was in the front row of the Tapestry, my work spread out on a very small table between me and the stage. Paolo was directly behind me.

"I'm telling you, it's like *Dawn of the Dead*," he said.

I turned to look again at the back of the house. There, lined up and smirking, or in the case of the guy on the far right, winking at me, was Herb's entourage of drag queens. This evening, Billy, Tommy, and Sid joined Andy and Mikey. I think it was Sid who was winking.

"The guy at the end keeps winking at me."

"The guy at the end is winking at everyone," Paolo said, and blew him a kiss.

"Stop it."

Never had a slope become slippery quite so fast. To humor Stacey, we had permitted the Two to attend rehearsals. That opened the door to Andy and Mikey, and now a posse the size of a basketball team. Naturally, I considered Roger and Paolo to be in a completely different category. I needed them to keep an eye on the others.

"I think the winker just waved a condom at me." Paolo looked again. "Yup, condom and a small pack of lube."

"Just pretend you're interested in the exercise, OK?" I shifted my attention back to the stage.

Marcus insisted that we stick to the established routine, allowing everyone to ease into working without Alex. Only Anna, Eduardo, Marcus, and I knew about the police raid. We'd decided to say nothing, hoping that the company would find a regular rhythm for rehearsal. So far, our efforts seemed to be succeeding. Rebounding vigorously, determined to show they could do their jobs in the face of tragedy, the Good Company was out in full force. Upstairs, Laura Schapiro and the mechanicals were fitting more costumes. In the house, Herb Wilcox and the actors playing the four young lovers waited their turn onstage. As always, we started with the *Daily News* exercise.

First up tonight were Eduardo Lugo and Stacey Rose, who now had not quite two weeks to create an onstage relationship as Puck and Oberon. They sat center stage, Marcus next to them.

"Her cat was lying..."

"...by the toaster..."

"...not breathing..."

Marcus and Eduardo had squeezed in two hours of work between the bottle debacle and the police search. Now, throwing himself into rehearsal, Marcus looked as if hidden booze, bloody sweaters, and police searches were the stuff of everyday life. Except that he wouldn't look at me.

"... CPR to the ..."

"... animal. 'The whiskers ..."

"... tickled,' she said, 'but ...'"

"Very good, guys." Marcus was beaming at his actors.

They read to the happy ending, when owner and pet both recovered fully.

"OK, I love my cat, but he dies before I kiss him," Eduardo said as they stepped away from the table.

Next up were Al Benning, who was replacing Eduardo as Lysander, and Peter Chang, playing Hermia, the other half of the couple.

"Is Roger with the Two?" I asked Paolo while Marcus and the actors chose another clipping from the pile on the table.

"Yes. He and the little freaks are in the dressing room, papering the walls. Something about the atmosphere and the energy."

"The yin and the yang?"

"More like the bull and the shit." Paolo looked at the back row again. "Oh, I think he has a dildo now."

"What?" I spun in my seat.

"No. My mistake. Just a cell phone." Paolo laughed.

"Not funny," I said.

"The angry man ..."

"... hit the canary trainer ..."

"... trainer ..."

"Let the rhythm flow, Al," Marcus coached gently.

Both actors took a breath.

"…with the dead…"

"…bird."

"The owner charged…"

"…the trainer,…"

"…Samuel Wilson, of…"

"Good. Keep going. Keep going."

"Where do you guys get these articles?" Paolo asked.

I didn't answer him. Instead, I checked over my notes for the evening. Despite everything that had happened, I still had a production to manage. Tonight we were jumping around in the script, hitting scenes that involved Eduardo and Al in their new roles. The night was all about giving the two of them a first crack at understanding the action.

We were starting with act 3, scene 2, and doing a series of scenes with the four lovers and Puck. These covered the part of the story in which Oberon orders Puck to use the love potion to separate the four young people into two distinct couples—no more ill-fated entanglements. Instead, Puck mistakenly applies the potion so that both young men are hopelessly in love with the same girl. Later, Oberon sends Puck to fix his error. Puck tricks the youngsters into running around the forest until they are exhausted. Once they've fallen asleep, he reapplies the love potion, guaranteeing that when the morning (and the final forest scene) comes, there will be two loving couples.

In most productions of *Midsummer*, the comedy comes right out of the confusion of identities and is the equivalent of a good old-fashioned door-slamming farce. Since the play takes place in a forest, instead of running in and out of hotel rooms and banging doors, everyone is constantly disappearing into and out of the moonlight.

Our forest was the chorus of six-foot hotties, who would keep re-arranging themselves to change the landscape. The combination of muscle boys in spandex and four guys playing the two young couples didn't add anything revelatory to Shakespeare, but it would make for some fun viewing.

"He waved the …"

"… dead canary …"

"Share the words. Breathe."

The story of Wilson, the now-notorious canary trainer, came to an end.

Next up were Herb and Eduardo, who was taking his second turn. Titania and Puck don't have a great deal of interaction in *A Midsummer Night's Dream*, but Marcus was insistent that the "fabric of the relationship between Oberon and Titania includes Puck."

This would be Eduardo's first direct stage time with Herb. I could feel the five guys in the back leaning forward in anticipation. I imagined Sid winking at high speed.

"The trees died …"

"… rapidly for no …"

"… no apparent …"

"Let the rhythm flow, Eduardo," Marcus coached gently.

"… no apparent reason."

"Poisoned by a …"

"… lakeside resident to improve …"

"… her view …"

"Good. Keep going. Keep going."

"Ah, poisonous divas. What's more fun?" Herb said, gratuitously stopping the exercise.

"Wouldn't want to be redundant, would we?" Eduardo said to no one in particular.

"Enough," Marcus intervened. "Let's begin again."

"I like your new Puck," Paolo said.

Onstage, it looked as if Herb had been about to object but then thought better of it. I didn't like that. With Herb, a nasty comeback deferred was nothing more than a time bomb.

"One at a time. Follow. Give."

Both actors took a breath.

"They had no right to …"

"… plant things in my …"

"… my view …"

"Share the words. Breathe."

Herb was terrifyingly sedate through the remainder of the exercise. Finally, we left the lady with the very skewered sense of self-importance behind. It was time to start rehearsal.

The young lovers don't know they are being watched by Oberon and Puck. Indeed, the entire forest is alive as Hermia struggles to understand what has happened. The love potion Puck wrongly applied has done its work: poor Hermia is without her Lysander. Both he and Demetrius now devote themselves to Helena.

So crazed with grief is Hermia, she even convinces herself that Helena prevailed because she is the taller of the two:

*"You thief of love! What, have you come by night and stolen my love's heart from him? Now I perceive that she hath made compare between our **statures**; she hath urged her **height**, and with her personage, her **tall** personage, she hath prevailed with him."*

Helena takes her advantage and leads the others in a verbal assault:

"Oh, when she is angry, she is keen and shrewd. She was a vixen when she went to school, and though she be but **little**, she is fierce."

Hermia is stung and beseeches Lysander to defend her:

"**Little** again? Nothing but **low** and **little**? Will you suffer her to flout me thus? Let me come at her."

Hermia launches herself at Helena, who immediately takes refuge behind the men. Lysander, whose only thought once revolved around Hermia, restrains her before she can reach Helena:

"Get you gone, you **dwarf**, you **minimus** of hindering knotgrass, you **bead**, you **acorn**."

It wasn't a bad first go-round for either Puck or Lysander. Sure, they needed work on their lines, but tonight wasn't the night to harp on that. Putting replacement actors into a play far along in production is no easy task. The new actors have to mesh with those who have already established relationships onstage, yet still be allowed to create something of their own. I'd done the rehearsing-understudies task myself on occasion, so I could see that Marcus was doing a good job of walking that fine line.

As they carefully worked through the scene, Marcus and the actors required my assistance with the blocking. Rita, then I, had recorded every movement made onstage. I typically used a system that involved character initials and different symbols for the action: crossing, entering, sitting, standing, kneeling, overacting (well, not that one). Even the occasional diagram for the really complicated scenes. Rita had not been as precise, but where possible, I'd been transcribing her notations into my own. By the end of the week, I'd have a complete and tidy prompt book. My romantic life might be a mess, I might not have been able to get myself to my rent-paying job in two days, and a woman I barely knew might be interested in filleting me with a kitchen knife, but no one was going to accuse me of disorganization.

I could even multitask. There was enough downtime as we worked to take care of a few housekeeping jobs. I flipped to the back of the prompt book. There, Rita had stored actor headshots. We needed to turn these eight-by-ten glossy pictures into a lobby display presenting the cast to the audience. Since there was always at least one actor who waited until the last minute to come up with a headshot, I double-checked who was already accounted for and who needed to be chased down.

I placed the stack in front of me, flipping each picture over as I checked off the name on my cast list.

"I thought directors didn't get their picture in the lobby," Paolo said, whispering in my ear so as not to disturb the action onstage.

"They don't," I answered, continuing to check off names.

"You just put his picture to the side. Over there." Paolo reached over my shoulder for the photo I'd placed face-down on my left. "This one." He turned it over. "Oh."

He was looking at a picture of Alex.

"Well," he said, "it looked like Marcus for a sec there."

He studied the picture.

"Nicky, you don't think that maybe someone got confused?"

"What? Like they killed Alex when they intended to kill Marcus?"

"Yeah, just like that."

I stopped to consider the possibility. The idea that someone wanted to kill my ex-lover but had instead killed an old friend was not one of the contingencies we studied in Stage Management 101.

"Alex was on his back," I said.

"This is not the time to discuss his sexual habits."

I took a deep breath. "He fell backward. That meant that who-ever killed him was looking at him. It's one thing to mistake them for a second when a picture flips by, it's another to mistake them face to face."

"What if the murderer was behind him? Maybe he was pulled, not pushed," Paolo said.

"You're sounding like Roger."

"It was just a thought." He leaned back in his seat.

Onstage, the work was progressing smoothly. It was my first full hour in the Tapestry Theater without someone complaining, shout-ing, or killing. It was almost enough to make me fall in love with theater all over again. Unfortunately, just thinking the thought was too tempting for fate.

Sean McGinn and the rest of the mechanicals appeared at the end of my row. "Nicky, I'm really sorry. Really. But we need to talk to you." He and the others looked like they'd love to complain, shout, and/or kill.

I felt badly for them. They'd become the bastard stepchildren of the production. As their leader, and the one Puck turns into a don-key, Sean gets plenty of stage time. And he was doing a great job with it. (Did I mention that I find talent erotic?) The others, however, af-ter an appearance early on, have to sit backstage for most of the play, waiting for the final act for their big moment. Given the goings-on over the past two days, they had pretty much been pushed aside.

"Can this wait until break?" I hated putting him off, but I didn't want to abandon rehearsal.

"Well, sorry, but no," Sean answered, backed by the nodding heads of his fellow actors.

In a happier production, I would have just told them to wait in the house until break. In a well-oiled rehearsal, I would have sat with my book, at the ready for any and every need onstage. In the Good Company's *Midsummer*, however, the only thing well oiled were the skids that were leading us off the edge. More unhappy actors might just tip us over. I had to take my chances. I slipped out of my seat and joined the guys.

"What's up, Sean?" I asked, finding myself standing perhaps just a bit closer than necessary, leaning in with my hand on his shoulder.

He fought back another one of those smiles. "It's the dressing room. And before you say anything, it's not the Two. Yeah, they're weird, but we can live with the walls covered in green paper. I mean, if it keeps the peace, it's OK. But I *would* like to know the difference between Lincoln green and deep running green. You know, they look the same to me." No doubt about it, very cute and very endearing.

"So what is the problem?" I asked to gently move him along.

"We think they've been in our stuff. All the makeup kits. Someone's been through them." Sean was visibly upset by this idea. It wasn't just the value of the material—though a well-stocked makeup kit didn't come cheap—it was the personal quality. A makeup kit was something an actor put together carefully over time: choosing the right bases, the brushes they loved best, the particular brands that worked for them.

"We don't want them pawing through everything, but we don't want to start any more fights around here," Sean said. "It'll be easier if you talk to them."

The others nodded in agreement.

Obviously, none of them had witnessed any of my previous exchanges with the Two.

I knew I wasn't to blame for the mess. In looking for the booze, I'd been very careful not to disturb anything, only lifting the lids of the makeup cases. Reluctantly, I filled them in on the day's police activity. I could see tension rising in the ranks as I spoke. So much for our peaceful rehearsal.

"Is anything missing?" I asked.

"No, but everything's been messed with. Mine is a total wreck." Sean spoke for all of them, everyone looking completely disgruntled.

"I'm not really sure what we can do about this," I said. "I don't think any of us wants to draw any more attention from the police. Not if Suege is in trouble."

They agreed, but I could see that my answer was unsatisfying. I didn't blame them.

"Look, why don't you all double-check to see if anything is gone? Make a list. There must be some kind of procedure with the police for this sort of thing. Are the Two still up there?"

"Yes. With your friend. Who," he rushed to add, "seems very nice. No complaints. You have nice friends." There he was being endearing again. "But I think Roger is enjoying this way too much."

If he only knew.

"Lysander, speak again ..."

All heads turned toward my work table. The action onstage stopped. Paolo was leaning over the front row of seats, reading from my script.

"And I know it says cross left, but he really should wait another line—"

"Paolo." I used my sharpest stage manager's voice, the one reserved for stopping all action and noise as quickly as possible.

"What? He needed to know his line. He was lost." Paolo looked at all of us, truly bewildered.

"I didn't call for a line." The actor playing Demetrius repeated himself to Marcus: "I did not call for a line."

"And I didn't call for an assistant director," Marcus said.

While I was talking to the mechanicals, Paolo had appointed himself prompter. Apparently, he'd also decided that he didn't much like the blocking.

"Can we get on with this, please?" Marcus snapped the words out. "Why is he on book?"

"I'm sorry. The guys wanted to know why their makeup kits were disturbed. I told them about the police search." Since I was standing in the aisle, I had to say this loud enough for Marcus to hear me onstage. Unavoidably, that meant everyone in the back row also heard. Another blow for productivity.

"What? What search?"

Herb and his boys were completely quiet for the first time all evening.

I repeated the info about the police and Suege's homegrown. Herb and his groupies huddled. I did not like the look of that.

Marcus was not happy. "Can we get on with this? There's nothing we can do about it now. We're wasting time."

"Yeah, OK." I turned back to Sean. "Guys, maybe we can figure out something later, OK? We should get back to work."

Now Sean smiled openly. "OK. Later it is." For a moment, I thought he was going to kiss me again. Instead, he turned and led the mechanicals back up the aisle. *Great*, I thought, *another first: a romantic tryst fueled by police intervention.*

As I settled in, Paolo whispered in my ear, "That actor needs help."

"Not now," I muttered.

"All right, but trust me, the entire NYPD isn't going to help this guy find his character."

The forest is shrouded in mist, the clear moonlight suddenly cut off by the swirling white tendrils of fog. Through the haze, a young lad stumbles, calling to his challenger:

"Where art thou, proud Demetrius? Speak thou now."

From a distance, he hears the sound of his rival's voice:

"Here, villain, drawn and ready. Where art thou?"

Lysander rushes off toward the voice, anxious to fight for the heart of his beloved Helena, who is lost somewhere in the woods.

A moment later, Demetrius appears, calling for action:

"Lysander, speak again. Thou runaway, thou coward, art thou fled?"

And so it goes throughout the night, both led astray by the mischievous Puck until, worn out, they collapse from exhaustion. But Puck isn't done yet. Why should he be? He is that wandering spirit of the night, capable of feints and shadows and sleights of hand beyond belief.

He beguiles Helena round and round until she too, worn from searching, curses the weary night and surrenders:

"And sleep that sometimes shuts up sorrow's eye, steal me from mine own company."

She lies down upon the soft ground. Finally, Hermia is led into the grove by Puck, who has now gathered all four together. Once they are asleep, he applies the magic potion that will undo the confusion.

Each lover will awake, once again in love with the true object of his affection.

We worked through the remainder of the scene without incident. As peace descended, I kept an ever-closer watch on Marcus. Four days ago, he was just a memory of a failed romance; now I saw him as sober, looking good, and, until this afternoon, unmistakably interested in taking up with me again. I watched him direct the lovers. I saw again the grace in his movements, the self-assurance he hadn't possessed since our freshman year. Now, as then, part of me wanted to be nearer, not only to touch the fine dark hair on his forearms, but to come within range of the emotional charge he possessed.

The scene ended with the young lovers on the verge of reconciliation. We took a break.

The actors fled to quiet corners to run over their lines or make notes on new blocking. Marcus marched passed me without a word, heading toward the lobby.

Anna plopped down next to me. "Don't worry about him. He'll come around."

"Where have you been?" I asked.

"In the box office. The computer still isn't working. Is Roger here?" she asked Paolo.

"I have him watching the Two in the dressing room to prevent damage," I answered.

"We need that. We need the computers." She considered how to get Roger in two places at once.

Paolo looked around. "Where's the lighting designer? Sucking it back at the local bar?"

"She's in the light booth, sulking."

"You know," I said, "you can't really stop her from drinking if she's determined. She'll sneak it somehow."

"I know that." Anna rubbed her eyes. "I'm just hoping to slow her down."

"Come on," Paolo said, putting his hand on my shoulder. "You get a break too."

Anna slumped deeper in her seat. "I'm going to sit here and wish I were on tour. One of those fifty-cities-in-sixty-days things. You never know where you are, you never get any real sleep, you end up having an affair with someone completely inappropriate, and you don't manage to save any money because you drink too much." She closed her eyes.

"OK." I got up and carefully stepped away from her. Anyone desperate enough to go on tour was desperate enough to avoid.

"I'll get Roger to talk to you," Paolo said. He patted her on the head as he sidled his way out of the row.

I stepped onto the stage and made a direct line for the rear exit.

"How far along do you think they are up there?"

I assumed Paolo was asking about the dressing room. "We're not going up there," I said, pushing open the black curtains. The double metal doors leading to the alley stood directly in front of us.

"We're not going out there," Paolo said, tugging on my arm.

"Yes, we are. Time to confront this head-on." I was only partially referring to Alex's murder. I also wanted to clarify my thoughts about Marcus. I wanted to push away the gloom that had settled over the Classmates. I couldn't help but think that a good look at the alley, the epicenter of this disaster, was necessary to achieving any of this.

Before I could open the door, Roger and the Two came bounding down the stairs from the dressing room. Two #2 pulled the black curtain aside. Two #1 stepped through the opening and announced to the house, "We have finished. It is now safe to go into the dressing room."

They bowed.

Roger and Stacey applauded.

The Two beamed with delight. Then, seeing Herb and his crew in the house, they snatched defeat from the jaws of triumph, hissing at the back row. This drew sharp rebukes from Stacey and Anna. The Two spun abruptly about and beelined their way toward their lover.

"Well, how's it look up there?" I asked, watching the Two scuttle for safety.

"I have to admit," Roger said, "it looks pretty cool."

Paolo laughed. "You're not converting to the church of color, are you, baby?"

"No. It just looks cool."

"Come on." I pushed the doors open. We stepped outside.

The alley was isolated from traffic and the direct effects of car exhaust. As a result, spill from the streetlamp glinted off still-white snow. This provided most of the light, since the fixture over the door was broken—another testament to Suege's particular non-management style. Low hanging clouds glowed with the reflected brilliance of Midtown. The way was narrow, barely more than two car widths wide. There were no windows in the back of the Brewery until the third floor. No fire escape. The building on the other side presented an equally blank wall, lacking even the loading-dock doors that gave access to our stage. I could see the lock on the gate to the street, the barbed wire covering the fencing.

I couldn't help but look at the spot where Alex died. Forty-eight hours of fresh snow and wind had covered all traces of blood. There were no footprints, but that meant nothing now. Where I could see cobblestones, they appeared to be discolored, but I had no way of knowing whether these stains were from Sunday or some long-past event.

The alley was surprisingly quiet, and damningly secluded. We stood in silence for a few moments. The lighting, the cold air, the high, close walls, the gate sitting like a metal curtain across the proscenium formed by the Brewery and the next building—all combined to give the open-air space a closed, theatrical feeling. There was no way to get out here except from the stage, unless, of course, you had a key to the gate.

Anyone who reads the papers knows that most murders are committed by someone close to the victim. Even given the existence of a key, the most likely possibility was that a member of the Good Company had been in the alley with Alex. The odds were that one of us had come through the door from the stage Sunday afternoon. Whether they'd come to deliberately kill or just found themselves in a fight gone bad didn't make any difference to the question of opportunity.

I summed up my thoughts. "It doesn't look good for the home team."

"Why are we out here?" Roger asked.

"So he can think about something other than Marcus," Paolo answered.

Leave it to Paolo. Under all the humor and sarcasm, he was sharp, missing very little about his friends.

"In that case, what do we know?" Roger asked, gathering himself up for a summation.

"This time it's your fault for setting him off," I said, bumping Paolo with my shoulder.

"Please. It was inevitable," he replied.

Roger forged on. "We know that Stacey *said* he was in the dressing room. We know the Two didn't like Alex. Probably because of his history with Stacey. We know Stacey loves the Two and they worship him. Any chance one of the three of them would hurt Alex on behalf of the other two?"

"I have real trouble," I said, "seeing Stacey working up to attacking Alex after all these years."

"But the Two..." Paolo hung the comment out to freeze in the night air.

I disagreed. "Seems to me, if they're going to hate someone from Stacey's past, it would be Anna."

Anna and Stacey. Stacey and Alex.

What else didn't I know about my dear old friends? How would I ever find it out even if I wanted to?

"Hanging out here in the cold isn't going to help," Paolo said. He put his hand gently on my shoulder. "Let's go inside, Nicky."

"What I don't understand," I said, ignoring him and focusing on Alex instead, "is the license or the icicle."

"There's still the rage angle. The guy who did this is so angry at Alex that having him on the ground bleeding to death isn't enough. He grabs an icicle and stabs him," Roger offered.

Paolo shuddered. "God, you have a grisly imagination."

Roger shrugged off the comment. "I'd say it points to Eduardo. That guy has anger issues."

"And I don't understand the phone call," I said.

"What phone call? Why do you keep holding out on us?" Roger asked.

"Alex called me Saturday night and left a message. He said he had great news but didn't want to tell it to my machine."

"So what was it?" Paolo was now squeezed between Roger and me.

"I don't know. We never got a chance to talk about it."

They gave me the same look that Detective Sanchez had Sunday afternoon.

"I'm sorry," I said. "We were busy. I was a little hung over. Anyway, he was distracted, remember? It got away from me."

Paolo snorted his disapproval.

"Well, what do you think it was about?" Roger asked.

"I have no idea. He didn't have any news when he left rehearsal."

Roger soldiered on into the obvious. "So something must have happened between then and when he called. What time was that?"

"He called at 2:45." I tried to recall the tone of the message. "Whatever it was, it was good news."

"Well, that's not much help." Roger moved on to his next suspect. "Let's get back to Eduardo. He has a real temper, doesn't he?"

It was getting colder as we stood there. The occasional car passed on 11th Avenue, heading deeper into Midtown.

"Yes, but he and Alex were always close."

"Oh. Oh. How about this?" Roger was excited. "Alex is out here on break. Eduardo comes out, they argue over ... what? A guy? Yes.

Jealousy. Were they ever interested in the same man? Jealousy is a great motive. And it could make Eduardo angry enough to jam an icicle in him."

"Yeah, it's a great motive, except Eduardo is straight," I said.

"Really?" Roger asked.

"He's straight?" Paolo raised his eyebrows.

"Yes. There are straight men in theater," I said.

Paolo shrugged. "Someone should talk to him about the way he dresses."

"Nice. Could we focus here?" I myself was having trouble keeping my mind from drifting back to Marcus. I'd been behaving like a high school kid: letting him talk me into raiding Alex's apartment, flirting, defending him against all reason, and then accusing him without real cause. And what was he up to? First he was flirting with Alex (I don't care what he said about that), and then with me. Was he serious about a second round? After what we'd been through, how could he possibly expect ...

I stopped myself. I was on the verge of one of those imaginary conversations, the kind you have with someone who's not actually present. Tempting as it was to win by taking both sides of the argument, I knew it wouldn't help. Maybe I did need that closure Paolo so abhorred. I shook myself back to the moment.

"We still have Herb and Suege," Roger said, "and whatever they're up to. Remember, Suege has a key to that gate."

"Oh, right," Paolo said. "You don't know yet." He dived into the business of the great pot bust with real enjoyment.

"Well, that's it, then," Roger said once he had the details. "Suege and Herb are growing and dealing. Alex gets in the way and—wham—dead on his back with an icicle in his neck."

"Oh, please," I protested. "There is no way Suege has set up anything big enough to warrant committing murder."

"Doesn't mean Alex didn't stumble onto something. Maybe Suege is laundering money through his art business," Roger insisted.

Paolo shook his head. "Maybe Alex stabbed himself, then tossed himself backward. That would make as much sense."

A memory triggered by an amber streetlight and the cold: Marcus and I, sitting together on the rim of the fountain outside the Fine Arts building at Baldwin. It was late fall, at night, after a show. We were huddled together against the chill, laughing, probably waiting for someone (Anna?) before we headed off for a drink. It wasn't a particularly important or special memory, or even a detailed one, but more of an impression: light, shadow, cold. One of the many simple impressions that bind two people together.

As the memory faded, so did my desire to spend any more energy on Alex's murder. Let the police deal with it. I had the right to mourn without responsibility. I wanted to spend my time reaching some balance with Marcus. I wanted to sort out things with Sean, who was taking up ever more space in my thoughts. I wanted everything to be just like it had been before I'd had lunch with Anna last Friday and decided to join this circus.

"Do we know anything?" Roger asked.

"We know a lot," Paolo answered. "But none of it adds up."

We stood in silence for another minute.

Paolo was the first to crack. "I'm cold."

"Me too." Roger put his arms around his lover.

"OK, OK. We're out of time anyway." I led us back inside.

Marcus and Stacey huddled center stage, speaking in low, angry whispers. I couldn't hear what they were saying, but I would have bet my job with the Good Company that the topic was Herb. Then again, who would want my job? I swung wide of them on the way to my work table.

I didn't really need to check the schedule. Unless Marcus had a new plan, it was time to bring Oberon and Titania back onstage. We were going to do the final scene in the forest between the fairy king and queen. This was a morning-after scene of love's reconciliation, where Oberon puts everything to rights with Titania. The last time we'd worked on it, Stacey and Herb had gone at it like Abbott and Costello imitating the Stooges doing Tracy and Hepburn. A dash of Roseanne and the anti-romance would be complete.

"OK, we're ready." Marcus nodded in my direction, all business.

I glanced around the theater. The Two were sitting house right (suspiciously quiet, I thought). Paolo had reinstalled himself in the row behind me. Actors were scattered around, interspersed between chairs that held coats, scarves, and various personal luggage. I didn't see Roger or Anna. I assumed they'd already gone to the box office. In the dim house light, the place looked like it was a perfectly ordinary night at rehearsal.

I called out for the actors we needed onstage. "Let's have Puck, Titania, Oberon, and Bottom, please." Another rule of Stage Management 101: always say "please" and "thank you," and never lose control of your voice.

"Suege." The shout, an equal mix of relief and dismay, had come from Herb's personal chorus in the back row.

The landlord, looking simultaneously pleased at the greeting and uncertain as to whom Suege might be, stood just inside the house door. Herb jumped from his seat and ran back to speak to him. Once there, he snapped at his boys, silencing them. He and Suege slipped into the lobby, leaving the Draggettes disgruntled in the back row.

"Can we get started, Nicky?" This time Marcus actually spoke directly to me.

Herb's team began a sotto voce chant: "Free Suege. Free Suege. Free Suege. Free Suege."

I tried to silence them. "Quiet, please." Actors never chant protest slogans in rehearsal, and they usually respond well to stage managers asking them to do something. The Greek chorus in the rear wasn't interested in such theatrical niceties.

Paolo tried to contain his laughter. "Cheerleaders. Everyone has cheerleaders except me. How come I don't have cheerleaders?"

"I don't," I said. I weighed my choices. Storming up the aisle with premeditated intensity and a fierce scowl on my face seemed to be the best option. It was that or start throwing things at them.

"You have me," Paolo said.

I did a quick calculation: no, it just wasn't possible to toss him all the way to the back row. I started walking.

I was halfway to the chanting when Suege and Herb came backing into the house. Anna had a finger at Herb's chest. She turned to glare at the boys in the back row. "That's enough." Even Sid was immobilized by the look. No winking now.

"If you want to stay, you are quiet," she said. "If you are not quiet, you go. Understand?"

There was no response.

"That is a yes-or-no question. Understand?"

Andy let out a tentative answer. "Yes?"

She rounded on Suege. "What are you doing here?"

"I ... I ..." For a moment, it looked as if Suege were going to start thinking again. We certainly didn't have the time for that.

"Then get out. You are not safe company. I don't want any more shit." Anna turned to Herb. "Break's over. Onstage."

I'd arrived at the action by then. I could see Roger peering wide-eyed over Anna's shoulder.

"Come on, Herb. We're doing act 4, scene 1: the morning after," I said.

"OK, OK. Damn, you people are nothing but theater fascists."

Unfortunately, Suege found a coherent thought. "You can't throw me out. I own the building."

"We'll see how long that lasts. Nicky. Marcus. Stacey." Anna barked out our names.

None of us were any more interested in being on the wrong side of Anna's anger than the now-quiet quints in the back row. Marcus and Stacey obediently trotted up the aisle to join me.

"I said, OK. We're done anyway." Herb raised his hands in surrender.

"We are?" Suege asked.

Herb pushed past all of us to start toward the stage.

Suege began shouting at Anna. "I don't want you here. You need to go. Why isn't murder enough to get rid of you?"

"God damn ..." Stacey tried to push past me. Marcus and I blocked him—no easy task considering his size and strength.

"That's a very good question." This came from the uniformed policeman in the doorway.

Anna and Roger jumped aside as two officers entered the house.

"Suege Nethevy?" The lead officer asked.

"Yes, what?"

"Suege Nethevy, you are under arrest for possession of a controlled substance with intent to distribute. You have the right to remain silent…" In the shock of actually seeing Suege arrested, the rest of the warning was lost on me, and I suspect most everyone else. We watched as the police whisked Suege away.

Anna immediately went after Herb.

"What the hell was he talking about? Was he threatening us?"

"How should I know?" Herb was back in diva mode, looking as insulted as if we had asked him to go onstage in flats. "I hardly know him. Isn't break over? Let's get this done." He continued on his way to the stage.

Stacey started after him with much too much intensity for my taste. I grabbed his elbow to slow him down.

"Let's just rehearse now, OK?" I said. "We need to get our work done. We can deal with all of this later."

He looked at me, then at Anna.

"That's a good idea, Stacey," she said.

Marcus nodded his assent.

"This is not going to be easy." Stacey took a deep breath and followed Herb at a more controlled pace.

The scene involved four actors: Sean as Bottom, Eduardo as Puck, Stacey as Oberon, and Herb as Titania. It was a brief exchange that undid the trick Oberon and Puck had played upon Titania. The king and queen's reconciliation followed, the last peacemaking of the play. Under normal circumstances, we would not have expected it to take more than half an hour. We'd left normal long ago.

Herb was crazed with an inability to focus. He argued with Stacey over the blocking:

"You shouldn't be anywhere near me. I'm the queen."

"And I'm the king."

"Well, if you say so."

He questioned the interpretation of lines:

"But she says, 'What visions I have seen.' It's obvious she's been liberated by her night of animal love," and "He says, 'There lies your love.' Why would he say that if he didn't understand how the beast called me forth?"

He even wanted to debate the words themselves:

"I thought it was supposed to rhyme. 'Sad' and 'shade' don't rhyme," and "Doesn't 'dotage' meant old age? Why the hell isn't this written in English?"

He raised objection after objection. Thirty minutes later, the rest of us were worn out.

"I am not going to explain every syllable to you, Herb," Marcus said, having lost all pretense of trying to reason with his actor. "It *is* in English, and you will say it the way it's written."

"All right, all right. I was just asking. Lord, I thought you wanted us to ask questions. I'm just trying to understand the part. Don't crucify me."

The stage tableau was intended to evoke joy: Bottom sleeping peacefully, a smile on his face; Oberon and Titania hand in hand; Puck scampering about laughing. They were as far from this pastoral bliss as possible.

"Someone should have stuck an icicle in you." Stacey said this with such low menace, I was tempted to call out a break.

"Oh, Princess, I wouldn't be as easy a mark as little Alex."

"Are you accusing me?" Stacey stepped into Herb, who, realizing that his rail-thin person was outmuscled by at least thirty pounds of Stacey, stepped back.

Tension rose throughout the house. Anna was on her feet again. I didn't look, but I heard the shuffle of feet and seats as the back row rose. The Two began to move toward the stage.

Marcus started shouting at Herb. "That's enough. That's it. I am so fucking tired of this shit. Do you want to look like an idiot onstage when this show opens?" He was right in Herb's face.

"I—"

"I don't give a shit. I don't care if you're offended. I don't care if the munchkins in the back row are offended. We are taking ten minutes. When we come back, be ready to work, or I *will* fire you." Marcus didn't wait for an answer. He disappeared through the up-stage curtains. We heard him pounding his way up the stairs to the dressing room.

Finally, Herb had nothing to say. In the silence that followed Marcus's exit, the actors onstage drifted toward their separate spots in the house.

"I'll talk to him," Anna said to me, climbing onto the stage. "Stay here and keep them from killing each other."

Roger sat down next to me. Paolo started singing quietly to himself: "There's no people, like show people..."

The three of us were alone down front. The house filled with the whispered murmurs of cast and hangers-on trying to determine exactly what the director's outburst meant for each of them.

"I know a joke," Roger said.

"Will you give it up, already?" I responded.

"This one is good. I promise."

Paolo stopped singing "Another Opening, Another Show" long enough to interject, "As good as that groundhog thing? That turned out real well."

Roger ignored us. "So the Pope—"

"Whoa." Paolo sat up, suddenly engaged. "You can't tell a Pope joke."

"Why not?"

"Because you were raised Methodist. Only ex-Catholics can tell Pope jokes. Right, Nicky?"

I was only half-listening. By turning in my seat to see Paolo, I'd inadvertently obtained a clear shot of Herb and his boys. They were heads-down in an intense conversation.

"What?"

"Only ex-Catholics can tell Pope jokes, right?" Paolo repeated.

I looked at the two of them, shaking my head slightly. "There are eight million people in this city. I could have made friends with any of them. Really. Any of them."

"Anyway, the Pope lands at JFK. He goes outside and finds his limo. Now, the Pope really loves to drive, but he never gets the chance—"

"That's a ridiculous setup," Paolo said.

"*So*, it's been a long time since he's been able to drive himself, so he tells the driver to move over and gets behind the wheel. He takes off. He loves it. Forty—fifty—sixty miles per hour. It's great. Seventy—eighty—ninety."

I saw Herb pass Sid a package. Maybe our little adventure in small-farm agriculture wasn't quite over.

"Suddenly, there are red lights flashing behind him, so he pulls over. The cop comes to the window, and the Pope says, 'What can I do for you, my son?' Well, the cop is stunned. I mean, it's the Pope."

Paolo snorted.

Herb's groupies filed out of the row. Herb followed them to the house exit. As the five disappeared into the lobby, Herb, looking pale and worried, watched each depart, his eyes sweeping back and forth along the line of them.

"So the cop tells the Pope to wait one moment, goes back to his car, and radios in to his sergeant. 'Sarge,' he says, 'I have a problem. I pulled this guy over for speeding, but he's big. Really big.' 'Well, who did you get,' the sarge asks, 'the mayor?' 'No, bigger than that.' 'You pulled over the governor?' 'No, bigger than the governor.' 'Well, who is it?' 'That's the problem—I don't know, but the Pope is his driver.'"

It was funny. I laughed. Paolo laughed too, if a bit grudgingly.

"Not bad," he said.

"Thank you. Apology accepted." Roger stood to bow.

Anna returned from the dressing room. Everyone in the house went quiet at once, as if they'd been talking about her. She stopped center stage, curtsied, and said, in her best Scarlett O'Hara, "Oh, now, you weren't all talkin' 'bout little ol' me, were you? Gracious, but you must get a life, bless your little hearts."

Her brief improv sparked a round of nervous laughter.

"So what's happening?" I asked when she joined us.

"He'll be down in a minute. He's composing himself. He's a little embarrassed."

"Why?" Paolo asked. He hadn't blushed since he was three.

"I said the same thing. I think it was long overdue." She leaned toward me, patting my arm. "I put in a good word for you. You guys should talk after rehearsal."

Paolo couldn't resist. "Again, I ask why?"

A few minutes later, Marcus returned to the stage. His demeanor was more subdued than when break had started. He was also considerably nicer toward me.

"Nicky, let's start from the top of that again, OK?" He didn't smile, but the words were warmer.

"OK," I called out. "Top of the scene again, please."

No mention was made of Marcus's reprimand. What anyone may have thought of his outburst, no one said. But the results were evident. He'd hit a vulnerable spot when he went for Herb's vanity. It was one thing to get jollies out of tormenting the other actors and director; it was another to look like a fool in front of an audience. The rehearsal proceeded without incident.

About ten minutes before the end, Sean sat down next to me.

"Hey," he whispered.

"Hey, yourself."

"So, this thing with Marcus, you going to settle it tonight?" he asked.

I lost my place in the script.

"Hey," he said, "I'm not stupid. What are you guys fighting about?"

"It's complicated," I said.

"Ah."

"Sean—"

"It's OK, Nicky. I'm going home, and I expect to have a drink with you later this week. You do what you have to do with him. I'll be around."

"How can you say that?" I marveled at his calm.

"I figure you're going to do what you're going to do anyway. No use in me making us both miserable."

He kissed me on the cheek, a simple kiss anyone might have interpreted as one of friendship. "And then we'll do what we have to do," he whispered directly into my ear, sending a shiver down my back.

He was definitely growing on me.

At eleven, we called it a night. A theater can become claustrophobic after hours of intense rehearsal. After an evening of torturous rehearsal, the Tapestry Theater was beyond unbearable. Everyone fled. The actors, the entourages, Anna, Roger and Paolo—each grabbed their belongings, pulling on winter armor as they rushed the exits like a crowd trying to get into the first day of a basement sale at Macy's.

Marcus and I danced around each other in silence for a few minutes. I made a great show of collecting my paperwork and packing up my supplies (which grandly consisted of pencils, spike tape for marking the stage, and the prompt book). I turned the three-minute operation into seven. Marcus was equally industrious. He managed to take even longer wrestling his copy of *A Midsummer Night's Dream* into his backpack.

He broke the silence. "This is stupid."

"Yeah."

"OK, look. I'm sorry," he said. "I know you have every reason to be suspicious. But, Nicky, I swear, I am sober. I swear it."

He was standing downstage right, the lover's corner. This was the space that basic directing texts will tell you is the hot spot for playing romantic scenes (as opposed to downstage left, where the best conspiracies are hatched). I don't think that had anything to do with my reaction. He had apologized first (hey, who doesn't like to get that now and then?), but even that bit of ego stroking couldn't compare with the look on his face. He was standing there, dressed in his jeans, boots, and one of those big wool sweaters he loved, looking so much like I remembered him looking all those cold winter nights in Philly. I loved that look.

"You know what?" I stepped onto the stage and crossed to him. "I believe you."

He kissed me. This time I kissed him back.

It wasn't like a first kiss, which is all erotic and emotional expectation. This kiss was a long-overdue homecoming, interweaving the thrills of memory, anticipation, and, most definitely, trepidation. I silenced the voices in my head—one of which sounded suspiciously like Paolo—that were telling me to run away. For the moment, Sean vanished from my thoughts. If this was closure, I was all for it.

———————

It being small, very little effort was needed to mess up my apartment. Still, we'd vigorously and joyously trashed it like it hadn't been trashed since I'd moved in. Afterward, bedding and clothing mixed together on the floor, we wrapped around each other on the futon. The tawny amber streetlight, not quite reaching through the entire room, illuminated our heads and upper bodies.

"So." Marcus looked around for the first time since we'd arrived. "This is where you live?"

"Hope so. Otherwise, someone's going to be really pissed."

He rolled over on his side, his left hand lightly stroking my chest. "Want to hear a joke?"

"Is it funny?"

"Oh, that hurts. Yes, it's funny."

"OK. Tell me." I rolled over so that we were face to face. I used to get more conversation, but tonight he'd skipped the warm-up. He was probably as nervous as I about what we'd just done. Was he picking up on my confusion?

"The Pope lands at Kennedy Airport. And when he gets to his limo, he says…" Of course, my first post-sex Marcus joke in seven years and it was one I'd just heard. What could I say? He was so happy, and so beautiful. His skin was pale white flushed with pink. I ran my finger along the curve of his bicep. I didn't have the heart to stop him. He looked so eager to make me laugh. Nor did I have the heart to send him home right then, though looking back I should have. Maybe I just wasn't brave enough.

I let my mind wander, careful to nod and "hmm" every now and then.

I'd been more right than I realized when I'd expressed my ambivalence to Roger and Paolo, and then to Anna. Even as I traced the pale greenish-blue vein on the back of his hand, I knew that this was not the beginning of something, but rather the long-awaited end. At school, we'd moved from nasty breakup to a forced friendship so quickly we'd never indulged in the usual transition markers: no tentative reconciliations, no bitter conversations, no chance to just plain-old trash each other to our friends.

"I don't know, but he has the Pope for a driver!" Marcus wrapped the joke. I laughed right on cue. So did Marcus. He always laughed at his own jokes.

I traced the line of his pecs. The feel of him in my arms was so familiar. Should I be reading anything into my preference for the memory of Marcus in those first years over the flesh and blood in the here and now? Maybe I was finally growing up. Or maybe I was just over Marcus.

"I don't think you were really listening."

"I was too," I said.

We kissed again. OK, so there was still room for more growth.

My eyes jerked open.

My heart pounded as if I'd been running.

I looked at the clock.

4:32 a.m.

I'd been dreaming, but it was gone. I looked over at Marcus. He was sleeping on his side, his back toward me. I could hear the soft sound of his breathing. I touched the back of his neck, where his hair tapered away to skin.

I sat up. My heart rate slowed. Carefully, so as not to wake him, I slipped out of bed, wrapped myself in my robe, and sat down on the armchair next to the futon. Something, barely a hint of a something, had worked its way through my sleeping brain. Now the thought poked at me, demanding attention. Had I been alone, I would have turned on the TV, searching for an oft-repeated sitcom to distract myself, trusting that whatever idea wanted my attention would assert itself as soon as I was busy elsewhere.

I was thirsty. I crept quietly to the kitchen. Cracking the fridge open, I pulled out a bottle of seltzer and chugged without benefit of a glass. As I enjoyed this perk of living alone, I thought of Aliza, swilling gin during rehearsals.

Rehearsals.

I knew why I was awake.

I leaned back against the sink. I ran over it in my head. I played it backward. I tried to write it in a different sequence. I put the line in different mouths, imagined it spoken with multiple intonations, placed it in contexts each wildly different from the other. Nothing changed. No matter how I looked at it, the end result was the same.

There were plenty of reasons for him to have lied, all but one of them not very sinister. Nor was there an automatic connection to homicide. It was just that I didn't believe a lie that big, so close to a murder, could be just a coincidence.

At that moment, I couldn't prove it, but I could feel it. I knew who had killed Alex.

ACT III

WEDNESDAY MORNING

THE FIRST DAY OF the first week of our freshman year, onstage at a podium surrounded by the faculty, the department chairman greeted the new term. He welcomed us to Baldwin University, home to one of the nation's foremost theater conservatories.

The details we saw from our seats in the front showed the effects of years of benign neglect that even a nationally ranked theater program can suffer. The little signs of corner cutting were all around us: theater seats just a few years past replacement, a fresh coat of paint over a wall instead of a real repair job, a floor mopped clean yet long overdue for refinishing.

The chairman, a towering figure with a booming voice and two Tony Awards in his past who was keenly aware of his school's outstanding reputation as well as its declining physical state, was performing a well-rehearsed dissembling for our benefit.

"Wealth stifles creativity at a young age. We must look toward the creativity of the mind, as it is challenged by the limits of physical resources. Your time here at Baldwin will be one free of the constraints of commercialism. Here, let inspiration spread its wings, free of care for the material world."

"I think we're going to be very, very 'free' here," someone whispered in my right ear.

The voice came from over my shoulder. I turned my head, trying not to draw the attention of the chairman, onstage only a few feet away, and slid my eyes tightly to one side. In that way I got my first glimpse of Marcus Bradshaw. After whispering to me, he'd settled back in his seat, looking completely relaxed, as if he hadn't moved since the speech started. All that I saw of him in that first constrained peek was a swatch of black hair, one blue eye, half a mouth, a great chin, and the collar of what I assumed was a button-down cotton shirt. I happily filled in the missing details. He grinned at me. I sighed. The girl sitting next to me, whom I had not yet met, poked me with her elbow.

"Slut," she said, with dry, good humor. I smiled as I blushed.

When the convocation was over, she introduced herself as Anna Mikasa, from Long Island, New York. Marcus was from Boston. They spoke with regional accents not yet wiped out by voice and speech training. Anna talked fast: Philadelphia was nice, but not New York, which she casually referred to as "the City." She'd seen almost everything on and off Broadway in the last four seasons. Marcus, strolling easily through the sunny September afternoon, just kept smiling at me as we made our way to a café on the ground floor of the building next to the theater.

Now that he was in full view, I was completely smitten. Marcus was taller than me by about two inches. His skin was pale while mine was a Sicilian olive tone; he was solid where I was slight. Mostly, he was beautiful. More importantly, he seemed interested in me. It was my fourth day away from home. I was from a small town on the Ohio-Pennsylvania border where this sort of thing never happened. Not to me, anyway.

That particular September day was just an extension of August. It was eighty-seven degrees in the shade, and we were nowhere near the shade. We sat on a flagstone terrace, looking out on a large, well-tended rectangle of lush grass overrun by Frisbee players and lounging students. The campus surrounded us, a mix of modified Tudor and Gothic Revival tied together by the acres of thin mullioned and small-paned windows that fronted every building.

Sitting just a few tables away was someone else I'd seen at convocation—a tall, beautifully made blond who I assumed was a classmate, since he'd been sitting in our section. I don't think he saw us; he never looked up from whatever he was trying to read in the glare of the direct sunlight.

Marcus did a very funny impression of the department chair. "Your time here at Baldwin will be free of constraints. We will not provide you with costumes or scripts. We believe in the imagination. We shall not even give you a stage."

"Please," I said. "It's too humid to laugh."

"I so need something cold to drink," Marcus said.

Anna fixed her most determined look first on me, then on Marcus.

"That's not what you need. You know what we really need?" she asked.

I didn't know it then, but I would never hear Anna ask that question without a ready answer of her own.

"Portable fans?" I answered.

"A party. It's our first week together. We need a party. We need to bond. Friday night."

Between that Monday and the Friday-night party, the week had been stunningly sunny. I had met them one after another: Alex, Sean, Eduardo, Stacey, and Rita. I'm sure my memory painted it brighter than it really was, but in the middle of the night, sitting in the dark, winter brooding outside my window, I needed something bright.

I watched Marcus sleep. I couldn't wake him. What would I say? I had to be absolutely certain before I said anything to anyone. Even then, I was completely in the dark as to the "why" of it. I couldn't risk destroying long-standing friendships for no good reason. Anna, Marcus, Rita, Stacey, Eduardo, Sean—none of them would ever forgive me. I wouldn't forgive me if I was wrong. If I was right—well, if I was right, friendship wouldn't matter.

The long night turned into 6:30 in the morning. I decided on my first step. After that, I'd have to improvise. No matter what, I'd need the day to myself.

I woke Marcus. Given the circumstances, I decided to put off telling him there would be no repeat of last night. I didn't want to spend the time going through it with him right then. I'd just send him on his way, claiming the need to get to work.

"Good morning." He reached to pull me close.

"Easy, tiger. I need to get to work," I lied. Like I said, there are a lot of reasons to lie.

"What time is it?"

"6:30."

"You get up at 6:30?"

"Every day," I lied again.

"That's not right. Come on, stay home. Call in sick."

"I stayed home the last two days. I'll be living in the streets soon."

"You can live with me." He smiled.

"Oh yeah, you and me and Rita in her bedroom. Very cozy. Get up."

"No." He rolled over.

"Don't you have anything to do today? Shouldn't you be out making the magic for *Midsummer*?"

"All I have is the sound designer at one o'clock," he said, voice muffled by the pillow he'd pulled over his head.

"Must be nice." I ripped the bedding off of him and went to the kitchen. The smell of fresh-brewed coffee coaxed him out of bed.

He left at 7:15, complaining that twenty bucks would get him a warmer sendoff from a stranger.

As soon as he was gone, I picked up the phone. I thought of waiting a bit longer—it was risky calling so early—but the empty space where my phone machine used to sit echoed with Alex's voice. On the fifth ring, Paolo answered.

"You had better be in an emergency room bleeding from your eyes."

"Good morning to you too, sunshine," I said.

"It's not morning. It's the middle of the night. Go to bed."

"It's almost 7:30. Is Roger there?"

"I should hope so. Hold on." Paolo put the phone down—not gently.

"Hello?" Roger was more awake.

I asked my question.

"It was Herb," he answered. "What's going on?"

Yes. Herb would fit nicely.

I wasn't willing to lay out what few details I had just yet. "I'll tell you later," I said. "Once I know more."

I figured it was too early to call Herb. Not that I was all that versed in his personal habits, but if anyone was truly not a morning person, I was willing to place my money on Herb Wilcox. I paced around my apartment, which is to say I walked six feet in one direction, then six feet back. I drank a pot of coffee. I turned on the morning news. I showered, made more coffee, and fed Sushi. I got online and checked the cost of flights to the Caribbean, hoping it would make me feel warmer. No luck there. All of this took me only as far as nine a.m. Probably still too early.

Finally, driven by the belief that the coffee is always smoother on the other side, I bundled up and headed out for a change of scenery. There was a Starbucks at World Wide Plaza, near the corner of West 49th Street and 8th Avenue.

Mrs. Wizniski was waiting in the hallway.

"Good morning, Nicky," she said, smiling and holding up one hand in greeting.

"Good morning, Mrs. Wizniski." I was delighted to hear something come out of her mouth other than a demand for groceries. Her cheery hello reminded me of the way she'd been when I'd first moved in. I could see it was going to be a good day for her.

"Are you dressed warm enough? It's supposed to be very cold outside."

"I'm all set," I said. How pleased my mother would be if she knew there was someone to check on me before I left the house.

"Nicky, the strangest thing has happened."

265

"What's that?" I stopped, unwary in the face of her coherent conversation. She even looked better today than when Marcus and I had seen her last. Her hair was neatly combed, the housedress she wore crisply pressed.

"Just yesterday, the nicest young man helped me buy a lottery ticket at the store. But now I can't find it. Have you seen it? They sometimes wander off at night, you know. In search of warmer temperatures." She was still smiling, still speaking in whole sentences, still looking good—just suddenly making no sense.

She had such a happy, expectant smile, as if I were going to produce the errant ticket out of my coat pocket and all would be well. As much as it saddened me, I had no alternative but to disappoint her.

"I haven't seen it, no."

"Oh, that's too bad. Well, if you see the young man, ask him to stop by. He was very nice." She said good-bye, closing the door to her apartment.

I stood in the hallway a moment, wishing I could help her or at least sit with her for a bit. Not today.

I pulled at my scarf as I pushed my way through the front door and into the cold morning. As I walked toward 9th Avenue, I thought about poor Mrs. Wizniski and her "secret desire" to buy land. That made me think about the bodega clerk, who was certain that the state was lying about someone buying a winning ticket from him. But then he was also certain that the government was lying about the Apollo space program. He was wrong. Neil Armstrong had walked on the moon. Sometimes the extraordinary is true. I stopped to lean on the low wrought-iron fence separating the building next to mine from the sidewalk, a new idea bouncing around in my head. I pictured Alex as he stood next to me Sunday afternoon, spacing out, staring at the stage before the Two stopped him. My new idea settled very tidily next to my 4:30 a.m. revelation. I had the motive.

This Starbucks was unusually spacious and bright. Plate-glass windows looked out on West 49th Street and on the courtyard at World Wide Plaza. I sat in a courtyard window. The concrete and brick surfaces of the plaza were dry and clear, lying exposed between bunches of snow at the bases of benches and trash cans.

The conversation with Mrs. Wizniski didn't alter my plan to approach Herb, but it did present another course of action. It also meant that I would have to let Anna in on my suspicions. I sat sipping my cappuccino, formulating how I wanted to ask for her help.

Ready to face her disbelief, I called.

She picked up almost immediately.

"Not a good time, Nicky. I just got into the office. I'll call you back."

"No. I need you to do something." I went right at the matter in just the way she herself would have. She laughed at me.

"Nicky, that's ridiculous."

"Just look, OK? You can probably do it this afternoon. If I'm wrong, I promise you can bitch me out for the next five decades."

"I can't believe you're asking me to do this. You know how much he means to me."

"And you don't think I care?"

"Until last week, you'd barely spoken to him since we graduated."

"Well, he didn't pick up the phone to call me either."

"Very mature. If you're wrong, I'm not going to bitch you out. I'm going to torment you."

She hung up.

Suddenly, Marina Isola, wrapped in her winter coat and holding a scarf but no gloves, was standing next to me. I'd been so intent on the call that I hadn't seen her approach my table.

"I hate this fucking town, you know that?" Her cherub face spouted profanity like a high-pressure faucet. She was hovering near tears.

"Mrs. Isola. Everything all right?"

"No, young man, everything is not all right."

I almost said, "I'm sorry," but then I remembered how well that didn't go over the day before. I just looked at her.

"I'm locked out." She jangled a set of keys in front of me.

"Of Alex's?" I asked.

"Where else? Would you please pay attention? You are hardly my first choice, but here you are, so try to help."

I could have sworn I was already paying attention. Apparently, Marina Isola required a great deal more than the average listener could supply. She was what Paolo called "hard work."

I figured it didn't really matter what I asked next. She'd be annoyed at anything. I kept it simple. "How'd this happen?"

She dropped into the chair opposite me. Opening her coat, she let it slide down her shoulders. She was in a floral pattern, a pale blue sweater with small daisies embroidered on it. She looked like someone's grandmother.

"All I do is walk in this city. I had to walk four blocks to find this place." She reached down and rubbed her ankles. "I can't wait to get back to my car. Are you going for more coffee?"

"Ah, sure. Would you like something?"

"Of course I want something, why do you think I brought it up? Get me a grande double latte, skim with extra foam and cinnamon."

She closed her eyes and started rubbing her temples. I snatched up my cell and headed for the counter. Apparently, the universe was never going to forgive me for entering Alex's apartment uninvited.

I returned warily, coffees in hand. "Here you go." I placed her cup in front of her.

She didn't bother to thank me. "The damn landlord of his changed the locks on me. A mother in mourning."

"Can't you get the super—"

"Yes, I can get the super to let me in. He did yesterday. When I left, I took your keys so I wouldn't have to call him again. Now they don't work and I can't find him." She held the keys up, jingling them. "Worthless."

The keys in her hand may have come from Alex's apartment, but they weren't mine. My set was in the possession of the NYPD, specifically in the keeping of Detective Marissa Sanchez. Apparently, they weren't Alex's keys either. I had a pretty good idea to whom they belonged.

She treated me to twenty minutes of the gross shortcomings of New York superintendents, New York subways, and New York landlords, as well as commentary on the tragic absence of 7-Elevens in the City. I was finally able to interrupt the flow of her complaints, convincing her to try calling the super one more time. I considered it more my luck than hers that she reached him. Offering one last comment on the evils of the big city, she hauled herself back outside to trudge the four blocks to Alex's. By the time she left, I felt a real compulsion to rush out and buy an "I ♥ NY" bumper sticker.

My phone vibrated. It was 9:50.

"Nicky, honey. How are you?"

(Translation: "You could have called and let me know you were still alive.")

My mother was the definition of healthy parenting in the wake of Marina Isola.

"I'm sorry I didn't call. But I'm OK, Ma. I took the day off."

"That's good. You need to take care of yourself."

(Translation: "Have you considered moving to another city?")

"I am, Ma. I'm perfectly safe here."

"Good. Do the police have any news yet?" she asked.

(Translation: "Like I believe that.")

"Nothing yet, Ma," I said.

"How's his mother? Poor woman, she must be devastated."

(Translation: "Be careful, unless of course you want to kill me by getting hurt.")

I thought of Marina, knife in one hand and keys jingling in the other, cursing out all of New York. Everyone grieves differently.

"She seems to be handling it," was the kindest response I could manage.

"I just wanted to check in and see how you were holding up."

(Translation: "Thank God you are still alive.")

"Thanks, Mom. I'm still here."

"Are you sleeping? You sound tired."

(Translation: "I've been up for two nights with worry.")

"Yes, I'm sleeping. Don't worry, OK?"

"Ha. I know what that tone means. Fine. I won't ask anymore. Just tell me, is the show still on?"

(Translation: "Please tell me you are not crazy.")

Good question. As of that moment, yes. After I heard from Anna? Hard to say.

"Yeah, we're still on." There was no way to explain it on the phone.

"I don't know how you people do it," she said.

(Translation: "How did I manage to raise such a lunatic?")

"We muddle on. Hard as it may be to believe."

"Fine. But you're not fooling me. Get some rest."

(Translation: "I may never sleep again.")

We exchanged our love and hung up.

I took a deep breath to clear my mind. It was time to call Herb Wilcox.

Whatever he did to support himself, I was lucky that he wasn't doing it just then. When I reached him, he said he'd be home all day. It took some persuading to get him to see me. In the end, I appealed to the same vanity that Marcus had so effectively played on the night before. I offered to run lines with him, convincing him that, as his stage manager, I wanted to help him look his best come opening night. Thank God he didn't have enough experience to know how completely out of place my offer was. What I really wanted was to see him at home, where he'd be most comfortable. I didn't want to tip him off to my suspicions. I needed to get him to tell me the answer to my question without him knowing he was doing so. That was only going to happen if he was relaxed and unwary.

The mid-morning F train to Delancey Street was not crowded. The twenty distraction-free minutes forced me to consider what I was doing. Sure, it might look cold-hearted on the outside, hunting down a Classmate like this, but then I thought about Alex and his phone call. If I'd spoken to him about it, everything might have turned out differently. Maybe I could do something about that now.

Herb lived on the edge of Chinatown, just east of Sarah Delano Roosevelt Park. I pushed his buzzer at eleven o'clock.

A dog started barking, followed by Herb speaking soothingly to the animal. Finally, the door opened. He wore sneakers, brown socks, baggy shorts, and a muscle tee made for someone with considerably more flesh. The fans of his drag alter ego, Anita Nutha, would not have recognized him. The dog, a dull gray German shepherd, peered at me suspiciously from behind Herb's legs.

"Snowball needs to smell you. Here, Snowball. Sniff." Herb shoved the dog at me.

I managed not to flinch. If I was going to pump Herb for info, I didn't want to start off by insulting his pet.

Swallowing my natural terror (which I have always viewed as a perfectly reasonable defense mechanism against creatures with lots of teeth and strong jaws), I said, "Snowball, aren't you a cutie?"

"Come on in. I'll put him in the bathroom."

The apartment was a second-floor walkup with a tiny living room, a small kitchenette, and what was probably an equally small bedroom. He had more rooms than I did, but less space. The apartment must have been remodeled in the not-too-distant past. The kitchen was new; the wood floors had a glossy finish. The only thing not bright and shiny was Herb's domestic style. The main window in the living room was covered with a blanket. The sink was half filled with dirty dishes. I imagined a bedroom strewn with clothes. I looked for someplace to toss my coat, settling on the back of one of two magazine-covered love seats. Both seats faced what I assumed was the most valuable object in the space: a flat-screen TV framed in silver.

"So what is this about?" Herb asked. He cleared a stack of magazines from the space next to my coat and settled himself on the other seat. He didn't offer anything to drink.

"Just what I said, Herb." I made my way through the clutter. "We open in less than two weeks, and you're having line trouble—which is perfectly understandable. You're not used to Shakespeare. Part of my job is to help."

"Really? Huh. That's it?"

"Scout's honor." I decided against the salute.

"Oh, Princess, who would let you into the Boy Scouts?"

His comment didn't say much for Herb's originality, but it did provide the perfect opening.

"Alex said the same thing to me on Saturday." I let my expression settle into one of momentary sadness, sighing softly as I sat.

"You know, despite what Mary Ménage says about me, I am sorry your friend is dead. He was actually OK."

"Thank you," I said, a little surprised by the warmth in Herb's voice. "I wouldn't have thought—"

"No, you wouldn't. None of you would. Christ, you are such a bunch of fucking pricks. So I didn't go to some big-shit prestigious"—and here he mocked the word, pronouncing it with a short "i" sound—"acting school. You all behave like I have a fucking STD."

"And Alex didn't?"

"Have an STD? I wouldn't know."

"Treat you badly," I said. Any other day I would have appreciated the joke.

"You think you're the only one who can reach out and touch someone? I had breakfast with the Puckster on Sunday morning. I

273

took him your basic New York peace offering: bagels, cream cheese, lox. We had a very nice chat. Buried the hatchet."

Not too surprisingly, Herb picked up on my complete amazement.

"Look, Princess, I want this play to work too. I have a lot riding on this shit. You think I want to spend my life doing drag at tiny hole-in-the-wall bars? I'm not getting any younger."

Was it really possible that Herb had been asking annoying, stupid questions and raising objection after objection in an honest effort to improve his performance? If I had in fact misjudged him so completely, was it possible I was on the wrong track now? The only way to find out was to finish what I'd come to do.

"He must have been pleased," I said.

"Oh, fuck no. I was the last person he wanted to see, but, being endlessly charming, I wooed him with witty conversation and excellent lox. Look, why are you here? I mean, you are going to run lines with me—you promised—but I am not slop-stupid. What do you want to know?"

Now that the time had come, I wasn't at all certain I did want to know. I considered for a moment, plucking at the upholstery.

"Easy, it's all I have," Herb said, trying to stop me from ripping a hole in the cushion.

"OK," I said. "The police told Alex's mother that someone spent the night with him Saturday—"

"Oh, that."

"He told you?" I couldn't believe that Alex would spill this to Herb for the price of a bagel.

"And yet again you are wrong. No, he did not tell me, but I can smell the freshly fucked a mile away. Your boy was all twitchy with afterglow. The muscle queen must be good in bed."

"Stacey?" This was getting interesting.

"Oh, please. Don't tell me you didn't see it. All that tension and the little looks when they thought no one was watching? Not to mention the nasty shit they said. And it *was* nasty. The whispered conversations? I found them twice, heads together, hands balled up like they were going to swing at each other. A guy can only work up that much animosity for two people in his life—his mother or the man he's screwing."

Stacey and Alex.

Herb misread the expression on my face.

"Jealous?"

"No," I said. "If he didn't tell you ..."

Herb leaned back and gave me another once-over. He shook his head. "And everyone says you're the smart one. He would never tell. That would spoil the fun of it being secret. You need to keep your eyes open."

I played for sympathy. "It's hard when you don't get to say good-bye, you know? I just ..." I looked down, tried to think of nothing, and counted to three. "I just want to know, was he happy Sunday morning?"

Herb bought my act. His expression softened from hostile to unfriendly. "Ecstatic," he said. "He was happy enough about getting laid, but there was something else. You may not realize this, but I am a very good observer of human nature. You have to be to work out a good drag act. It's all about catching the reality of what's going down and then twisting it. Little Alex was all dishy and chatty, telling stories about your years as wannabe prima donnas in Philly. Oh, don't worry, there was no serious dirt on you, but our director—quite the little druggie, wasn't he? And the Puckster's mother? Thank Christ he tells a good Pope joke, it washed the taste of her right away. No, trust me, he may have been all atwitter with the prospect of being Mrs. Muscle Queen, but there was something else making him purr. He was even talking about moving downtown into a bigger place. Maybe he and Billy Rose were going to shack up."

"*Stacey* Rose."

"Whatever."

Could that be why he'd called me Saturday? I couldn't picture Stacey leaving the Two. Even if that wasn't why Alex had called, Herb was giving me plenty to think about.

I tried a sudden change of topic to throw him off. "Tell me about Suege."

"Nice try, but sympathy only gets you so far. Suege is nothing. And I had nothing to do with his little pot farm. Are we running lines or what?"

I wasn't put off. "You know, we found out yesterday that Aliza was drinking at rehearsals. Anna has her on the short leash—threatened to fire her if she did it again." I left it to Herb to make the transference.

He took his time responding. "The lights are hung," he said. "I'm sure, Princess, you are smart enough to make it work from here on out. But could you really replace *another* actor? We only have eight days." He paused, but I didn't respond. "Don't worry. Like I said, I want more. You know, this play was supposed to be the first step. Let's see what we can save of it, hmm?"

He plucked his script from the table next to him and tossed it to me.

As I leafed through the pages, I tried to sort through what he'd said. Some of it was a lie, some of it the truth, and some of it misunderstanding. I just wasn't certain which part was which, except for one bit of information that I'd expected to hear and one bit that didn't surprise me at all. I took those for the truth. And each bit of info was leading inexorably to the next, each step more depressing than the last.

Audiences are always asking actors, "How do you memorize all those words?" The actors will tell you they don't—they learn the action of the play, and the lines follow. Unfortunately for Herb, he had only the dimmest understanding of *A Midsummer Night's Dream*. After more than two hours, we were barely ahead of where we'd started.

My phone vibrated. The timing was right for Anna. I couldn't take not knowing.

I swallowed my fear of dogs. "I need to use your bathroom."

Herb dragged Snowball into the bedroom.

The stabbing scene from *Psycho* filled the clear plastic shower curtain. I looked at Janet Leigh screaming, then checked out my caller ID: Anna had called. I punched her speed-dial number.

"Hello." She was using her crisp, at-the-office voice.

"Hey," I said. "I have to make this quick."

"Why are you whispering?" she asked.

"I'm in Herb's bathroom."

"No, Nicky. Not three of them."

"Stop it. It's not that. I'll explain later. And get that look off your face." I turned on the water.

"You can't see me."

"I don't need to. So?"

"I did what you asked. I didn't find anything. I feel like a real shit. Not my favorite feeling in the world. You owe me a full explanation." She was Anna in full producer mode, brusquely efficient.

"Not on the phone. Meet me at the theater early."

"I should have stage-managed the damn thing myself. I'll see you at 5:45." She hung up.

———

It was 2:30 when I left Herb's.

I called Paolo.

"You do realize that I work during the day, don't you? Even as you ring and ring and plan one endlessly diverting bit of mayhem after another, I am actually trying to create something." Paolo never answered the phone with "Hello."

I was standing at the corner of Canal and Mulberry, between Chinatown and Little Italy. The day had only gotten colder. This was not the time to listen to Paolo define his work habits.

"I'm in Little Italy. What are you doing?"

"Why am I surrounded by men who never hear anything I say?" he asked.

"I've just had a conversation with Herb. I have a really bad feeling about what's going to happen tonight. I need to talk to you." I threw in a sweetener, just in case. "And I have dirt."

"Good dirt?"

"Great dirt."

"I could take a short break."

———

"Please don't tell me you eat leftover Chinese for breakfast too?"

Paolo plopped down the freshest lunch his microwave could supply: a bowl of rice with chicken and cashews. "Did you interrupt my day to make fun of my cooking, or do you have news?"

We sat at the counter island that formed one side of his kitchen. I laid out my theory of Alex's murder. He was so impressed he thought I was wasting my time gathering more information. I finally convinced him that a few more hours weren't going to kill anyone—literally. I wasn't going to risk accusing the wrong person. Before leaving, I extracted his most solemn promise (for whatever that was worth) that he and Roger would be at the theater no later than six o'clock. I had no idea what was going to happen, but I wanted backup.

I took the Number 1 train uptown. That train runs local, always offering plenty of time to think—not exactly the best choice for me right then. I still couldn't prove anything, but I could see the sequence of events from the first action to Alex's death. The unresolved question was whether or not it was premeditated. When I reached the 50th Street station, I didn't feel like going home. I wasn't ready to go to the theater either. I drifted back to my neighborhood Starbucks. After all that I'd consumed, a little more caffeine wouldn't hurt.

Another call came in before I could even order. I pushed answer without looking.

"Hello?"

"Nicky. It's Stacey. We have a problem. I need to see you at the theater. Right away."

This could not be good.

WEDNESDAY EVENING

Stacey Rose and the Two were waiting for me in the lobby. He stood, scowling, arms crossed over his chest. They sat on the bench in the center of the room, eyes down, casting the occasional glance at the big guy. It was nearly five.

"What's up, guys?" I tried not to assume the worst.

"I'm really sorry about this, Nicky. I had no idea what they were up to, or I would have stopped them." Stacey looked me directly in the eye as he apologized for whatever it was he hadn't done. He then yielded the floor to the Two. "Guys?"

They stood, shuffling their feet, eyes still down. "We're sorry too," they said together.

"Fine," I said. "I accept. Can you tell me what you're all apologizing for?"

"Show him," Stacey commanded.

"Follow us," Two #1 mumbled. They started walking, none too quickly, toward the front stairs.

"After you." Stacey gestured for me to precede him.

We climbed to the top floor. There, we stopped at the door to one of the art studios. I looked along the length of the hallway. From what I could see, it didn't look as if anyone had been up here in a long time. Suege must have been growing his pot in a space on another floor.

"Go ahead. Open it," Stacey said.

"We just want to say ..."

"... that we only wanted to help."

They pushed the door open, stepped in, and moved aside.

At first I had no idea what was so important. Clearly this was prime studio space. High up and facing north, the windows provided abundant natural light of the type painters preferred: flat, even, neither hot nor cold. Yet the studio was unused. Storage shelves along one wall were empty, the racks opposite them devoid of canvas. Dust clung to every surface. The space was well prepped for use, but no one had painted in here in recent memory.

The exception to all this lay in the middle of the studio. There, more than a dozen squares of colored silk were neatly set out in two rows, arranged for maximum exposure throughout the day to the light coming through the window.

"This is ... I have no idea what this is. Anyone?" I opened the floor to explanations.

"It's absent healing," Two #1 said, as if he had expected the project to speak for itself.

"It's very helpful," Two #2 added defensively.

"Then why are you apologizing to me?" Oh, how I longed for Roger speaking film noir. That, at least, I knew was eventually translatable.

Stacey ordered them to tell me how it worked.

"You take a personal object from someone…"

"… place a piece of colored silk over it…"

"… and place all of that in natural light."

"Then you can transmit the benefits of the color to the person."

"We set it up yesterday."

Stacey waited a moment, cast another angry look at his lovers, and added, "Using items they took from the makeup kits in the dressing room."

The Two were suddenly all eyes downward, not looking at either Stacey or me.

Now I wanted an apology. "You two went through everyone's makeup kit? When?"

When they didn't respond right away, Stacey gave them another verbal push.

"While you were at lunch with the nice pale one…"

"… and the nasty dark one."

"The police came and searched everywhere."

Two #2 was particularly incensed. "They made us take down all the paper we'd put up. We had to start over."

I couldn't fault them on character judgment, but we did seem to be getting away from the point. "Tell me when you did this," I insisted.

"Right after the police left," Two #1 answered.

"When we saw Suege's cannabis farm, we thought of this." Two #2 was very proud. "We only wanted to help."

"What did you take?" I asked.

"Nothing. Strands of hair, tissue."

"Things like that. Nothing valuable."

"Show me," I said.

"But that will ruin—"

Stacey interrupted. "Show him."

It was true. Under the silk squares was a collection of garbage and cast-off junk that no one would actually miss. I suppose their hearts were in the right place.

"All right. But you're going to have to apologize to the cast," I said.

Two #1 rounded on Stacey angrily. "You said he would take care of it."

"We told you he'd tell her." As usual, Two #2 was having more of whatever Two #1 was experiencing.

"Her?" I asked Stacey.

"Anna. The guys are afraid she'll be angry at them. I was sort of hoping we could just deal with this. I mean, it's really nothing valuable." Stacey turned abruptly from stern to softhearted.

Apparently no one was worried about me being angry. I tried to find this thought in some way complimentary. I failed.

I decided to put the apology question on hold. "Why don't you tell me how you got in here? Where's the person who rents this studio?"

Stacey laughed. "Are you kidding? Suege couldn't run a business with six MBAs helping him. The only reason he's able to rent the Tapestry is that theater companies are so desperate."

"All these studios are empty?" I was amazed. What a waste. I could think of any number of people—Paolo in particular—who could put this facility to better use.

"Almost all," Stacey answered.

"And they're not even locked?" How careless could Suege be?

"Oh, it was locked, but that wasn't a problem…"

"… we're good."

I turned to look at the Two: color therapists, theater critics, and second-story men?

"It's true." Stacey offered them this one compliment, perhaps to soften the tension between the three of them. "I locked us all out of the apartment the other day. They got us back in."

"We did," Two #1 said.

"We're good," Two #2 said, repeating his earlier assertion.

"And we took care of making him new keys."

"We are good at helping. You just never let us." Two #2 finally looked at me.

Stacey just smiled at them.

I had no faith in absent healing. Still, the entire exchange clarified one more piece of the puzzle. I should have thought of it earlier, but under the circumstances, I wasn't holding anything against myself. I was, however, pretty certain that I now knew where I would find the proof I needed to corroborate my theory about Alex's murder.

I felt generous—almost. "OK. Let me *think* about the apology."

Stacey made the Two pack everything up. ("It's not your space and they're not your objects.") He collected it all in a garbage bag and headed outside.

Having dispensed with the color voodoo, I left the Two to mope in the lobby. In the theater, I coaxed the space to life, turning on the house lights, the work lights onstage, the ventilation fans. Like every empty stage, the Tapestry held the promise of taking the audience and actor to any place, to any time. For just a few hours, everyone conspired to forget themselves, to suspend their disbelief long enough to inhabit a make-believe world. This thought, usually cheering, did nothing for me. I took that as a sign of just how rough the night was going to be.

I followed my regular routine. I figured having everything set up for rehearsal as usual would arouse the least suspicion, give us the most room to maneuver.

Anna showed up promptly at 5:45.

"Why are those two sitting in the lobby looking like someone stole their scooters?"

"It's complicated. And a little odd," I said.

She parked her coat in the second row and joined me onstage. "Save me the bullshit. What's going on?"

I explained what I believed to be the entire chain of events leading up to and away from Alex's murder, including what I'd surmised in the art studio. She went silent. I got a folding chair for her to sit on. I waited. It was a lot to take in.

"It makes logical sense. I don't know." She went quiet again.

"Just tell me this: he did lose his keys, didn't he?"

"Yes." She thought a bit longer. "Shouldn't we call the police?"

I shook my head.

"We can't just turn him in unless we're a hundred percent certain. Right now all we have is a theory that, let's be honest, failed its first test."

"Then you're wrong." She made this statement as if it exhausted the topic. Clearly, Anna preferred to move on.

I felt the same urge tugging at me, but I could also hear Alex's voice on my answering machine. "We have to try. We know where it is, we just need to get to it."

The Two decided to join us. They strolled down the aisle as if nothing had happened upstairs. They smiled at Anna. They ignored me.

Opportunity doesn't always come in the prettiest package.

"You know what we need?" I asked, smiling at the Two.

"Don't smile at us."

"It makes us nervous."

I ignored the snarky comments. "We need a color-therapy session to help cleanse the company and lift everyone's spirits. Doesn't that sound good, Anna?" I challenged her to disagree with me in front of them.

"Maybe." Anna looked at me with grave suspicion.

The Two backed off the stage, into the front row. They would have made a killing as synchronized swimmers.

"Why are you saying this?" Two #1 demanded.

"I think it's a good idea. You said you wanted to help."

Two #2 almost fainted. He leaned on his counterpart, clutching his own shirt collar as if fingering a string of pearls he wore around his neck. "Do you mean it?"

"Of course I do. How about tonight?"

"Tonight?" Anna was really worried now. "Let's talk." She tugged at my sleeve.

"I don't think we have time, Anna. People will be here soon. We need to plan."

"We need more warning than this. Everyone does." Two #2 had recovered his composure.

"They need to bring things from home." Two #1 started outlining what I assumed would be their standard preparatory tasks.

"We need to coach them on the purpose and method so they can make a useful choice."

Anna jumped to their defense. "You do. We need to prepare properly. We can't possibly do this tonight. Tomorrow, or the day after." She gave me her most evil cease-and-desist look.

I ignored her, pretending that no obstacle could stand in our way. "Oh, please. It's almost all guys. They'll all have wallets. What's more personal than a wallet? Right, Anna?"

We stood just downstage of center, directly under a work light that cast harsh shadows on our faces. I watched her closely. I was counting on her to realize where this was heading.

The Two, standing at the edge of the stage, were oblivious to the looks Anna and I were exchanging. They teetered between the bliss of leading us into color balance, and unhappiness at my choice of object.

"Wallets aren't any good. They have no color."

"We need color," Two #2 announced, as if this was news to anyone.

"But guys, wallets can be full of things with color. Photos, business cards, IDs, even credit cards come with nifty backgrounds now." Once again, I checked on Anna's expression. This time, I could see realization creep into her eyes.

The Two cocked their heads to one side and said, in unison, "It won't work."

Anna was all the way home now. This only made her unhappier. "It'll have to work," she said. She looked at me as if to say, "I've known you and trusted you for years, so I will do this, but if it doesn't work, we stop now." Or maybe she was thinking I was insane. It was a tough read.

"But, Anna—," the Two protested.

"No. We do it tonight. We won't have time later. We will use the wallets."

"But you said we could do it tomorrow." Two #1 was very confused.

"Or the day after. You did. You just said that." Two #2 raised the indignation level.

"*Sorry*, guys," I said, stressing the "sorry." "But if we don't do this tonight, I'm sure we'll all be saying how *sorry* we were. Of course, if we did pull it off, there'd be no need to *apologize*."

They were many things, the Two, but they were not that slow, and they understood that I had just set the price for letting them off the public hook for ransacking the makeup kits. For my efforts, I received a look that confirmed I'd never be Anna's equal in their affections.

This was a problem too complicated for nonverbal communication. They huddled, whispering. Anna gave me another this-had-better-be-worth-it look. I just shrugged my shoulders. I thought I was right, but I wouldn't really object to being proved wrong.

The Two continued to confer. The only word I could make out was "carnivorous." I didn't want to know.

Finally, they reached a decision. Two #1 spoke for them. "Very well. We will do this. We will do this with wallets. We will do this for the good of the Good Company." Here, I swear, they both stood a bit taller. Nice face saving, I thought.

"Great. Now go and get yourselves ready. Do whatever it is you do to read the colors." I imagined them boiling everyone's wallets and straining them like tea leaves.

"We don't have to prepare."

"We are always ready."

I couldn't have them jumping the gun. This farce, like any other, would be all about the timing.

"Then go sit quietly. This has to be a surprise, doesn't it, Anna?"

"Apparently."

"And if it isn't, if anyone knows, especially Stacey,"—here I slowed down to drive the point home—"the deal is off. Understand?"

The Two were not happy about this last condition, but I counted on their pride outweighing their loyalty this one time. After all, it was already 6:10. They would only be keeping their little secret for less than an hour.

"OK. We're going to go somewhere else," Two #1 said.

––––––––––

Roger and Paolo rolled in late, just past 6:30. I took them aside, but before I could say a word, Paolo started talking.

"It's not my fault," he said, peeling off his scarf and coat.

"Well, it's not mine," Roger protested.

"Who bought the strange gizmo thingy from the TV that crushes ice, sharpens knives, and eats cats?"

"I did, but—"

Paolo did not let him finish. "No. Don't even try. This time—"

As certain as I was that this was going to make a funny story when we were sitting around in our eighties at the Old Homo Retirement Home, I really needed their attention.

"Guys, focus. Please?"

They stopped bickering and looked at me. I had the uneasy realization that, if fully investigated, the line dividing Roger and Paolo from the Two would, in fact, be much finer than any of us might hope.

"Of course," Paolo said. "After all, she's safe with the vet."

"And I am so glad for that. No one wants to kill a cat. We don't have a lot of time. Did you fill him in?" I asked Paolo.

Roger assured me he was up to speed. "I told you you couldn't trust—"

"Could we please do the I-told-you-sos later? Here's what we do now. Roger, you are going to the dressing room. Paolo, the lobby. I want you to stay there no matter what. If he comes through, don't stop him, just don't let him out of your sight. We'll be right behind. Promise."

"Wouldn't it be easier to just dry-gulch him and frisk him when he gets here?" Roger asked.

"If you mean attack him, no, it wouldn't be. Not if we're wrong," I said.

"Always Mr. Finesse," Paolo snorted.

"Oooh, French. I love it when you're urbane."

"Cat killer."

"Please. Just go. And stay put." I pointed toward an exit.

With one last snarl, they went in opposite directions.

I had one phone call to make, and then I'd be ready.

The Good Company gathered once more. The actors came straggling in by ones and twos. Call was for 7:00. It was 6:45. I started putting chairs into a circle onstage. Anna helped. Eduardo Lugo pitched in when he arrived.

"What's up?" he asked, placing two chairs stage left. "Not another meeting? I hate meetings."

"Nope, not a meeting," I said. "Anna has an announcement, and then we'll get started."

Anna dropped a chair, still folded, onto the stage. "Give us a second, will you?" she said to Eduardo, dragging me upstage.

"I have an announcement?" she whispered to me. "What announcement do I have? Stop making shit up."

"Once everyone is here and seated, you and I—"

She interrupted me. "*You.*"

"*I* am going to tell Marcus what we're doing. If we're going to pull this off, he has to be with us on the color-therapy session. Then you announce it to everyone else and we start—no delays."

"Are you drunk? Are you completely fucking drunk? Where is Aliza's stash?"

"Anna, we have to know. And he has to have no idea we ever suspected anything if we're—"

"*You.*"

"*I'm* wrong. Oh, and there is one other thing."

I gave her the final detail of my plan.

"Do you know how much I'm hating you right now?" She walked away.

We directed the company members to take a seat onstage. The Two had returned and placed themselves at the farthest upstage point of the circle, the twelve o'clock spot. Stacey sat to their right. The four lovers filled in to their left. I stood, leaning on the back of the next chair. Marcus stood with me, wondering what was happening. All I told him was that we needed to talk to Anna in a moment. The designers took the six o'clock position. Tonight, the chorus of gym boys joined us, filling in between five o'clock and three o'clock. Herb

Wilcox and his squad were the last to arrive. The quints took seats in the second row. Herb sat next to the designers, the mechanicals acting as a buffer between him and Stacey. Everyone had gathered.

I took one full look around the circle. I checked my watch: 7:01. I'd left us thirty minutes before the next phase kicked in.

"Hello," I said, with enough punch to get everyone's attention. "We'll be with you in one moment. Anna?"

She was standing upstage, waiting. "Marcus?" She motioned for both of us to join her.

"What's going on?" he asked as we huddled. "You guys are freaking everyone out."

I dove into the deep end. "I know who killed Alex."

He went pale.

"What? Who ..." He couldn't even finish.

"Stacey," I said.

Anna closed her eyes.

"Excuse me?" Marcus looked from one to the other of us. "Are you serious? Why the hell would you think that?"

"Stacey and Alex spent Saturday night together, at least part of it. I have no idea how Stacey managed that with the Two around, but he did. Herb was at Alex's Sunday morning. He knew. He told me. He also told me that he'd seen the two of them together here at the theater."

"Herb was at Alex's Sunday? What did Alex—"

"We don't have time to go into the whole thing. Last night you asked me to trust you. Do you trust me, Marcus?" I asked.

He searched my face, then Anna's, for some sign we were joking.

"If you're serious, we need to call the police," he said.

"No. I mean, I am serious, but we need to be a hundred percent certain. We have a plan, but we need you to play along to pull it off. If he's innocent, no one will even know we suspected anything. Just back us up, OK?"

"What plan?" he wanted to know.

"We don't have time."

Anna stood quietly through all of this. She never opened her eyes, as if looking at us would blind her.

Marcus considered for a moment. "This is stupid. We're talking about Stacey. The police—"

"The police will never believe us. We have nothing to go on but a guess." I looked over his shoulder at the assembled company, most of whom were beginning to look restless. "We're running out of time."

"Marcus." Anna opened her eyes and looked at him, pleading. "Please, I need you to say yes."

He looked as shaken as she. "OK."

We turned toward the company. Their puzzled but trusting expressions greeted us. Why should they be suspicious? Most of us had a long, happy history. The scam I'd organized was well outside our normal routine.

"Here," I said to Marcus, as we walked downstage. "I saved you a chair near the main action." I offered him the empty folding chair at two o'clock. He sat down without speaking.

Anna called everyone to attention and began to explain that we were going to have a color-therapy session, casting it as a means of helping us move beyond the past few days. Aliza started to laugh, but Anna's expression silenced her. Laura Schapiro rolled her eyes. I think that after murder, drunks, and now this, she was finally giving up on the Good Company. Stacey, who under other circumstances would show pride in the sudden vindication of the Two, instead appeared more suspicious than happy. Other members, Sean included, nodded a baffled assent, reserving their full support. Marcus retained his stunned look, as if he couldn't understand what was happening. However, as arranged, he seconded Anna. Our united front stopped serious protest, at least for the moment.

"Everyone get out your wallets," Anna said. "Since we didn't give everyone warning, we figured this would be the best choice."

Now he knew exactly what we were aiming for, but it was too late to turn back.

"And," I jumped in, "no cheating. You can't take anything out before we look." I said this directly to Stacey, then turned and tried to convey a sense of "Got him!" to Marcus. I don't know if he caught my exact meaning. He certainly looked as unhappy as Anna.

"Guys?" Anna nodded at the Two, taking an empty chair next to the mechanicals.

The Two explained the idea behind the exercise: how they were going to look at the color of objects in the wallets, analyze them, and explain the good and bad qualities, how we'd discuss what people liked and didn't, how this affected them.

I could see the company hovering just short of rebellion. I trusted in my Classmates to go along for at least a bit; they were always willing to try. It was Herb I was worried about. He just smiled at me. I couldn't think of a more damning reaction. I was certain he would not play along when his turn came. The opportunity to throw a grand tantrum would be just too tempting. If I was lucky, we wouldn't get that far.

The Two were ready.

I offered one last instruction: "Clockwise."

Two #1 glared at me.

"Ooooops. *Sorry*," I said.

They blinked in unison.

"Of course," Two #1 said, and nodded his head. "Clockwise."

Al Benning was first. He dutifully dug out his wallet, apologizing that the only things in it were a driver's license, a ten-dollar bill, a library card, and an ATM card and receipt. "I can't even get a credit card. How lame is that?"

The Two zeroed in on the library card, specifically the band of red at one end. They were magnificent, in a sideshow-psychic kind of way.

"Red is the color best suited for fighting cold," Two #1 intoned.

"That you have red on you is a good sign. We recommend red silk socks to keep the blood moving through the body."

"Wouldn't wool be warmer?" Al asked. They didn't answer, just handed back his wallet.

Our target began to squirm. The Two noticed and asked him to stop fidgeting.

7:15.

It was a toss-up. Would the company rebel and end the session before the murderer cracked?

From the second wallet, the Two extracted a twenty-dollar bill and began to explain the reparative effects of green on stress-related problems. Green at the waist was OK, but what a person really needed was to lie on the ground with a green scarf over their chest. Someone to my left muttered something about the power of lots of money to relieve stress.

Anna's knuckles were white, her hands gripping the sides of her chair. I was sweating. My heart was pounding again, as it had done when I'd woken up that morning. We must have looked just like I felt, because Stacey was beginning to stare at me. He knew we were using the Two.

7:22.

A third wallet. Everyone was growing restless now. Sean was watching me closely, no doubt, along with everyone else, wondering what Anna, Marcus, and I were up to. To his credit, he gave me an encouraging nod. I was even more convinced that I needed to reevaluate how I chose the men I dated—out with the drunken charmers, in with the stable nice guys. Stacey's anger, focused exclusively on me, chased that stray thought away.

The Two were the only ones speaking, their untrained voices swallowed by the space. The ventilation system creaked overhead, whirling fans competing for attention.

They pulled a MetroCard from the wallet.

"Yellow is for combating fear …"

"… and for protection."

"We'll do a breathing exercise. Close your eyes …"

"… and visualize the yellow light."

"Now, breathing in …"

Almost no one closed their eyes other than the Two. Stacey had his eyes on me. I couldn't face him.

Herb began to mutter to himself. Eduardo was showing the strain of trying to play nice. Marcus's face betrayed no emotion at all—he sat staring at the floor. Stacey, eyes darting around the circle, was poised on the edge of his seat. Anna, her eyes closed, was gently rocking in her seat. It was frightening to see her like this.

He was standing before I even realized he was moving.

Anna stopped rocking.

"I'll be right back," he said, sprinting across the stage and up the aisle.

I jumped, immediately following, calling for the others to help. As I left the stage, I was aware that Anna had begun to cry.

When I reached the lobby, I found Paolo, cell phone open, standing in front of the box office and blocking the wastebasket.

The company gathered behind me, Eduardo on one side—"What the fuck is going on?"—and Sean on my other—"Nicky, are you all right?"

Marcus Bradshaw, whom I'd now always think of not as my former boyfriend but as Alex's killer, turned from Paolo to face the assembled Good Company and extras. In his left hand he held his wallet, and in his right a New York State driver's license. I didn't need to see the photo or name. It was certain to be Alex's.

"He ran right past me," Paolo shouted. "But I managed to get between him and the trash. He was trying to wipe it clean."

Just then, Roger came running out of the stairwell, cell phone in hand. He stopped, blocking the exit.

The Good Company waited on Marcus and me. I waited on Marcus. Marcus was silent. No one moved.

Finally, I couldn't take it. "What happened, Marcus?"

"Nicky, I didn't mean to. It was supposed to be a joke. That's all. But he was so angry. In the alley. He...I didn't mean it. It was an accident. I didn't..." He stopped. There was really nothing more to say.

Stacey Rose, letting out a sound that was part roar, part wail, broke through the crowd, lunging at Marcus. Quick responses from Eduardo and Sean prevented him from reaching his target.

I looked at my watch. Exactly 7:30. I thanked my stage manager's internal clock as the front doors opened. Man Wilson, Channel 3 News, pursued by his cameraman, came bounding into the lobby.

"This is Man Wilson, Channel 3 News, coming to you live from the Brewery Arts Center in Hell's Kitchen. Here tonight with the stunning and astonishing capture of a killer."

At least we wouldn't be lacking for witnesses.

WEDNESDAY NIGHT

You would think that having twenty-nine witnesses and a live broadcast of the confession would make for a shorter question-and-answer session with the NYPD. If so, you'd know as little about police work as I did. Marcus was in custody; Man Wilson, Channel 3 News, having finally run out of adjectives, was long gone. I wasn't really sure about the rest of the Good Company. As for me, I sat with Detectives Sanchez and Rampart onstage in the circle of folding chairs. I'd used the setup as a show-and-tell to explain the sequence of events that led to Marcus in the lobby, trying to ditch Alex's wallet and a lottery ticket.

"So you woke up in bed with the murderer and you just sat there looking at him until sunrise, then sent him on his way?" Detective Sanchez was now completely convinced that there were no limits to my insane behavior. I, however, have always thought *insane* too harsh a word. I prefer the small comfort of thinking that, at my worst, I am only *inane*. I know, it's a *very* small comfort.

"Could you just go through it one more time?" Rampart had scribbled furiously in his notebook but still wanted to verify everything. "We need to be certain that we have the basic details tonight."

"Fine. I went home with Marcus last night. We had sex. Afterward, he told me a joke."

"And this was routine?" Sanchez asked.

I had the urge to say there was nothing routine about sex with Marcus, but I managed to control myself.

"Yes. He liked to tell me a joke after sex. He said he liked to hear me laugh. Anyway, he told me a joke that my friend Roger had told me earlier, at the theater."

"How did you know he didn't have sex with Mr. Parker and tell him the joke?" When Sanchez asked this question, Rampart stopped writing.

"Well, I'd never want to guess who Marcus would or wouldn't have sex with, but I can definitely tell you Roger would not have sex with Marcus, if you know what I mean."

Rampart's only response was a grunted "Huh."

I was getting impatient. After all, I wasn't the murderer, I was the guy who'd caught him. "Can I tell this story, please?"

Sanchez motioned for me to continue.

"So he told me the joke. About 4:30-ish, I woke up. At first I didn't know why, but then I remembered that I'd heard a line from the joke on Sunday morning: 'No. Bigger than the Governor.' I couldn't remember who was telling it—there were a lot of people talking all at once in the theater that day. But it started me thinking.

"Marcus said he went to a late AA meeting Saturday night. That he had nothing going on with Alex, even though I know I picked up on something between them. He told me that Anna would confirm that he'd come home, hadn't spent the night out. That's true as far as it goes, but it didn't say anything about where he'd been *before* he got home, did it? But I believed him, until I heard the joke.

"See, Marina Isola thought someone had spent the night with Alex. I just couldn't stop thinking that it was all too coincidental. If I could trace that joke back to Alex on Sunday morning, then I was pretty certain that Marcus was lying about having sex with Alex Saturday night. Why would he do that?"

"Well," Rampart said, "if he wanted to get into bed with you, why wouldn't he lie?" Under other circumstances, his clumsy effort at delicacy would have made me laugh.

"Maybe, but we have a long history. He might just as easily have fessed up. He didn't. He chose to lie, and that made me suspicious. A lie so close to a murder is just too coincidental."

"So you just decided that this lie—if he'd even told a lie—meant he was a murderer?" Sanchez said this as if she were trying to figure her way through string-theory physics. "Why didn't you call us?"

"Listen to the tone in your voice. It could have been something else. I mean, I'd just spent the night with him."

"So you decided to spend the day trying to trap him, rather than turn him in? You have a strange code of ethics, Mr. D'Amico."

When she put it that way, I could see how it might look odd to others. But she wasn't the one who hadn't returned Alex's phone call. Maybe my actions were pretty cold-hearted, but they were nothing compared to the icy-cool performance Marcus had put on for the past three days.

"Anyway, I called Roger, who told me he heard the joke from Herb Wilcox. Now, before I could get to Herb, I ran into my downstairs neighbor, Mrs. Wizniski."

"We'll need to speak with her." Rampart made another note.

"Uh, yeah. That might not be so easy. Thing is, she doesn't always remember everything. This morning, she didn't remember that I'd bought a lottery ticket for her yesterday, and she couldn't even remember where she'd put it.

"And that started me thinking again. First about Mrs. Wizniski, who wanted to buy property with her winnings, then about the guy who sold it to me—who lived right on Alex's corner—and finally about Alex on Sunday afternoon. He'd dismissed the business of fixing the computers, saying it was just money. Alex was always very conscious about money. He didn't have much. Plus, his license was missing. So what if Alex was the guy who won on Saturday? And what if Marcus had taken the ticket? Maybe he figured that he could use the license to claim the prize. They sort of looked alike."

"That was unlikely to work." Sanchez took my theory as further confirmation that all of the Baldwin Classmates were round the bend.

"Well, I don't think he was thinking all that clearly, what with the murdering and all. I think he took the ticket on the fly and then, when Alex's confrontation with him in the alley turned deadly, he was left holding a signed lottery ticket. He decided to grab the license as well. I'm guessing he came back inside, went upstairs to hide the sweater, then pulled Alex's license from his wallet. He was doing *everything* on the fly. Even the icicle. Which, when you think about it, was a pretty clever way to confuse things—trying to make everyone look for motives that didn't exist."

Sanchez sighed. She was not so impressed. "So you asked Ms. Mikasa to look through his belongings for the license and ticket?"

"Yes. I asked her to do that while I talked to Herb, who did tell me that Alex told him the joke Sunday morning. He also thought that Alex had spent the night with someone."

Rampart nodded in agreement. "He told us the same thing, but he said it was Mr. Rose."

"Herb Wilcox wouldn't know who was sleeping with who even if they were sleeping with him. He isn't exactly the best judge of character, is he?"

"You woke up with the murderer, Mr. D'Amico. You tell us." Detective Sanchez was not having me in any way, shape, or form.

Rampart got us back on track. "What else did he tell you?"

"He said Alex was really happy about something else. That Alex was even talking about moving downtown to a bigger place. Where would he get money for that? If he saw the lottery numbers Saturday night, Marcus would know, because he was there, and it would explain his phone call to me at 2:45 in the morning. But when I saw Alex at the theater, he was definitely not happy. I think he discovered that the ticket was missing after Herb left. Since the only person who knew about it was Marcus, it wouldn't be too hard for Alex to figure he'd taken it."

"You were assuming that Mr. Bradshaw was with Mr. Isola when he found out he had the winning numbers?" Rampart asked.

"Yeah, I guess so," I answered.

Rampart flipped through his notebook. "Mr. Jasper and Mr. Bud claim that Alex Isola was bothering Stacey Rose on Sunday afternoon."

I had no idea who he was talking about. "Who are Jasper and Bud?"

Sanchez and Rampart exchanged glances. "What do you mean, who are they? They're here every day at your rehearsals."

"I've never heard of them," I said honestly.

"What do you mean, you've never heard of them?" Sanchez had that look again, the one she'd given me on Sunday when she'd decided I drank too much.

Rampart coaxed me along. "They follow Stacey Rose everywhere he goes? They look very similar, but aren't related? This ringing any bells for you?"

"Oh," I said, finally catching up. "The Two. I didn't know their names. No idea."

They both stared at me, not speaking. Finally, Rampart asked, "Who helped you?"

"What?" I asked.

"Who. Helped. You?" he repeated. It was obvious that neither of them believed that I could find my way to the restroom, much less figure out who committed a murder.

"I guess I was pretty lucky."

Rampart made a note about my good fortune.

"Look, the Two were wrong," I said. "Alex wasn't staring at Stacey on Sunday, he was staring at Marcus. Are we done here?"

"Almost. Tell us again about this color-therapy thing," Sanchez said.

"Fine. He had to have the license and ticket somewhere, didn't he? Anna didn't find them at her place. Then I thought, well, why would he keep them there? It was possible Anna might stumble onto them. Why not at the theater? But then, while I was talking to Stacey and the Two this afternoon, it really hit me that a lot of people were searching this place. If I were him, I'd keep everything on me."

"Then why agree to your color-therapy scheme?" Rampart was scribbling furiously.

"He thought we were after Stacey. He knew that wouldn't get us anywhere. And he didn't know we were going to use wallets until after we started. It was too late then."

They looked at me in silence.

Sanchez spoke. "Mr. D'Amico, I'm a little surprised at your attitude. You seem rather casual about having caught someone you were sleeping with committing murder."

"I wasn't sleeping with him. It was just once. It was more of an accident than a thing, you know?" How could they? As I said it, I didn't even know for certain what it had been, though I was sure it wasn't a real-live, full-blown "thing."

"You accidentally had sex with him?" Rampart asked. He did not write that down.

"Were you in a blackout?" Sanchez asked.

I ignored the question. "I told you, we were involved a few years ago, and these things happen. Call it closure, OK? And no, I'm not that thrilled about any of this."

Sanchez just shrugged. These things never happened to her. Then she said something that took me completely off-guard. "Closure is a fine thing, Mr. D'Amico. But from what you've told us about your past relationship with Mr. Bradshaw, I wonder if you would have been so suspicious of his joke-telling had he been nicer to you at school."

I started to object, then caught myself. She had to be wrong. There was Alex to consider. I would have been on my guard no matter what. At least I hoped that I would.

She took my silence as the end of my story. "OK, we're done here. We'll need you tomorrow to make a more formal statement."

We all stood. Then I remembered the keys.

"One other thing," I said. "Marina Isola has a set of keys that don't fit to Alex's apartment. They're actually keys to Anna Mikasa's. Marcus pretended to me on Monday that he'd left them at home, but actually he left them at Alex's Saturday night. That's why he wanted us to get in there. He wanted to get his keys back."

They didn't say anything, just nodded their heads.

"Right," Sanchez said. "Tomorrow."

———

As I entered the lobby, Sean was laughing at something that Roger and Paolo were telling him. This I did not like.

"Whatever these two are telling you, it's all lies," I said to Sean after Sanchez and Rampart, offering the barest of good-nights, left the building.

"So what happened in there? It took forever." Sean was flashing his sweetest, most encouraging smile at me, looking directly into my eyes. A look that contained more desire than curiosity.

Roger was very excited. "Are you going to get a medal?"

"More likely a referral to rehab," I said.

Paolo gave Sean a knowing look.

"Let's just say that when Detective Sanchez thinks of this, and she will, she won't be kind."

They laughed uneasily.

"Where's Anna?" I was surprised not to see her.

"She said she'd catch up to you later," Sean answered. "She's pretty broken up."

"But she did say something about having spent the goddamn money, so you're doing the goddamn show," Roger added.

I just shook my head.

"Hey." Sean put his arm around me.

I didn't duck his gesture. Doing that in front of Paolo and Roger seemed pretty harsh. I knew we'd eventually have to talk, and sooner rather than later. Sweet smile aside, this wasn't going to be our time. Not until I stopped hearing Alex's voice asking me to call him back.

"What I want to know is, why?" Roger loved a tidy denouement. "Do you really think it was a joke?"

"I think it was just a prank when he took the ticket. But that didn't matter once he decided not to call for help after knocking Alex down and cracking his head open. Even if it was just because he panicked. Then the thing with the icicle and hiding his sweater? He was well over the line past prank."

Paolo interrupted. "So are you going to tell it to us from the beginning?" he asked.

"I'm hungry," I said.

"We'll feed you—both of you." Paolo was already putting on his coat.

"Chinese again?" I asked.

"It's all he knows how to cook," Roger said, also bundling up. "How do you figure Anna plans to get this show up?"

"You know what?" I said. "I'd rather you tell me what happened to the cat."

CURTAIN CALL

THE WEDDING GUESTS ARE departing. The young lovers excuse themselves of their elders. Hand in hand, two by two, they stroll out of sight,
heads together, giggling as they go. The palace itself seems to dissolve
as the king of Athens and his new bride bid all to bed.

At last the mortals are gone. Oberon lays his blessing upon the
house.

"Now until the break of day, through this house each fairy stray.
To the best bride-bed will we, which by us shall blessed be. Every fairy
take his gate, and each several chamber bless, through this palace, with
sweet peace. And the owner of it blest, ever shall in safety rest."

And then away, all but Puck.

Puck, alone now in the empty space, looks out at the audience and,
with a sly smile, discharges the last obligation of the night.

"If we shadows have offended, think but this and all is mended:
that you have but slumbered here while these visions did appear. Give
me your hands, if we be friends, and Robin shall restore amends."

The small—very small—closing-night audience applauded politely—very politely. The actors took the stage for curtain call.

Everyone was moving as fast as possible, trying to get the entire company onstage before the audience gave up clapping. The gym-boy chorus hustled out center, bowed, and quickly made room for the mechanicals. As one, the remainder of the cast entered. The young lovers, wigs in hand to reveal their faces in full, were center. Eduardo took one side of the lovers. All considered, he'd been a great Puck. Stepping in late and without a director (Anna, Stacey, and I had coached him) was an uphill climb without a summit. Sean took the other side of the stage. He'd patiently listened to me explain why we were not going to date. Then he'd patiently continued to bring me coffee, make me laugh, and generally be the nicest not-boyfriend I'd ever had. I had no idea what to do next. Last onstage were Herb and Stacey, as far from each other as possible. The police had never connected Herb to Suege, so we didn't lose our Titania. As for Stacey and the Two, whatever shadow Alex cast upon the threesome was something they were keeping to themselves. Outwardly, all was a hazy pink bliss.

In the light booth, Anna, Rita (who'd finally made it home from Detroit), and I watched as the applause died quietly, fading all too quickly as the Good Company exited—except for the Two, who stood cheering in the back left; the quints, screaming in the back right; and Roger and Paolo ("We deserve a closing-night party, thank you"), who clapped dutifully, if not energetically, from mid-house.

I called the last cue. The stage lights faded to black as the house blazed more brightly.

ACKNOWLEDGMENTS

In matters medical and legal, I had the generous advice of Dr. Alan Baldridge of St. Christopher's Hospital for Children in Philadelphia, Dr. Robert Bettiker of Temple University, and Lt. Paul Walsh (Ret.). If there are errors, you can be certain they are mine, not theirs.

My thanks to Maxine Kalkut-Knox, who read every draft, and to Angela Zito, whose comments on an early draft were invaluable.

At Midnight Ink, I am indebted to my editors, Barbara Moore and Wade Ostrowski, to Brian Farrey for getting the word out, and to Kevin Brown for the beautiful cover art.

Read on for an excerpt from the next
Nicky D'Amico Mystery by Chuck Zito

Deck the Halls

COMING SOON FROM MIDNIGHT INK

———————————————————

"WHY DON'T YOU HAVE ice?" Paolo Suarez demanded, gin bottle in hand.

I countered. "Why don't I have my clipboard?" The first scene was starting in fifteen minutes, and I couldn't find my notes.

"In a real hotel, we'd have ice. I need ice to make a decent martini."

I searched through the dresser one more time. I wasn't expecting to find anything; I was just getting desperate.

"This is a real hotel. This just isn't a real guest room." This came from Jimmy Dolan, the nineteen-year-old grandson of one of my current employers. Jimmy, who'd been a wrestler in high school, was as short as me (five feet seven inches) but carried twice as much muscle. He'd squeezed himself into a small Victorian chair in the far corner of my room. Tight as the fit was, dressed in costume he looked like he belonged there. He was wearing a single-breasted brown sack suit with a high collar and a bow tie. He looked like a respectable turn-of-the-century workingman, ready to uphold the family honor. "And doesn't a martini have vermouth, too?"

Paolo didn't respond. He just stared at Jimmy as if he were something a bird had dropped on his shoulder.

Paolo's partner, Roger Parker, lay sprawled across the twin bed that was pretending to be suitable adult accommodation. Without even bothering to look up from his paperback, he said, "Paolo thinks of vermouth the same way he of thinks of Santa Claus. He's pretty sure no one has really ever seen either of them."

"I just don't see any reason to bruise the gin," Paolo said.

I stopped what I was doing. "Could at least one of you help me look?" I considered the three of them: Jimmy in the chair, Roger on the bed, and Paolo at the windowsill.

"What's this about?" Roger asked. "You never lose anything."

That was an all-purpose question. What *was* this all about? My current job—nursemaid to a Christmas-themed murder-mystery weekend—was not exactly what I'd had in mind when I'd spent tens of thousands of dollars on a degree in theater. Yet here I was in the lake district of upstate New York on a Friday night, getting ready to start the game.

The idea was simple enough. The innkeepers, Frank Swinney and Ray Dolan, had taken an old Victorian building, once the highest of high-end resorts, restored it to its 1889 glory, and were now cashing in on the infamy of two twentieth-century murders that had occurred on the property. For well over a decade, they'd been doing themed mystery weekends, each year working their way through the holiday calendar.

Imagine *Holiday Inn* without Irving Berlin, Bing Crosby, or Fred Astaire and with a really sick, twisted sense of humor. What does that leave? Murder House. Specifically, at the very moment when it all first started to go wrong, it left me in a room on the third floor of Murder House, Paolo Suarez grousing about the lack of ice. Which, considering the very nasty blizzard raging outside, was probably the entertainment high point of the evening.

The Christmas murder played each weekend between Thanksgiving and Christmas. The very first scene of the very second weekend was about to start. The mystery took its basic idea from the Naked Trunk Murders of 1905. That year, Harriet and Arthur Wainwright checked into what was then the Skylark Resort. Joshua Stokes, Harriet's lover, took a room that same week. Together, Harriet and Joshua lured Arthur into Stokes's room, where they bludgeoned him to death, stuffed him into Stokes's trunk, and, once Stokes checked out, left him with the luggage at the train station. They might have gotten away with it if Stokes had done as originally planned and taken the trunk to New York City. Instead, he panicked. He left the trunk at the local station, where the smell eventually attracted police attention. In the days before DNA and trace evidence, a trunk with a naked body packed inside might very well have led nowhere in New York City. But in the upstate region where the Skylark was located, Arthur Wainwright was the only missing person on record. Harriet got life in prison for her involvement. Joshua, as the person who actually did the killing, got the death penalty. The Skylark got its local nickname: "Murder House." And Frank and Ray got a great marketing ploy.

"All right, I'm just going to have to go without the notes," I said, giving up. They weren't that extensive anyway, and there was nowhere else in the room they might be. While the second-floor guest rooms were spacious, my room, tucked under the eaves of the third floor, was nothing more than it had ever been—servants' quarters. Then again, considering the knife and hatchet collection under glass in the Axe Room and the presence of the supposedly real trunk into which Arthur Wainwright was stuffed (complete with bloodstains) in the Trunk Room, my little retreat was not really so very unwelcoming. Certainly, there were few enough places to lose anything. With the exception of the one chair, the room was sparsely furnished with plain, sturdy country furniture. The owners reserved the period pieces for the rooms of paying guests. "Let's get going," I said.

Roger slapped his book shut. "Finally."

He was the first one into the hallway. Paolo followed his lover, more dutifully than enthusiastically. Jimmy was right behind me.

"He's very excited," Jimmy said in my ear as Roger rushed down the stairs.

"Yeah, well, he loves a mystery," I said.

"You know what I love?" Jimmy grabbed my ass.

I swatted his hand away. "Stop that." I had no intention of succumbing to the charms of my boss's grandson. Murder House may not have been much of a job, but it was the only one I had, and I intended to keep it.

"Oh, come on. We'll have a quick one after the first scene. No one will know." Jimmy was grabbing me again as we reached the second floor.

The third-floor stairs led us to the long central hallway of the second floor. There were four themed guest rooms on this floor: the Axe, the Trunk, the Cell, and the Piano rooms. Each contained memorabilia from Murder House's sordid past. The contents of these rooms contrasted sharply with the abundance of Victorian Christmas decorations covering every wall, shelf, and mantel. Adding to the overall strangeness of the effect were pieces of contemporary Christmas kitsch tucked away among the holly.

"Why couldn't we get the kind of old queens who have taste?" Paolo was staring at a mechanical Santa doll sitting on a small table along the banister.

"I love these things," Roger said, pushing the button at Santa's base. The doll started swaying and singing "Santa Claus Is Coming to Town."

"Is it Sunday yet?" Paolo continued down to the first floor.

"Dance with me," Roger called after him, enjoying the torment.

"They're kind of a strange couple, aren't they?" Jimmy asked.

He had no idea. They were my closest friends, and I was as baffled as everyone who knew them. I was even the one who had introduced them. Roger Parker, a tall, strawberry blond Midwestern systems analyst, and Paolo Suarez, a small, thin, wiry New York native and sculptor, had taken to each other instantly in some combustible, opposites-attract way. Six months after meeting at a showing of Paolo's work, they'd moved into Paolo's SoHo loft (funded by the family trust), and six years later they were still captivating each other and mystifying the rest of us.

Jimmy reached for me again.

"Look. You cannot grab at me every time we are alone. Understand? Stop it." I turned to face him, hoping that taking a firm stand now would put an end to his pursuit. I did not need any temptation from this kid. Particularly since he looked really good in his sack suit—and anyone who looked good in a sack must look spectacular out of one.

"Kiss for good luck?" He leaned in.

"Break a leg," I said, turning away.

A wide hall running the length of the inn evenly divided the first floor of Murder House. To one side were a spacious library and sitting room, both with fireplaces; to the other, the dining room and the pantry/kitchen combination. A covered porch wrapped around the outside of the building along the sitting room and library. The Great Hall was done up more lavishly than the second floor. Holly with red and white berries wrapped itself around the banister of the main stairway. Along the walls, the light fixtures dripped holly and silk tassels. Yet more holly—this time with red berries and white bows—circled the chandelier in the center of the hall. Dangling randomly from all this greenery, and adding a whimsical "don't get too serious" quality, were mechanical mistletoe. When anyone pulled the strings hanging from them, they played "Holly Jolly Christmas."

The exception to all the Christmas glitz was the Naked Trunk diorama. This wax-museum display sat to the right as you entered Murder House. It was a recreation of Harriet Wainwright and Joshua Stokes stuffing the naked, bloody (yet still tastefully rendered) body of Arthur Wainwright into a trunk. Not *the* trunk—that was supposedly in the Trunk Room upstairs. In a show of restraint, not one of the three was wearing a Santa hat. The overall effect of the Great Hall was just as creepy as any proprietor of a murder-mystery inn could hope for.

"How could this have happened?" Ralph Masters, captain of industry, leans against the bookshelf, dazed. His world is collapsing. His business empire is a mighty engine of capitalism. He spent years building it. How could it have come undone so quickly? "Eustace, what shall I do?"

Eustace Truly, Masters's loyal and excessively devoted personal secretary, fights back his tears. To see Mr. Masters in this state is almost more than Eustace can bear. "I don't know, sir, but I will stand by you no matter what."

Eustace moves toward his employer. For a moment, Masters thinks that his secretary intends to embrace him. But men do not do such things, not in Ralph Masters's world. And though it is 1905, a new century and a new era of enlightenment and tolerance, there are limits.

"Eustace. Do not forget yourself, young man."

Eustace stops, shaken by the sudden flash of realization that he is in fact what Masters thinks him to be. How shall he cope? What will he do?

The library offered a respite from the murder theme. The two walls lined with bookshelves sported sprigs of the ever-present holly. On the fireplace mantel, white and red pillar candles nestled in layers of fir greenery. The lit fire provided the perfect contrast to the snow outside, falling in thick sheets of large, wet flakes, the sort of snow that piles up so fast it reaches several feet in just few hours.

I was the only one enjoying the snowfall. Everyone else watched Jimmy Dolan and Frank Swinney play out their scene. Five couples, including Roger and Paolo, had signed on to play "whodunit" for the weekend. When the guests had arrived that afternoon, they'd received clue cards with bits of information, a packet with a fake newspaper article about the mystery, and a scorecard. The structure of the game was simple: Murder House's makeshift company of actors, comprised of staff and friends, would perform a series of short vignettes on both Friday and Saturday night. These would be scenes from the life of the fictional Masters family, who were themselves spending Christmas at a country inn. The game opens with the report of the murder of Pritchard Masters, heir to the family fortune. Between scenes, fortified with the hints on their clue cards, guests have the chance to ask one question of each of the characters. The game ends Saturday evening after dinner with the revelation of the murderer.

Frank and Ray had opted for this version of the mystery weekend (as opposed to the type where the guests themselves play the characters) mostly because of Ray's theater background. He'd spent decades as a high school drama teacher. There was no way he was going to let any of this out of his control. He even reserved for himself the role of Mary Masters, matriarch of the family.

The scene ended and the questioning began. My job just then was to mingle and keep the pace moving. Along with Ray, who was not in costume, I was to watch out for guests trying to break the one-question rule.

Almost immediately, I overheard Jimmy saying, in what little trace of character he had mustered as Eustace, "That's two questions, madame."

The inquisitive madame was Caroline Durst. She and her partner, Denise Shuman, were booked into the only guest room on the third floor, the Executioner's Room, with its lithographs of hangings and torture devices. Not my idea of a home away from home.

Denise and Caroline were a complementary set. Denise was a compact dark-haired woman who seemed to radiate intensity. Caroline, a willowy blonde, gave off a more relaxed vibe. In this case, looks were deceiving. In the few hours since meeting them, it was apparent that Denise deferred in most matters to Caroline. Caroline not only took the lead but charged ahead with great zeal.

"It was only one question. It had two parts," she said to Jimmy.

"Hi," I said, approaching. "How're we doing?"

"What are you, the ward nurse? We're doing fine. Little E.T. here won't answer the question," Caroline barked. Denise giggled at the wordplay on "Eustace Truly."

I sighed. "Of course, Eustace can answer your questions for you," I said. "But we do encourage everyone to ask only one question per round of each character. That keeps the playing field level." Then, because I knew the competitive type when I saw them, I added, "And you wouldn't want to win with an unfair advantage, would you? What kind of victory would that be?"

I had no experience in the hospitality business or with weekend murder mysteries, but I knew all about cajoling cranky actors and designers into playing nice with everyone else in the sandbox. I'd hit the right note with the ladies. They moved on to speak with Frank/Ralph.

As Jimmy/Eustace turned to speak to another guest, Ray Dolan, his grandfather and half-owner of Murder House, slid up next to me and offered his appreciation.

"That was very nicely done, Nicky," he said.

Ray was a soft-spoken man with a round face and rimless glasses now in his mid-sixties. He and his partner, Frank, had cashed in their chips—Ray's teacher's pension fund and Frank's Wall Street earnings—over fifteen years earlier to move upstate and open Murder House. From the look on his face, he was still enjoying himself.

"I've seen their type before. Most people come here for the fun of it. Some people come to win. People like Caroline and Denise come to crush the opposition." He laughed as he said this to me. "It's a mystery to me why they make so much of it. It's just a game."

323

He smiled at me again and then strolled over to chat with a middle-aged couple, Robert and Priscilla Hall, whom I'd only met in passing earlier in the day.

I looked around the room. Roger was happily chatting it up with two guys named Stephen and Ryan, a couple in their early thirties who, like Roger, apparently lived for technology and mysteries. Roger could not have been happier. Even though the three of us had already been dragged into two real-life murder investigations, he still got excited over a good puzzle. Once I'd taken the four-weekend gig at Murder House, Paolo had booked the second weekend as an early Christmas gift for his lover.

The other guests, Tinkey Lee and Walter Carter, were just finishing up with Frank/Ralph.

I estimated that I had another ten minutes while everyone socialized before we started again. Next up was a scene between the Masters's daughter, Rose, and her best friend, Lilly. Trish Eaton, a friend of Jimmy's, and Susan Lukazic, the inn's maid, played the parts. I figured I had just enough time to run to the third floor, make a quick check to see that the girls were ready, and then take a fast look at the costume and prop storage room to see if my notes were there.

ABOUT THE AUTHOR

Chuck Zito has spent most of his adult life working in theaters. A graduate of Carnegie Mellon University Department of Drama, he recently left his post as executive director of Diversionary Theatre in San Diego. He now lives in New York City.